'SPEAK IF YOU CAN,' SHE IMPLORED: 'JUST ONE WORD!'

from 'The Five Senses' by Edith Nesbit

THE
DREAMING
SEX

THE DREAMING SEX

Early Tales of Scientific Imagination by Women

Edited by
MIKE ASHLEY

PETER OWEN
London and Chicago

PETER OWEN PUBLISHERS
73 Kenway Road, London SW5 0RE

Peter Owen books are distributed in the USA by
the Independent Publishers Group,
814 North Franklin Street,
Chicago, IL 60610, USA

This collection first published in Great Britain 2010 by
Peter Owen Publishers

ISBN 978-0-7206-1354-4

A catalogue record for this book is available from the British Library

Printed and bound in the UK by
CPI Bookmarque, Croydon, CR0 4TD

SOURCES AND COPYRIGHT ACKNOWLEDGEMENTS

Front cover illustration by J.H. Bacon from *Cassell's Family Magazine*, May 1897, accompanying the story 'The Blue Laboratory' by L.T. Meade

Frontispiece illustration by Fred Leist from *The London Magazine*, December 1909, accompanying the story 'The Five Senses' by Edith Nesbit

'The Blue Laboratory' by L.T. Meade, first published in *Cassell's Family Magazine*, May 1897

'The Mortal Immortal' by Mary Shelley, first published in *The Keepsake*, 1834

'The Moonstone Mass' by Harriet Prescott Spofford, first published in *Harper's Monthly*, October 1868

'A Wife Manufactured to Order' by Alice W. Fuller, first published in *The Arena*, July 1895

'Good Lady Ducayne' by Mary Elizabeth Braddon, first published in *The Strand Magazine*, February 1896

'The Hall Bedroom' by Mary Wilkins Freeman, first published in *Collier's Weekly*, 28 March 1903

'The Curious Experience of Thomas Dunbar' by G.M. Barrows, first published in *The Argosy*, March 1904

'The Sultana's Dream' by Roquia Sakhawat Hossein, first published in *The Indian Ladies' Magazine*, 1905

'The Five Senses' by Edith Nesbit, first published in *The London Magazine*, December 1909

'Lady Clanbevan's Baby' by Clotilde Graves, first published in *Off Sandy Hook* (London: Heinemann, 1915)

'Monsieur Fly-by-Night' by Muriel Pollexfen, first published in *The Grand Magazine*, October 1915

'The Ultimate Ingredient' by Greye La Spina, first published in *The Thrill Book*, 15 October 1919

'The Miracle of the Lily' by Clare Winger Harris, first published in *Amazing Stories*, April 1928

'The Earth Slept: A Vision' by Adeline Knapp, first published in *One Thousand Dollars a Day: Studies in Practical Economics*, Boston, Massachusetts: Arena Publishing, 1894

CONTENTS

INTRODUCTION

AT THE END of the Victorian era, from around 1890, there was a considerable rise in the number of stories that looked at the potential benefits, or dangers, of the wealth of technological and scientific advance that had been gathering pace during the previous forty or fifty years. This was the dawn of what would later be termed 'science fiction' (often abbreviated to the objectionable 'sci-fi'), although that phrase was not coined until 1929. These earlier works, notably those by H.G. Wells, were known by the more charming phrase of 'scientific romance' – romance being used in its original meaning of something exciting and adventurous.

This anthology brings together a selection of such stories, all by women.

It has become a common-held belief that it was not until after the Second World War that women turned to science fiction, when writers such as Judith Merril, Kate Wilhelm, Anne McCaffrey, Ursula K. Le Guin and Alice Sheldon (James Tiptree, Jr) began their trade. Before 1939 science fiction appeared to be solely a male domain, untouched by female hands.

This anthology will prove that wrong. One thing that science fiction sets out to do is to speculate on what new advances in science and technology might achieve, and there were many women just as interested in that prospect as men. However, the women laboured under a major handicap. Early in the first story, 'The Blue Laboratory', a male scientist says to the young woman who has come to serve as governess to his children, 'Is it possible that you, a young lady, are interested in science?' You can almost hear the amazement in his voice. This story was published in 1897, just a year before Marie Curie established her reputation with the discovery of radium. Yet thirty years later that view still prevailed. Hugo Gernsback, publisher of the world's first science-fiction magazine, *Amazing Stories*, was delighted but surprised when one of the prize-winners in a contest he had run in 1926 was a woman. 'As a rule,' he wrote, 'women do not make good scientifiction writers because their education and general tendencies on scientific matters are usually limited.'

Were they limited? If they were it was because the scientific establishment imposed the barriers. It was almost impossible for women in the Victorian or Edwardian era to gain a scientific education. Elizabeth Garrett managed to qualify as a doctor in 1865 but only because she found a loophole in the regulations of the Society of Apothecaries. No sooner had she qualified than the society changed its regulations, banning women from entering. It was not until 1911 that Elizabeth Davies-Colley became the first British woman member of the Royal College of Surgeons.

It was not as if women were not interested in science. Caroline Herschel, for instance, the sister of the Astronomer Royal, Wilhelm Herschel, was an excellent astronomer in her own right, discovering several comets and producing an important catalogue of nebulae. The Royal Astronomical Society awarded her its Gold Medal in 1828, but it would not go to another women until 1996.

Then there was Ada Lovelace, the daughter of Lord Byron. She became a first-class mathematician and worked with Charles Babbage on his famous 'Difference Engine' and 'Analytical Engine', now considered the prototype of the world's first computer. She even wrote the equivalent of a program for the machine, with the result that she is considered the world's first computer programmer – back in 1843!

Marie Curie, the discoverer of radium and polonium, went on to win the Nobel Prize not once but twice – for physics in 1903 and chemistry in 1911. And yet the French Academy of Sciences refused to elect her as a member.

The interest of women in science may be traced back many years in Britain, certainly to the time of Margaret Cavendish (1623–73) who, through marriage, had become the Duchess of Newcastle. What is interesting about Cavendish is that not only did she debate science and philosophy with the best of them – she attended meetings of the Royal Society although was not allowed to be a member – but she wrote one of the earliest works of science fiction. This was *The Description of a New World, Called the Blazing World*, first published in 1666, the year of the Great Fire of London. It is a unique and highly imaginative work, unlike anything else of its day, creating a neighbouring world to the earth to which a woman travels, becoming the ruler or goddess of one of them. The story is self-indulgent but full of wonderful scientific ideas.

We can add to that. In his excellent study of the history of science fiction, *Billion Year Spree* (1973), Brian W. Aldiss, while recognizing earlier works, identified the novel *Frankenstein; or, The Modern Prometheus* as the point at which true science fiction was born. Because of its interpretation by the cinema, *Frankenstein* is usually regarded as a work of horror fiction, but its core deals with the fundamental scientific process for the creation of life. *Frankenstein* was written by Mary Shelley, who was only twenty when the book was published anonymously at the end of January 1818. So not only is it clear that women were interested in the study of science; they were also interested in speculating on its potential in the new world of technological marvels that the industrial and scientific revolutions were creating. It was a woman who created the field of scientific fiction, and this anthology celebrates that by looking at other contributions by other women during the century following *Frankenstein*.

There were plenty of other women producing similar works during this century. I have concentrated on short fiction, but it is worth highlighting some women novelists to emphasize – if it were necessary – just how many women were writing scientific fiction. There was Jane Webb (1807–1858), best known for her works on horticulture and the Victorian kitchen garden but who, in *The Mummy! A Tale of the Twenty-Second Century* (1827), took *Frankenstein* a step further by creating a scientifically advanced future in which it was possible to revive the dead. Then there was Mary Griffith (c. 1800–1877), another horticulturalist, who wrote *Three Hundred Years Hence* (1836), describing a utopia where women are emancipated and slavery is abolished. There is more hope for the future in *A Vision of Our Country in the Year Nineteen Hundred* (1851) by Jane Ellis, while in *Mizora* (1881) Mary Bradley Lane reveals an ideal society within a hollow earth – ideal, that is, if you don't like men or animals. Women were strong in suggesting utopias, either in the future or elsewhere on earth. Catherine Helen Spence (1825–1910), who became Australia's first female political candidate in 1897, presented one such in *A Week in the Future* (1889). So did Anna Blake Dodd in *The Republic of the Future* (1887). The best known of them is probably *Herland* (1915) by Charlotte Perkins Gilman (1860–1935).

There were many other themes. *Poseidon's Paradise* (1892), by the Californian writer Elizabeth Birkmaier, is a genuine adventure romance set in Atlantis just before its destruction. Christabel Coleridge (1843–1921), granddaughter of the poet Samuel Taylor Coleridge, produced an interesting novel of telepathy in *The Thought-Rope* (1909). Most remarkable of all, in my view, is *Around a Distant Star* (1904) by the French writer Jean Delaire (real name Elisa Touchemolin, 1868–1950), in which a scientist creates a spaceship-drive that can travel at two thousand times the speed of light. He also invented a super-telescope. He travels to a far-distant planet and through his telescope looks back and sees earth at the time of the crucifixion of Jesus.

Few of these names will be known today, and that only underlines the point that, despite there being a significant amount of scientific fiction written by women in the nineteenth and early twentieth centuries, it has been forgotten. Women had considerable interest in what science might bring, as the following stories show. Here you will find thoughts on how to slow down the ageing process, how to photograph thoughts, how to enhance our natural senses, whether we can become invisible, whether there might be another dimension around might be satisfied with synthetic wives and so much more. Apart from the first and final stories, the contents are arranged in the order in which they were first published, so as to follow the emergence of ideas.

Mike Ashley, 2010

L. T Meade

THE BLUE LABORATORY

Elizabeth 'Lillie' Thomasina Meade (1844–1914) was a prolific Irish novelist once best known for her books for adolescent girls. Few of these are remembered today, although her work is highly prized by a small coterie of collectors. As she wrote around 280 books, plus many magazine essays and stories and edited the magazine Atalanta for six years, there is plenty to collect. What she is best remembered for are her volumes of detective and mystery stories. These came about when Arthur Conan Doyle decided to kill off Sherlock Holmes, and The Strand, *which had published the stories and seen its circulation quadruple as a result, was desperate for something to take their place. Lillie Meade was one of the more creative writers who helped plug the gap. In order that she could draw upon expert knowledge she often consulted a medical expert, and in this instance it was Eustace Robert Barton (1854–1943), who went under the name of Robert Eustace. His role was predominantly in providing the scientific expertise and double-checking the final story, but it was Meade who did the writing. Similar stories are included in the collections* A Master of Mysteries *(1898),* The Brotherhood of the Seven Kings *(1899),* The Man Who Disappeared *(1901) and* The Sorceress of the Strand *(1903). Many of these stories have plots that hinge on some new scientific development.*

The following story formed part of a series entitled 'Tales of Other Cities' which was run in Cassell's Magazine *in 1897 with contributions by various authors. Meade's was the most unusual. She later included it in her collection* Silenced *(1904).*

The Blue Laboratory

WHEN I DECIDED to accept the offer of a situation as governess in a Russian family, I bought, amongst other things, a small silver-mounted revolver, and fifty cartridges.

But before proceeding to tell this story, I had better say one or two words about myself. My name is Madeline Rennick; I am an orphan, and have no near relations. When Dr Chance, an Englishman, but a naturalised Russian, offered me a hundred pounds per annum to educate his two daughters, I determined to accept the situation without a moment's hesitation. I bade my friends adieu, and reached St Petersburg without any sort of adventure. Dr Chance met me at the station. He was somewhat handsome but near-sighted man on quite the shady side of fifty. He was coldly polite to me, gave directions about my luggage, and took me straight to his house on the Ligovka Canal. There I was received by Mrs Chance, a lady in every respect the antipodes of her husband. She was of mixed Russian and German extraction, and had a manner full of curiosity, and yet thoroughly unsympathetic. My pupils were rather pretty girls. The elder was tall, and had the dark eyes of her father; she had a fine open expression – her name was Olga. The younger was small in stature, with a piquante face – she was called Maroussa. The girls could speak English tolerably well, and the warmth of their greeting made up for their mother's indifference.

'You must find it dreadfully dull here,' said Maroussa, on a certain afternoon when I had been a month in Russia.

'Not at all,' I replied. 'I have long had a great desire to see Russia.'

'You know, of course, that father is English. He has lived here ever since he was thirty years of age. He is a great scientist. How your eyes sparkle, Madeline! Are you interested in science?'

'I took a science tripos at Girton,' I answered.

As I spoke I bent over the Russian novel which I was trying to read. The next moment a coldly polite voice spoke almost in my ear. I looked up, and saw to my astonishment that Dr Chance, who seldom or never favoured the ladies of his family with his presence, had come into the salon.

'Did I hear aright?' he said. 'Is it possible that you, a young lady, are interested in science?'

'I like it immensely,' I replied.

'Your information pleases me. The fact is this. I came up just now to ask you to grant me a favour. At times I have intolerable pain in the right eye. To use it on such occasions makes it worse. Today I suffer torture. Will you come downstairs and be my secretary for the nonce?'

'Of course, I will,' I answered. The moment I spoke, Dr Chance moved towards the door, beckoning to me with a certain imperious gesture to follow him. I felt myself, as it were, whirled from the room. In a moment or two I was alone with the Doctor in his cabinet. A gentleman's study in Russian houses is always called by this name. The Doctor's cabinet was a nobly proportioned room – two-thirds of the walls being lined from ceiling to floor with books – a large double window giving abundant light, and a door at the further end letting in a peep of a somewhat mysterious room beyond.

'My laboratory,' said the Doctor, noticing my glance. 'Some day I shall have pleasure in showing it to you. Now, can you take down from dictation?'

'Yes, in shorthand.'

'Capital! Pray give me your very best attention. The paper I am about to dictate to you is to be posted to England tonight It will appear in the *Science Gazette*. As you are interested in such matters I do not mind confiding its subject to you. Miss Rennick, I have discovered a *method of photographing thought*.'

I stared at him in astonishment; he met my gaze fully. His deep-set glittering eyes looked something like little sparks of fire.

'You do not believe me,' he said, 'and you represent to a great extent the public to whom I am about to appeal. I shall doubtless be scoffed at in England, but wait awhile. I can prove my words, but not yet – not yet. Are you ready? '

'I am all attention,' I answered.

His brow cleared, he sank back on his divan. He began to dictate, and I took down his words assiduously. At the end of an hour he stopped.

'That will do,' he said. 'Now, will you kindly transcribe in your best and fairest writing what I have been saying to you?'

'Yes,' I answered.

'And please accept ten roubles for the pleasure and help you have given me. Not a word of refusal. Be assured that you have my very best thanks.'

He gave me a long and earnest look, and slowly left the room.

It took me from two to three hours to transcribe what had fallen so glibly from the Doctor's lips. Having finished my paper, I went upstairs.

When I entered the salon, Olga and Maroussa rushed to meet me.

'Tell us what has happened,' they cried.

'But I have nothing to tell.'

'Nonsense, you have been away for five hours.'

'Yes, and during that time your father dictated a lecture to me, which I took down in shorthand. I have just transcribed it for him, and left it on his desk.'

'Please, Madeline,' said Olga, 'tell us what was the subject of father's paper.'

'I am not at liberty to do that, Olga.'

Olga and Maroussa glanced at each other.

Then Olga took my hand.

'Listen,' she said, 'we have something to say to you. In the future you will be often in the laboratories.'

'Are there more than one?'

'Yes. Now pray give me your attention. Please understand that Father will ask you to help him again and again. He may even get you to assist him with his chemistry. It is about Father's other laboratory, the one you have not yet seen – the Blue laboratory – that we want to speak. The fact is, Olga and I have a secret on our minds in connection with it. It weighs on us – sometimes it weighs heavily.'

As Maroussa spoke she shuddered, and Olga's olive-tinted face grew distinctly paler.

'We long to confide in someone,' said Olga.' From the moment we saw you we felt that we would be *en rapport* with you. Now will you listen?'

'Certainly, and I also promise to respect your secret.'

'Well then, I will tell you in as few words as possible,

'A couple of months ago some gentlemen came to dinner – they were Germans and were very learned. One of them was called Dr Schopenhauer; he is a great savant. When the wine was on the table, they began to talk about something which made father angry. Soon they were all quarrelling. It was fun to listen to them. They got red and Father pale, and Father said, "I can prove my words." I am sure they forgot all about our existence. Suddenly Father sprang up and said, "Come this way, gentlemen. I am in a position to make my point abundantly plain." They all swept out of the dining-room and went into the cabinet Mother said she had a headache, and she went upstairs to her boudoir, but Maroussa and I were quite excited, and we slipped into the cabinet after them. I don't think any of them noticed us. They went from the cabinet into the laboratory, a glimpse of which you saw today. He opened a door at the further end, and walked down a long passage. The scientists and Father, absorbed in their own interests, went on in front, and Maroussa and I followed. Father took a key out of his pocket and opened a door in the wall, and as he did so he touched a spring, and behold, Madeline, we found ourselves on the threshold of another laboratory, double, trebly as large as the one we had left. There was an extraordinary sort of dome in one of the corners standing up out of the floor. Maroussa and I noticed it the moment we entered the room. We were dreadfully afraid of being banished, and we slipped at once behind a big screen and waited there while Father and the savants talked their secrets together. Suddenly Maroussa, who is always up to a bit of fun, suggested to me that we should stay behind and examine the place for ourselves after Father and the Germans had gone. I do not know how we thought of such a daring scheme, for, of course, Father would lock us in, but we forgot that part. After a time he seemed to satisfy the gentlemen, and they left the room as quickly, as they had come in. Father turned off the electric light, and we were in darkness.

'We heard the footsteps dying away down the long corridor. We felt full of fun and mischief, and I said to Maroussa, "Now let us turn on the light."

'We had not gone half-way across the room when, oh, Madeline! what do you think happened? There came a knock which sounded as if it proceeded from the floor under our feet; it was in the direction of the queer dome which I have already mentioned to you. A voice cried piteously three times, "Help, help, help!" We were terrified, all our little spirit of bravado ran out of us. I think Maroussa fell flop on the floor, and I know I gave about the loudest scream that could come from a human throat. It was so loud that it reached Father's ears. The knocking underneath ceased, and we heard Father's footsteps hurrying back. There was Maroussa moaning on the floor and pointing at the dome; she was too frightened to speak, but I said, "There is someone underneath, away by that dome in the corner. I heard someone knocking distinctly, and a voice cried 'Help!' three times."

'"Folly!" said Father; "there is nothing underneath. Come away this moment."

'He hurried us out of the room and locked the door, and told us to go up to Mother. We told Mother all about it, but she, too, said we were talking nonsense, and seemed quite angry; and Maroussa could not help crying, and I had to comfort her.

'But, Madeline, that night we heard the cry again in our dreams, and it has haunted us ever since. Madeline, if you go on helping Father, he will certainly take you into the Blue laboratory. If ever he does, pray listen and watch and tell us – oh, tell us! – if you hear that terrible, that awful voice again.'

Olga stopped speaking; her face was white, and there were drops of moisture on her forehead.

I tried to make light of what she had said, but from that hour I felt that I had a mission in life. There was something in Olga's face when she told me her story which made me quite certain that she was speaking the truth. I determined to be wary and watchful, to act cautiously, and, if possible, to discover the secret of the Blue laboratory. For the purpose I made myself agreeable and useful to Dr Chance. Many times when he complained of his eyes he asked me to be his secretary, and on each of these occasions he paid me ten roubles for my trouble. But during our intercourse – and I now spent a good deal of my time with the Doctor – I never really went the smallest way into his confidence. He never for a moment lifted the veil which hid his real nature from my gaze. Never, except once; and to tell of that awful time is the main object of this story. To an ordinary observer, Dr Chance was a gentle-mannered, refined but cold man. Now and then, it is true, I did see his eyes sparkle as if they were flints which had been suddenly struck to emit fire. Now and then, too, I noticed an anxious look about the tense lines of his mouth, and I have seen the dew coming out on his forehead when an experiment which I was helping him to conduct promised to prove exceptionally interesting. At last, on a certain afternoon, it was necessary for him to do some very important work in the Blue laboratory. He required my aid, and asked me to follow him there. It was, indeed, a splendidly equipped room. A teak bench ran round three sides of the wall, fitted with every conceivable apparatus and appliance: glazed fume chambers, stoneware sinks, Bunsen burners, porcelain dishes, balances, microscopes, burettes, mortars, retorts, and, in fact, every instrument devoted to the rites of the mephitic divinity. In one corner, as the girls had described to me, was a mysterious-looking, dome-shaped projection, about three or four feet high, and covered with a black cloth that looked like a pall.

This was the first occasion on which I worked with the Doctor in the Blue laboratory, but from that afternoon I went with him there on many occasions and learned to know the room well.

At last, on a certain day, my master was obliged to leave me for a few minutes alone in the laboratory. I have by nature plenty of courage, and I did not lose an instant in availing myself of this unlooked-for opportunity. The moment he left the room I hurried across to the mysterious dome, and, raising the black cloth, saw that it covered a frame of glass, doubtless communicating with some chamber below. I struck my knuckles loudly on the glass. The effect was almost instantaneous. I was immediately conscious of a dim face peering up at me from beneath, and I now saw that there was an inner and much thicker partition of glass between us. The face was a horrible one – terrible with suffering – haggard, lean, and ghastly; there was a look about the mouth and the eyes which I had never before seen, and I hope to God I may never witness again on human countenance. This face, so unexpected, so appalling, glanced at me for a second, then my master's steps were heard returning, a shadowy hand was raised as if to implore, and the ghoul-like vision vanished into the dark recesses beneath. I pulled the covering back over the dome and returned quickly to my work. Dr Chance was near-sighted; he came bustling in with a couple of phials in his hand.

'Come here,' he said. 'I want you to hold these. What is the matter?' He glanced at me suspiciously. 'You look pale. Are you ill?'

'I have a slight headache,' I replied,' but I shall be all right in a moment.'

'Would you like to leave off work? I have no desire to injure your health.'

'I can go on,' I answered, placing immense control upon myself. The shock was past; it was an awful one, but it was over. My suspicions were now realities: the girls had really heard that cry of pain. There was someone confined in a dungeon below the Blue laboratory – God only knew for what awful purpose. My duty was plain as daylight.

'Dr Chance,' I said, when my most important work was over, 'why have you that peculiar dome in the corner of the floor?'

'I warned you to ask no questions,' he said; his back was slightly to me as he spoke. 'There is nothing in this room,' he continued, 'which is not of use. If you become curious and spying, I shall need your services no longer.'

'You must please yourself about that,' I replied with spirit; 'but it is not an English girl's habit to spy.'

'I believe you are right,' said Dr Chance, coming close and staring into my face. 'Well, on this occasion I shall have pleasure in gratifying your curiosity. That dome is part of an apparatus by which I make a vacuum. Now you are doubtless as wise as you were before.'

'I am no wiser,' I answered.

The Doctor smiled in a sardonic manner.

'I have finished my experiment,' he said; 'let us come away.'

I ran straight up to my room and shut and locked myself in. I could not face the girls – I must not see them again until I had so completely controlled my features that they would not guess that their suspicions were confirmed. I sat down and thought. No danger should now deter me on the course which I had marked out for myself. The miserable victim of Dr Chance's cruelty should be rescued, even if my life were the penalty. But I knew well that my only chance of success was by putting the Doctor off his guard.

Having planned a certain line of action, I proceeded to act upon it. That evening I dressed for dinner in my choicest. I possessed an old black velvet dress which had belonged to my grandmother. The velvet was superb, but the make was old-fashioned. This very old fashion would, doubtless, add to its charm in the eyes of the Doctor; he might, when he saw the dress, remember some of the beauties he had met when he was young. Accordingly, I put on the black velvet dress, pinned a lace kerchief in artistic folds round my throat, piled my hair high on my head, and then daringly powdered it. I had black hair – black as ink – a clear complexion, a good deal of colour in my cheeks, and very dark eyes and eyebrows. The effect of the powdered hair immediately removed me from the conventional girl of the period and gave me that old-picture look, which men especially admire.

When I went into the salon, Olga and Maroussa rushed to meet me with cries of rapture.

'How beautiful you look, Madeline!' they exclaimed; 'but why have you dressed so much?'

'I took a fancy to wear this,' I said; 'it belonged to my grandmother.'

'But why have you powdered your hair?'

'Because it suits the dress.'

'Well, you certainly do look lovely. I wonder what Mamma will say?'

When Mrs Chance appeared, she stared at me in some astonishment, but vouchsafed no remark. We all went down to dinner, and I saw Dr Chance raise his eyes and observe my picturesque dress with a puzzled glance, followed immediately by a stare of approval.

'You remind me of someone,' he said, after a pause. 'My dear,' turning to his wife, 'of whom does Miss Rennick remind you?'

Mrs Chance favoured me with her round, curious, unsympathetic stare.

'Miss Rennick is somewhat like the picture of Marie Antoinette just before she was guillotined,' she remarked after a pause.

'True, there is certainly a resemblance,' answered the Doctor, nodding his head.

I drew my chair a little closer to him and began to talk. I talked more brilliantly than I had ever done before; he listened to me in surprise. Soon I saw that I was pleasing him; I began to draw him out. He told me stories of his early youth, of a time when his fat German wife had not appeared on the horizon of his existence. He even described his conquests in those early days, and laughed merrily over his own exploits. Our conversation was in English, and Mrs Chance evidently could not follow the Doctor's brilliant remarks and my somewhat smart replies. She stared at me in some astonishment, then, gently sighing, she lay back in her chair and began to doze. The girls talked to one another; they evidently suspected nothing.

'Shall we go up to the salon?' said Mrs Chance at last.

'You may, my dear,' was the Doctor's quick reply, 'and the fact is, the sooner you and the girls do so the better, for Miss Rennick has to get through some work this evening for me. Did I not tell you so, Miss. Rennick? Will you have the goodness to follow me now to the cabinet? If you finish your work quickly, I will do something for you. I see by your manner that you are devoured by curiosity. Yes, don't attempt to deny it. I will gratify you. You shall ask me this evening to tell you one of my secrets. Whatever you ask I shall do my best to comply with. The fact is, I am in the humour to be gracious.'

'Miss Rennick looks tired,' said Mrs; Chance; 'don't keep her downstairs too long, Alexander. Come, girls.'

'The girls smiled and nodded to me, they followed their mother upstairs, and I went with the Doctor to his cabinet. The moment we were alone he turned and faced me.

'I repeat what I have just said,' he began. 'You are full of curiosity. That which ruined our mother Eve is also your bane. I see this evening defiance and a strong desire to wring my secrets from me in your eye. Now let me ask you a question. What has a young, unformed creature like you to do with science?'

'I love science,' I said; 'I respect her; her secrets are precious. But what can I do for you, Dr Chance?'

'You speak in the right spirit, Miss Rennick. Yes, I require your services: follow me at once to the Blue laboratory.'

He tripped on in front, genial and pleased. He opened the door in the wall, switched on the electric light, and we found ourselves in the ghastly place with its ghastly human secret. I went and stood close to the dome-shaped roof on the floor. Dr Chance crossed the room and began to examine some microbes which he was carefully bringing to perfection.

'After all,' he said, 'this experiment is not in a sufficiently advanced stage to do anything further tonight. I shall not require you to help me until tomorrow. What, then, can I do for you?'

'You can keep your promise and tell me your secret,' I answered.

'Certainly: what do you want to know?'

'Do you remember the first day I helped you?'

'Well.'

'I wrote a paper for you on that day; the subject was "The Photography of Thought". You promised your English public that in a month or six weeks at farthest you would be able to prove your words. The time is past. Prove your words to me now. Show me how you photograph thought.'

Dr Chance stared at me for a moment. Then he grinned from ear to ear. His glittering teeth showed, then vanished. His eyes looked like sparks of living fire; they contracted and seemed to sink into his head, they shone like the brightest diamonds. His emaciated, pale, high forehead became full of wrinkles. He stretched out his hand and grasped me by my shoulder.

'Are you prepared?' he asked; 'do you know what you ask? I *could* tell you that secret. God knows I would tell it to you, if I thought you could bear it.'

'I can bear anything,' I said, steadying myself. 'At the present moment I am all curiosity. I have no fear. Is your secret a fearful one? Is it a terrible thing to photograph thought?'

'The ways and means by which these secrets have been wrung from Nature are fraught with terror,' was the slow reply; 'but you have asked me, and you shall know – on a condition.'

'What is that?'

'That you wait until tomorrow evening.'

I was about to reply, when a servant came softly up the room, bearing a card on a salver.

He presented it to the Doctor. Dr Chance looked at me.

'Dr Schopenhauer has called,' he said abruptly; 'he wants to see me on something important. I shall be back with you in a few moments.'

He left me alone. I could scarcely believe my senses. I was by myself in the Blue laboratory. Such an unlooked-for opportunity was indeed providential. I went straight like an arrow shot from a bow to the dome-shaped roof. I withdrew the covering and bent over it, peering into the utter darkness below. Of course, I could see nothing. I rapped with my knuckles on the glass; there was no sound, no reply of any sort. Had the victim been removed into a still further dungeon? I did not despair. I knocked again. This time my efforts were rewarded by a faint, far-away, terrible groan. I was desperate now, and, in spite of the risk I ran of being heard by Dr Chance, began to shout down through the glass.

'If there is anyone within, speak!' I cried.

A voice, faint and hollow, a long way off – dim as if these were its last and dying utterances – answered me.

'I am an Englishman – unjustly imprisoned.' There was a long pause; the next words came fainter: 'Put to torture.' Another silence; then the voice again: 'In the shadow of death – help, save!'

'You shall be released within twenty-four hours: I swear it by God,' I answered back. My next act was indeed daring, and the inspiration of a moment. I ran to the door, took out the key, and, hurrying to the bench where Dr Chance's large microscope stood, took one of the pieces of hard paraffin which he used for regulating the temperature of his microscope stage and, taking a careful impression of the key, returned it to its place, slipping the paraffin impression into my pocket. Having done this, I wandered about for a moment or two, trembling violently and trying to resume my self-control. The Doctor did not return. I resolved to stay in the Blue laboratory no longer. I turned off the electric light, took the key out of the lock, went up the long passage, and knocked at the door of the other laboratory. It was quickly opened by the Doctor. I gave him the key without glancing at him, and hurried to my room.

How I spent that dreadful night I can never now recall. I had no personal fear, but each thought in my brain was centred upon one feverish goal. I would rescue that tortured Englishman, even at the risk of my life. At the present moment I could not determine clearly how to act, but before the morning two steps became clear to me. One was to have a duplicate key made immediately of the laboratory, the second to go and see the English Consul. I did not even know the name of the Consul, but I was aware that the Ambassador and Consul were bound to protect English subjects. Dr Chance was himself a naturalized Russian, but the imprisoned man was an Englishman. I would appeal to my own country for his release.

Having nerved myself to this point, I dressed as usual and attended to my duties during the morning hours. All my splendour of the night before was laid aside, and I was once again the plain, sensible-looking English governess. At half-past twelve we all assembled for the mid-day meal. Dr Chance sat at the foot of his table. He was particularly agreeable in his manner, but I observed that he gave me some stealthy and covert glances. For a moment I thought he might suspect something; then, believing this to be impossible, I tried to remain cool and quiet. Towards the end of the meal, and just when I was about to rise from the table, he laid his hand on mine, and spoke.

'I am sorry to see you looking so pale,' he said; 'are you suffering from headache?'

'Yes.'

'Ah, Miss Rennick, you allow your emotions to get the better of you. That headache is due to excitement.'

'I have no cause to be excited,' I replied.

'Pardon me, you have cause. You remember what I promised to tell you tonight?'

I stared him full in the eyes. 'I remember,' I answered.

'It grieves me to have to disappoint you. An unexpected matter of business calls me from St Petersburg. I shall be absent for a couple of days.'

'But, my dear Alexander, I know nothing of this,' said the wife.

'I will explain the matter to you later, my dear,' he said. 'The principal thing now is that I am unable to fulfil a promise made to Miss Rennick. See how she droops; her passion for science grows with what it is fed upon. Miss Rennick, I must leave home at eight o'clock this evening; I shall not be back before Saturday, but for the greater part of this day I shall require your services. Will you meet me in my cabinet not later than half past two?'

I promised, and left the room with the two girls. At this hour we always went upstairs and devoted ourselves to lessons: we generally sat in the salon. It was all-important, all essential to my plans, that I should have an hour on this occasion, the one precious hour left to me – for it was now half-past one – at my disposal.

The moment I was alone with the girls, I locked the door and turned and faced them.

'Listen to me,' I said. 'I have something most important to do. I mean to trust you, but only to a certain extent; I have no time to tell you everything.'

'Oh, Madeline, Madeline! have you discovered something?' cried Olga.

'Yes, but I cannot breathe a word now; you can both help me to an invaluable extent.'

'I shall be only too delighted,' said Maroussa, beginning to skip about

'Try to keep quiet, Maroussa; this is a matter of life or death. It is now half-past one. In an hour's time I must be in your father's cabinet; in the meantime I have much to do. I want to visit a lock-smith's; he must make me a key. I shall ask him to have it ready by the afternoon, and will beg of you, Olga and Maroussa, to call for it when you go out later in the day. Do not let anyone know; contrive to do this in secret, and bring the key carefully back to me.'

'Nurse will come with us,' said Olga; 'we can easily manage. What locksmith will you go to?'

I mentioned the name of a man whose shop I had noticed in a street near by. Olga took a little pocket-book and made a note of the address, looked at me again as if she wanted to question me further, but I told her I had not a moment to spare. She kissed me, and she and Maroussa ran to their own rooms.

Now, indeed, I must put wings to my feet. I sat down and wrote the following letter to the Consul.

Chance House, Ligovka Canal.

SIR, – I urgently implore your immediate assistance. I have discovered that an Englishman is imprisoned in an underground cellar in this house, and put to torture. I am an English girl residing here as governess. I have made up my mind to rescue the Englishman, but cannot do so without assistance. Dr Chance leaves Petersburg this evening at eight o'clock. At nine o'clock I shall be in the large laboratory in the garden, known by the name of the Blue laboratory. I will give one of the servants directions to bring you there, if you will be kind enough to come to my aid. In God's name do not fail me, for the case is urgent. Both the Englishman and I are likely to be in extreme danger. I claim assistance for us both as British subjects.

Yours faithfully,

Madeline Rennick

This letter written, I hastily addressed it and slipped it into my pocket. I wrapped myself in my warm furs and went out. No one saw me go. At this hour Mrs Chance slept, and the girls and I were supposed to be engaged over our work. On my way to the Consul's house I stopped at the locksmith's, and gave him directions to make a key from the wax impression. I told him that the key must be ready in two or three hours. He objected, expostulating at the shortness of time, and stared me all over. I was firm, telling him that Miss Chance would call for the key between five and six o'clock that evening. He then promised that it should be ready for her, and I left him to hurry to the Consul's. The Consul's servant opened the door; I put the letter into his hands, charged him to take it immediately to his master, and hurried home. I had then in truth set a match to the mine. What the result would be God only knew!

At half past two o'clock I knocked at the door of Dr Chance's cabinet. He called to me to come in. I entered and went through my usual duties. The Doctor gave me plenty of work. I had letters to copy, to take down paragraphs for different science papers at his dictation, to transcribe and copy them – in short, to work hard as his clerk for several hours. Tea was brought to us between five and six, but at the meal he scarcely spoke, and sat with his back half-turned to me. At seven o'clock he left the room.

'I must prepare for my journey,' he said. 'I shall find you here for last directions just before I start.'

When he was gone I rested my face in my hands, and wondered with a palpitating heart what the Consul would do for the relief of the wretched victim whose life I was determined to save. At ten minutes to eight Dr Chance, dressed from head to foot in his warm furs, entered the cabinet.

'Good-bye, Miss Rennick,' he said. His wife accompanied him, and so did both the girls. 'You will have a couple of days' holiday while I am absent. This is Wednesday evening; I trust to be back by Saturday at farthest.'

He shook hands with me and went into the hall, accompanied by his wife and daughters. In two minutes' time Olga danced into my presence.

'Here is the key,' she said, dropping her voice. She glanced behind her. 'Madeline, how white you look – but it is all right: I called for the key, leaving Maroussa and Nurse outside. We often go to that shop to have locks repaired and altered, and no one suspects anything. Madeline, won't you tell me now what you have discovered?'

'Not yet, Olga. Olga, you have helped me much; and now, if you wish really to do more, will you and Maroussa, as you pity those in sore misery and given over unto death, offer up your prayers for what I am about to do during the next few hours?'

'I will,' said Olga, tears springing to her eyes. 'Oh, Madeline, how brave and good you are!' She flung her arms round my neck, kissed me and left the cabinet.

I went up to my room, resolving to visit the Blue laboratory between eight and nine o'clock. At nine o'clock, if all went well, the Consul would come to my aid. I had already prepared one of the servants to receive the Englishman on his arrival and to bring him to me straight to the Blue laboratory. The man said he quite understood. I slipped three roubles into his hand; his countenance became blandly agreeable, he put the money into his pocket and promised to attend faithfully to my directions. When I reached my room I glanced at the clock on my table; it pointed to five-and-twenty minutes past eight. The time had come. I hastily slipped my revolver into my pocket and, with the duplicate key also concealed about my person, ran downstairs. I did not meet a soul; I went into the cabinet, passed through the first laboratory, sped down the stone passage, and reached the door in the garden wall. Would my key open it? Yes, the lock yielded smoothly and easily to the touch of the duplicate key. I swung the door back and did not even trouble to shut it. I felt no fear whatever now. Dr Chance was miles away by this time. I switched on the electric light and walked across the room. My difficulties were, however, by no means over. It was one thing to have entered the laboratory, but it was quite another to go down into that dim dungeon where the victim was incarcerated. His face had peered at me through the glass dome, but how was that dome opened? By what means was the dungeon reached? I carefully examined the floor, and quickly perceived a trap-door concealed by a mat. In the centre of this door was a ring. I tugged at it with all my might and main; the door gave way. I saw that it was shut down by a spring and was only capable of being opened from the top. The moment I opened the door I saw steps underneath. I had provided myself with a candle and some matches. I now lit the candle and went slowly and cautiously down the stone stairs. There were about seven or eight stairs in all. My candle gave but small light, and I was rather in despair how to act, when a button in the wall attracted my attention. Doubtless this place was also lit by electricity. I pressed the button, and lo! a small incandescent globe shone out on the wall beside me. I now saw that I was in a somewhat large underground chamber, the deep arches of its groined roof receding farther and farther away into total darkness. Not a living soul could I see. I looked around me much puzzled, and then a faint, very faint, groan fell upon my ears. I directed my steps in the direction of this sound, and I saw the dim outline of further groined arches and deeper shadows. I went on a few more steps, and then discovered the object of my search. A man, tightly bound, lay upon the floor. His eyes stared fully at me; his face was cadaverous, of that yellow hue which one has seen now and then on the face of a corpse. His hands were tied, so were his feet; he could not move an inch. His lips moved, but no sound came from them. Only the eyes could speak, and they told me volumes. I fell on my knees and touched him tenderly.

'I said I would rescue you,' I cried, 'and I have come within the time. Now, fear nothing. I shall soon manage to untie your bonds and set you free.'

The lips again moved faintly, and the eyes tried to express something negative: what I could never guess. I laid my hand on the man's brow – it was wet with perspiration. My blood began to boil. Why had I ever worked for such a demon as Dr Chance? But surely Providence had set me this task in order to rescue the miserable creature who lay at my feet? I was just about to raise the head of the wretched man when I felt a touch on my shoulder. Had the Consul already arrived? Surely it was not yet nine o'clock. The next moment I started upright as if I had been shot. Dr Chance stood before me. There was not the least surprise in his gaze, neither was there the faintest touch of anger in his small, deeply set, short-sighted eyes. He peered forward as if he would examine me closely, and then stepped back.

'Miss Rennick,' he said, 'when I began my journey, the thought came over me that it was cruel to disappoint you. I had faithfully promised to impart one of my graver – my very gravest – secrets to you tonight. After all, a gentleman's word to a lady ought to come before every other consideration. I have therefore postponed my journey. Mr servant told me that I should find you in the Blue laboratory. I came straight here. The moment I entered the room I saw that the trap-door was raised; the faint light beneath further guided my footsteps. I have found you: I am now prepared to tell you my secret.'

I did not reply, but my heart beat loud and hard in great heavy thumps which must surely have been heard; the man was a monster – his very civility was laden with omen.

'You are doubtless overpowered by my polite consideration for you,' he continued. He never once glanced at his victim. I tried to moisten my lips – I tried to say something, but not a word would escape me.

'You are anxious to know how I photograph thought. I am prepared to enlighten you. Stand here, will you?'

He came forward and pushed me into a different position. From where I now stood I could see both the victim and the devil in human shape who had tortured him.

'By means of that man who lies on the floor at your feet,' continued Dr Chance, 'I have photographed thought. He was once my secretary. I quickly perceived that his character was feeble. I used mesmerism to get him into my power. By slow degrees he became my servant, I his master. By still slower, but also sure, degrees he became my slave, and I his tyrant. He is now absolutely subjective to my will, and consequently of immense use to me. By means of that bodily frame of his I have been able to peer deeper into certain secrets of Nature than any other man of my day. Yes, Miss Rennick, I am the greatest scientist at present in existence. What are the tortures of one man in comparison with so stupendous a result? Now listen. I always knew that you were inspired with the vein of curiosity to a marked degree: you are a clever girl, and might have done well, but as you sow, you must reap. When I left you in the Blue laboratory for a short time yesterday, I did so without suspicion, but the moment I returned I guessed that you had discovered something. Your face was full of wonder, despair, incredulity, horror. I then carefully laid a trap for you. It would never do for you to know my secrets, and then to go abroad and possibly divulge them. I took you into the laboratory again in the evening; I desired my servant to announce Dr Schopenhauer; he never really came at all. I left the room, and from the passage outside watched you. I heard you cry out to that man; I saw you take an impression of the key. I determined that you should have your way. Today I kept you by my side on purpose, for I did not really require your services. I went away tonight more completely to blind you. I came back when I thought I had given you sufficient time to enter the laboratory. All has happened as I expected. Never for a single moment did you really deceive me. Now listen. I will keep my word: I will tell you my secret.

'It is a known scientific fact in physiology that in the dark the retina of some animals displays a pigment called the "visual purple". If, for instance, a frog is killed in the dark, and the eye after death is exposed to an object in the light, the image of this object becomes stamped on the retina, and can be fixed there by a solution of alum. Proceeding upon this basis, I have further discovered that by fixing my own gaze for a lengthened time on an object, and then going into a dark room and gazing at an exposed photographic plate, the object I have been looking at appears on the negative when developed. Do you follow me so far?'

I nodded. My tongue was dry, cleaving to the roof of my mouth; not a word could I utter.

'I doubt if you will understand me further,' continued Dr Chance, 'but I will try to make the matter as plain to you as I can. I have conceived on a sound scientific basis that even *thought itself* may thus be photographed. This is what really takes place. Subjective impressions of thought cause molecular changes in the cells of the brain; why, then, may these not also be capable of decomposing this "visual purple", and then giving a distinct impression on a negative when exposed sufficiently long to its influence? I have made experiments and discovered that such is the case. In dreams especially this impression becomes terribly vivid. No more fascinating problem has ever absorbed a scientist than this. Behold my victim! Ought he not to congratulate himself on suffering in so vast a cause? Night after night I fasten back his eyelids with specula, and as he sleeps his eyes are wide open, staring straight for many hours in the dark at an exposed plate. This plate is destined to receive the impressions made by his dreams. Night after night I make different experiments. These can be easily done by giving my victim certain drugs, such as cocaine, Indian hemp, opium, and others. It is well known that the action of these drugs causes vivid and extraordinary dreams. This is my secret. During the day time I am merciful. I feed my patient well; he is not likely to die, although there is a possibility that he may reach madness owing to the sufferings which I cause his nervous system. Now, would you like to see some of the developed photographs?'

I shuddered and covered my face with my hands. A short scream burst from my lips.

'Nothing more,' I cried. 'I pray and beseech of you not to say another word. You are a devil in human shape. I will not listen to any more.'

Dr Chance came close to me.

'Women are hyper-sensitive,' he said in a low tone. 'Remember you wished to know. Remember I warned you that the secret was fraught with terror, with horror to many. I had hoped that you would rise above this horror, but I see that you are distinctly human.'

'I am, and I rejoice in the fact,' I replied. A small clock standing on a bench by my side showed me that it wanted seven minutes to nine. Would the English Consul come to my rescue? All now depended on him. Dr Chance noticed the direction in which my eyes were travelling.

'You are tired of this room,' he said: 'little wonder! But remember you forced your way in against my will. Now listen to me. You know my secret. I have taken pleasure in enlightening you. I could experiment on you. You are strongly imaginative, and would make a good victim.

'No, kill me rather,' I cried, falling on my knees.

'That is what I propose to do,' said Dr Chance in a slow calm voice. 'It would interfere vastly with my experiments were you to proclaim my secret to anybody else. Women, even the best women, are not to be trusted with such an important matter. I have no intention of having the grand dream of my life destroyed by the caprice of a girl. I propose, therefore, having imparted to you my secret, to seal it for ever on your lips by death. In five minutes you will die.'

'Five minutes?' I answered. His very words braced me. In five minutes it would be nine o'clock.

'In the meantime,' continued the Doctor, 'is there anything I can do for you?'

I thought. Awful as my predicament was, I yet was able to think. If only I could gain time! I looked at the victim on the floor. His eyes were shining dimly; they were full of tears. He tried to speak. Once I saw him writhe and struggle in his bonds.

'Never mind,' I said, bending over him. 'Remember while there is life there is hope. If I can rescue you –'

'That is impossible,' interrupted Dr Chance. 'It is unkind to raise sensations which can never by any possibility be realised. How shall we employ ourselves during the remaining minutes? You have now but four minutes to live. I should recommend you during the very short time which still remains to prepare your soul to meet your Maker. What, you will not?'

'My Maker will take care of my soul,' I replied. 'I am giving up my life in the cause of the oppressed. I have no fear of death. You can do your worst.'

'You really are a most interesting character. It is a sad pity that you cannot devote your life to the science you would so vastly help. Give me your hand. I should like to walk round this dungeon with you.'

He stretched out his hand and took mine. I did not refuse to walk with him. He took me from end to end of the dismal place. The little clock sounded nine strokes in a silvery voice.

'Your time is up,' said Dr Chance; 'come!' He turned, and then walked quickly, still holding my hand, across the room. What was he going to do! Oh great God! why was not the Consul punctual? I strained my ears to listen for a sound, but none came. I was standing exactly under the dome in the glass roof. I had just put out my foot to ascend the stairs when a sudden noise startled me. Before I could move a huge bell-shaped glass with great swiftness descended completely around me, and sank into a circular groove on the stone flags at my feet. What could this mean? Dr Chance was looking at me from outside the wall of glass. He was grinning with a fiendish expression of triumph. I shouted to him – he took not the slightest notice; he turned round and pressed a lever beside the wall. There was a sudden loud thumping as of a piston working to and fro, and a valve at my feet opened and shut rapidly with a hissing sound. The truth flashed across me in a moment. I was under the receiver of an enormous exhaust pump, which had fitted into the dome above my head. Dr Chance had told me that the dome was used for causing a vacuum. In a vacuum I knew no one could live. I gasped for breath and screamed to him for mercy, but the piston thumped on and on quicker and quicker. Frantic with terror, I dashed madly against the glass and tried with all my puny strength to burst it. It was very thick, and defied all my efforts. My eyes seemed to start from my head, my whole body seemed to be swelling. I fought for my breath madly. Suddenly there was a noise like the rushing of waters in my ears, my brain reeled and I fell. During the agonies of my death struggles I could just catch sight of the fiendish face of my master peering in at me. It was the face of a devil. What providential inspiration came to my aid at that last extreme moment I know not, but suddenly I remembered my revolver; with my last remaining strength I drew it from my pocket, and, pointing it upwards, pressed the trigger. There was a terrific crash of falling glass, a sudden in-rush of air, and I became unconscious.

When I came to myself a strange face was bending over me, and a kind hand was wiping something warm from my face, which doubtless was bleeding from the glass that had fallen upon it. I promptly guessed that the Consul had arrived, and that I was saved. I opened my eyes and caught sight of the face and figure of Dr Chance. Handcuffs encircled his wrists, a man in the dress of the police officers of St Petersburg was standing close to him; I further saw a shadowy figure – doubtless that of the victim whom I had come to rescue; he was supported by two other men.

'Don't speak, rest quiet; all your sufferings are over,' said the kind voice which I afterwards knew to be that of the English Consul. Then I passed into deep oblivion, and it was many days before I remembered anything more. It may have been a fortnight later when I came to myself in a pleasant bedroom in the Consul's house. His wife was bending over me. She told me in a few words what had occurred. The victim of Dr Chance's cruelty had been sent to the hospital, and was rapidly getting better. Dr Chance himself was imprisoned, and would doubtless be sent to Siberia for his crimes.

The whole place was talking of what I had done, of the horror which had been discovered in the Blue laboratory.

'Your letter came just in time,' said Mrs Seymour. 'My husband acted on it immediately; he went to see the Ambassador, who gave him a note to the Prefect of Police. But how did it come into your head to act so promptly, so bravely?'

Tears filled my eyes. I was too weak to reply.

I am now back again in England! I have not seen Olga and Maroussa again. I wonder what will become of them, what their future history will be? For myself, I can never return to St Petersburg.

Mary Shelley

THE MORTAL IMMORTAL

Mary Shelley (1797–1851) was the daughter of a remarkable couple, the noted philosopher and theoretical anarchist William Godwin and the early feminist Mary Wollstonecraft. Mary's mother died soon after her birth, and so Mary was raised by her father who imbued her with his radical ideas and independent thinking. It led to a strong-willed girl who often ignored the conventions of society. Her affair with the married poet Percy Bysshe Shelley when she was only sixteen was in itself a scandal, to which came the added complications of two children. Matters were made worse with the suicide of Shelley's wife in 1816, after which Mary and Percy married. They had two more children, but only one of their four offspring survived into adulthood. Percy drowned in 1822, and Mary never married again, although she had several offers.

Mary Shelley's Frankenstein *has been recognized by many authorities as the first genuine work of science fiction. But it was not her only scientific romance. Among her later novels is* The Last Man *(1826), in which a plague wipes out civilization, while among her contributions to the literary annals is this story, 'The Mortal Immortal' (1834). Both these works reveal her continued yearning for the now lost companionship with Shelley and friends, but both also show that she was aware that growth in scientific learning would bring as much peril as pleasure. This story also owes something to her father's novel,* St Leon *(1799), in which the protagonist likewise learns of the dangers of living too long.*

The Mortal Immortal

July 16, 1833. – This is a memorable anniversary for me; on it I complete my three hundred and twenty-third year!

The Wandering Jew? – certainly not. More than eighteen centuries have passed over his head. In comparison with him, I am a very young Immortal.

Am I, then, immortal? This is a question which I have asked myself, by day and night, for now three hundred and three years, and yet cannot answer it. I detected a grey hair amidst my brown locks this very day – that surely signifies decay. Yet it may have remained concealed there for three hundred years – for some persons have become entirely white-headed before twenty years of age.

I will tell my story, and my reader shall judge for me. I will tell my story, and so contrive to pass some few hours of a long eternity, become so wearisome to me. For ever! Can it be? To live for ever! I have heard of enchantments, in which the victims were plunged into a deep sleep, to wake, after a hundred years, as fresh as ever; I have heard of the Seven Sleepers – thus to be immortal would not be so burthensome: but, oh! the weight of never-ending time – the tedious passage of the still-succeeding hours! How happy was the fabled Nourjahad! But to my task.

All the world has heard of Cornelius Agrippa. His memory is as immortal as his arts have made me. All the world has also heard of his scholar, who, unawares, raised the foul fiend during his master's absence, and was destroyed by him. The report, true or false, of this accident, was attended with many inconveniences to the renowned philosopher. All his scholars at once deserted him – his servants disappeared. He had no one near him to put coals on his ever-burning fires while he slept, or to attend to the changeful colours of his medicines while he studied. Experiment after experiment failed, because one pair of hands was insufficient to complete them: the dark spirits laughed at him for not being able to retain a single mortal in his service.

I was then very young – very poor – and very much in love. I had been for about a year the pupil of Cornelius, though I was absent when this accident took place. On my return, my friends implored me not to return to the alchymist's abode. I trembled as I listened to the dire tale they told; I required no second warning; and when Cornelius came and offered me a purse of gold if I would remain under his roof, I felt as if Satan himself tempted me. My teeth chattered – my hair stood on end; I ran off as fast as my trembling knees would permit.

My failing steps were directed whither for two years they had every evening been attracted, – a gently bubbling spring of pure living water, beside which lingered a dark-haired girl, whose beaming eyes were fixed on the path I was accustomed each night to tread. I cannot remember the hour when I did not love Bertha. We had been neighbours and playmates from infancy, – her parents, like mine were of humble life, yet respectable – our attachment had been a source of pleasure to them. In an evil hour, a malignant fever carried off both her father and mother, and Bertha became an orphan. She would have found a home beneath my paternal roof, but, unfortunately, the old lady of the near castle, rich, childless, and solitary, declared her intention to adopt her. Henceforth Bertha was clad in silk – inhabited a marble palace – and was looked on as being highly favoured by fortune. But in her new situation among her new associates, Bertha remained true to the friend of her humbler days; she often visited the cottage of my father, and when forbidden to go thither, she would stray towards the neighbouring wood, and meet me beside its shady fountain.

She often declared that she owed no duty to her new protectress equal in sanctity to that which bound us. Yet still I was too poor to marry, and she grew weary of being tormented on my account. She had a haughty but an impatient spirit, and grew angry at the obstacle that prevented our union. We met now after an absence, and she had been sorely beset while I was away; she complained bitterly, and almost reproached me for being poor. I replied hastily, 'I am honest, if I am poor! – were I not, I might soon become rich!'

This exclamation produced a thousand questions. I feared to shock her by owning the truth, but she drew it from me; and then, casting a look of disdain on me, she said, 'You pretend to love, and you fear to face the Devil for my sake!'

I protested that I had only dreaded to offend her; while she dwelt on the magnitude of the reward that I should receive. Thus encouraged – shamed by her – led on by love and hope, laughing at my later fears, with quick steps and a light heart, I returned to accept the offers of the alchymist, and was instantly installed in my office.

A year passed away. I became possessed of no insignificant sum of money. Custom had banished my fears. In spite of the most painful vigilance, I had never detected the trace of a cloven foot; nor was the studious silence of our abode ever disturbed by demoniac howls. I still continued my stolen interviews with Bertha, and Hope dawned on me – Hope – but not perfect joy: for Bertha fancied that love and security were enemies, and her pleasure was to divide them in my bosom. Though true of heart, she was something of a coquette in manner; I was jealous as a Turk. She slighted me in a thousand ways, yet would never acknowledge herself to be in the wrong. She would drive me mad with anger, and then force me to beg her pardon. Sometimes she fancied that I was not sufficiently submissive, and then she had some story of a rival, favoured by her protectress. She was surrounded by silk-clad youths – the rich and gay. What chance had the sad-robed scholar of Cornelius compared with these?

On one occasion, the philosopher made such large demands upon my time, that I was unable to meet her as I was wont. He was engaged in some mighty work, and I was forced to remain, day and night, feeding his furnaces and watching his chemical preparations. Bertha waited for me in vain at the fountain. Her haughty spirit fired at this neglect; and when at last I stole out during a few short minutes allotted to me for slumber, and hoped to be consoled by her, she received me with disdain, dismissed me in scorn, and vowed that any man should possess her hand rather than he who could not be in two places at once for her sake. She would be revenged! And truly she was. In my dingy retreat I heard that she had been hunting, attended by Albert Hoffer. Albert Hoffer was favoured by her protectress, and the three passed in cavalcade before my smoky window. Methought that they mentioned my name; it was followed by a laugh of derision, as her dark eyes glanced contemptuously towards my abode.

Jealousy, with all its venom and all its misery, entered my breast. Now I shed a torrent of tears, to think that I should never call her mine; and, anon, I imprecated a thousand curses on her inconstancy. Yet, still I must stir the fires of the alchymist, still attend on the changes of his unintelligible medicines.

Cornelius had watched for three days and nights, nor closed his eyes. The progress of his alembics was slower than he expected: in spite of his anxiety sleep weighted upon his eyelids. Again and again he threw off drowsiness with more than human energy; again and again it stole away his senses. He eyed his crucibles wistfully. 'Not ready yet,' he murmured; 'will another night pass before the work is accomplished? Winzy, you are vigilant – you are faithful – you have slept, my boy – you slept last night. Look at that glass vessel. The liquid it contains is of a soft rose-colour: the moment it begins to change hue, awaken me – till then I may close my eyes. First, it will turn white, and then emit golden flashes; but wait not till then; when the rose-colour fades, rouse me.' I scarcely heard the last words, muttered, as they were, in sleep. Even then he did not quite yield to nature. 'Winzy, my boy,' he again said, 'do not touch the vessel – do not put it to your lips; it is a philtre – a philtre to cure love; you would not cease to love your Bertha – beware to drink!'

And he slept. His venerable head sunk on his breast, and I scarce heard his regular breathing. For a few minutes I watched the vessel – the rosy hue of the liquid remained unchanged. Then my thoughts wandered – they visited the fountain, and dwelt on a thousand charming scenes never to be renewed – never! Serpents and adders were in my heart as the word 'Never!' half formed itself on my lips. False girl! False and cruel! Never more would she smile on me as that evening she smiled on Albert. Worthless, detested woman! I would not remain unrevenged – she should see Albert expire at her feet – she should die beneath my vengeance. She had smiled in disdain and triumph – she knew my wretchedness and her power. Yet what power had she? The power of exciting my hate – my utter scorn – my – oh, all but indifference! Could I attain that – could I regard her with careless eyes, transferring my rejected love to one fairer and more true, that were indeed a victory!

A bright flash darted before my eyes. I had forgotten the medicine of the adept; I gazed on it with wonder: flashes of admirable beauty, more bright than those which the diamond emits when the sun's rays are on it, glanced from the surface of the liquid; and odour the most fragrant and grateful stole over my sense; the vessel seemed one globe of living radiance, lovely to the eye, and most inviting to the taste. The first thought, instinctively inspired by the grosser sense, was, I will – I must drink. I raised the vessel to my lips. 'It will cure me of love – of torture!' Already I had quaffed half of the most delicious liquor ever tasted by the palate of man, when the philosopher stirred. I started – I dropped the glass – the fluid flamed and glanced along the floor, while I felt Cornelius's gripe at my throat, as he shrieked aloud, 'Wretch! you have destroyed the labour of my life!'

The philosopher was totally unaware that I had drunk any portion of his drug. His idea was, and I gave a tacit assent to it, that I had raised the vessel from curiosity, and that, frightened at its brightness and the flashes of intense light it gave forth, I had let it fall. I never undeceived him. The fire of the medicine was quenched – the fragrance died away – he grew calm, as a philosopher should under the heaviest trials, and dismissed me to rest.

I will not attempt to describe the sleep of glory and bliss which bathed my soul in paradise during the remaining hours of that memorable night. Words would be faint and shallow types of my enjoyment, or of the gladness that possessed my bosom when I woke. I trod air – my thoughts were in heaven. Earth appeared heaven, and my inheritance upon it was to be one trance of delight. 'This it is to be cured of love,' I thought; 'I will see Bertha this day, and she will find her lover cold and regardless; too happy to be disdainful, yet how utterly indifferent to her!'

The hours danced away. The philosopher, secure that he had once succeeded, and believing that he might again, began to concoct the same medicine once more. He was shut up with his books and drugs, and I had a holiday. I dressed myself with care; I looked in an old but polished shield which served me for a mirror; methought my good looks had wonderfully improved. I hurried beyond the precincts of the town, joy in my soul, the beauty of heaven and earth around me. I turned my steps towards the castle – I could look on its lofty turrets with lightness of heart, for I was cured of love. My Bertha saw me afar off, as I came up the avenue. I know not what sudden impulse animated her bosom, but at the sight she sprung with a light fawn-like bound down the marble steps, and was hastening towards me. But I had been perceived by another person. The old high-born hag, who called herself her protectress, and was her tyrant, had seen me also; she hobbled, panting, up the terrace; a page, as ugly as herself, held up her train, and fanned her as she hurried along, and stopped my fair girl with a 'How, now, my bold mistress? Whither so fast? Back to your cage – hawks are abroad!'

Bertha clasped her hands – her eyes were still bent on my approaching figure. I saw the contest. How I abhorred the old crone who checked the kind impulses of my Bertha's softening heart. Hitherto, respect for her rank had caused me to avoid the lady of the castle; now I disdained such trivial considerations. I was cured of love, and lifted above all human fears; I hastened forwards, and soon reached the terrace. How lovely Bertha looked! Her eyes flashing fire, her cheeks glowing with impatience and anger, she was a thousand times more graceful and charming than ever. I no longer loved – oh no! I adored – worshipped – idolized her!

She had that morning been persecuted, with more than usual vehemence, to consent to an immediate marriage with my rival. She was reproached with the encouragement that she had shown him – she was threatened with being turned out of doors with disgrace and shame. Her proud spirit rose in arms at the threat; but when she remembered the scorn that she had heaped upon me, and how, perhaps, she had thus lost one whom she now regarded as her only friend, she wept with remorse and rage. At that moment I appeared. 'Oh, Winzy!' she exclaimed, 'take me to your mother's cot; swiftly let me leave the detested luxuries and wretchedness of this noble dwelling – take me to poverty and happiness.'

I clasped her in my arms with transport. The old dame was speechless with fury, and broke forth into invective only when we were far on the road to my natal cottage. My mother received the fair fugitive, escaped from a gilt cage to nature and liberty, with tenderness and joy; my father, who loved her, welcomed her heartily; it was a day of rejoicing, which did not need the addition of the celestial potion of the alchymist to steep me in delight.

Soon after this eventful day, I became the husband of Bertha. I ceased to be the scholar of Cornelius, but I continued to be his friend. I always felt grateful to him for having, unaware, procured me that delicious draught of a divine elixir, which, instead of curing me of love (sad cure! solitary and joyless remedy for evils which seem blessings to the memory), had inspired me with courage and resolution, thus winning for me an inestimable treasure in my Bertha.

I often called to mind that period of trance-like inebriation with wonder. The drink of Cornelius had not fulfilled the task for which he affirmed that it had been prepared, but its effects were more potent and blissful than words can express. They had faded by degrees, yet they lingered long – and painted life in hues of splendour. Bertha often wondered at my lightness of heart and unaccustomed gaiety; for, before, I had been rather serious, or even sad, in my disposition. She loved me the better for my cheerful temper, and our days were winged by joy.

Five years afterwards I was suddenly summoned to the bedside of the dying Cornelius. He had sent for me in haste, conjuring my instant presence. I found him stretched on his pallet, enfeebled even to death; all of life that yet remained animated his piercing eyes, and they were fixed on a glass vessel, full of roseate liquid.

'Behold,' he said, in a broken and inward voice, 'the vanity of human wishes! A second time my hopes are about to be crowned, a second time they are destroyed. Look at that liquor – you may remember five years ago I had prepared the same, with the same success; – then, as now, my thirsting lips expected to taste the immortal elixir – you dashed it from me! And at present it is too late.'

He spoke with difficulty, and fell back on his pillow. I could not help saying, 'How, revered master, can a cure for love restore you to life?'

A faint smile gleamed across his face as I listened earnestly to his scarcely intelligible answer.

'A cure for love and for all things – the Elixir of Immortality. Ah! if now I might drink, I should live for ever!'

As he spoke, a golden flash gleamed from the fluid; a well-remembered fragrance stole over the air; he raised himself, all weak as he was – strength seemed miraculously to re-enter his frame – he stretched forth his hand – a loud explosion startled me – a ray of fire shot up from the elixir, and the glass vessel which contained it was shivered to atoms! I turned my eyes towards the philosopher; he had fallen back – his eyes were glassy – his features rigid – he was dead!

But I lived, and was to live for ever! So said the unfortunate alchymist, and for a few days I believed his words. I remembered the glorious intoxication that had followed my stolen draught. I reflected on the change I had felt in my frame – in my soul. The bounding elasticity of the one, the buoyant lightness of the other. I surveyed myself in a mirror, and could perceive no change in my features during the space of the five years which had elapsed. I remembered the radiant hues and grateful scent of that delicious beverage – worthy the gift it was capable of bestowing – I was, then, IMMORTAL!

A few days after I laughed at my credulity. The old proverb, that 'a prophet is least regarded in his own country', was true with respect to me and my defunct master. I loved him as a man – I respected him as a sage – but I derided the notion that he could command the powers of darkness, and laughed at the superstitious fears with which he was regarded by the vulgar. He was a wise philosopher, but had no acquaintance with any spirits but those clad in flesh and blood. His science was simply human; and human science, I soon persuaded myself, could never conquer nature's laws so far as to imprison the soul for ever within its carnal habitation. Cornelius had brewed a soul-refreshing drink – more inebriating than wine – sweeter and more fragrant than any fruit: it possessed probably strong medicinal powers, imparting gladness to the heart and vigour to the limbs; but its effects would wear out; already they were diminished in my frame. I was a lucky fellow to have quaffed health and joyous spirits, and perhaps a long life, at my master's hands; but my good fortune ended there: longevity was far different from immortality.

I continued to entertain this belief for many years. Sometimes a thought stole across me – Was the alchymist indeed deceived? But my habitual credence was that I should meet the fate of all the children of Adam at my appointed time – a little late, but still at a natural age. Yet it was certain that I retained a wonderfully youthful look. I was laughed at for my vanity in consulting the mirror so often, but I consulted it in vain – my brow was untrenched – my cheeks – my eyes – my whole person continued as untarnished as in my twentieth year.

I was troubled. I looked at the faded beauty of Bertha – I seemed more like her son. By degrees our neighbours began to make similar observations, and I found at last that I went by the name of the Scholar Bewitched. Bertha herself grew uneasy. She became jealous and peevish, and at length she began to question me. We had no children; we were all in all to each other; and though, as she grew older, her vivacious spirit became a little allied to ill-temper, and her beauty sadly diminished, I cherished her in my heart as the mistress I idolized, the wife I had sought and won with such perfect love.

At last our situation became intolerable: Bertha was fifty –

I twenty years of age. I had, in very shame, in some measure adopted the habits of advanced age; I no longer mingled in the dance among the young and gay, but my heart bounded along with them while I restrained my feet; and a sorry figure I cut among the Nestors of our village. But before the time I mention, things were altered – we were universally shunned; we were – at least, I was – reported to have kept up an iniquitous acquaintance with some of my former master's supposed friends. Poor Bertha was pitied, but deserted. I was regarded with horror and detestation.

What was to be done? We sat by our winter fire – poverty had made itself felt, for none would buy the produce of my farm; and often I had been forced to journey twenty miles to some place where I was not known, to dispose of our property. It is true we had saved something for an evil day – that day was come.

We sat by our lone fireside – the old-hearted youth and his anti-quated wife. Again Bertha insisted on knowing the truth; she recapitulated all she had ever heard said about me, and added her own observations. She conjured me to cast off the spell; she described how much more comely grey hairs were than my chestnut locks; she descanted on the reverence and respect due to age – how preferable to the slight regard paid to mere children: could I imagine that the despicable gifts of youth and good looks out-weighed disgrace, hatred and scorn? Nay, in the end I should be burnt as a dealer in the black art, while she, to whom I had not deigned to communicate any portion of my good fortune, might be stoned as my accomplice. At length she insinuated that I must share my secret with her, and bestow on her like benefits to those I myself enjoyed, or she would denounce me – and then she burst into tears.

Thus beset, methought it was the best way to tell the truth. I revelled it as tenderly as I could, and spoke only of a *very long life*, not of immortality – which representation, indeed, coincided best with my own ideas. When I ended I rose and said, 'And now, my Bertha, will you denounce the lover of your youth? You will not, I know. But it is too hard, my poor wife, that you should suffer for my ill-luck and the accursed arts of Cornelius. I will leave you – you have wealth enough, and friends will return in my absence. I will go; young as I seem and strong as I am, I can work and gain my bread among strangers, unsuspected and unknown. I loved you in youth; God is my witness that I would not desert you in age, but that your safety and happiness require it.'

I took my cap and moved towards the door; in a moment Bertha's arms were round my neck, and her lips were pressed to mine. 'No, my husband, my Winzy,' she said, 'you shall not go alone – take me with you; we will remove from this place, and, as you say, among strangers we shall be unsuspected and safe. I am not so old as quite to shame you, my Winzy; and I daresay the charm will soon wear off, and, with the blessing of God, you will become more elderly-looking, as is fitting; you shall not leave me.'

I returned the good soul's embrace heartily. 'I will not, my Bertha; but for your sake I had not thought of such a thing. I will be your true, faithful husband while you are spared to me, and do my duty by you to the last.'

The next day we prepared secretly for our emigration. We were obliged to make great pecuniary sacrifices – it could not be helped. We realized a sum sufficient, at least, to maintain us while Bertha lived; and, without saying adieu to any one, quitted our native country to take refuge in a remote part of western France.

It was a cruel thing to transport poor Bertha from her native village, and the friends of her youth, to a new country, new language, new customs. The strange secret of my destiny rendered this removal immaterial to me; but I compassionated her deeply, and was glad to perceive that she found compensation for her misfortunes in a variety of little ridiculous circumstances. Away from all tell-tale chroniclers, she sought to decrease the apparent disparity of our ages by a thousand feminine arts – rouge, youthful dress, and assumed juvenility of manner. I could not be angry. Did I not myself wear a mask? Why quarrel with hers, because it was less successful? I grieved deeply when I remembered that this was my Bertha, whom I had loved so fondly and won with such transport – the dark-eyed, dark-haired girl, with smiles of enchanting archness and a step like a fawn – this mincing, simpering, jealous old woman. I should have revered her grey locks and withered cheeks; but thus! It was my work, I knew; but I did not the less deplore this type of human weakness.

Her jealousy never slept. Her chief occupation was to discover that, in spite of outward appearances, I was myself growing old. I verily believe that the poor soul loved me truly in her heart, but never had woman so tormenting a mode of displaying fondness. She would discern wrinkles in my face and decrepitude in my walk, while I bounded along in youthful vigour, the youngest looking of twenty youths. I never dared address another woman. On one occasion, fancying that the belle of the village regarded me with favouring eyes, she brought me a grey wig. Her constant discourse among her acquaintances was, that though I looked so young, there was ruin at work within my frame; and she affirmed that the worst symptom about me was my apparent health. My youth was a disease, she said, and I ought at all times to prepare, if not for a sudden and awful death, at least to awake some morning white-headed and bowed down with all the marks of advanced years. I let her talk – I often joined in her conjectures. Her warnings chimed in with my never-ceasing speculations concerning my state, and I took an earnest, though painful, interest in listening to all that her quick wit and excited imagination could say on the subject.

Why dwell on these minute circumstances? We lived on for many long years. Bertha became bedrid and paralytic; I nursed her as a mother might a child. She grew peevish, and still harped upon one string – of how long I should survive her. It has ever been a source of consolation to me, that I performed my duty scrupulously towards her. She had been mine in youth, she was mine in age; and at last, when I heaped the sod over her corpse, I wept to feel that I had lost all that really bound me to humanity.

Since then how many have been my cares and woes, how few and empty my enjoyments! I pause here in my history – I will pursue it no further. A sailor without rudder or compass, tossed on a stormy sea – a traveller lost on a widespread heath, without landmark or stone to guide him – such I have been: more lost, more hopeless than either. A nearing ship, a gleam from some far cot, may save them; but I have no beacon except the hope of death.

Death! mysterious, ill-visaged friend of weak humanity! Why alone of all mortals have you cast me from your sheltering fold? Oh, for the peace of the grave! The deep silence of the iron-bound tomb! That thought would cease to work in my brain, and my heart beat no more with emotions varied only by new forms of sadness!

Am I immortal? I return to my first question. In the first place, is it not more probably that the beverage of the alchymist was fraught rather with longevity than eternal life? Such is my hope. And then be it remembered, that I only drank *half* of the potion prepared by him. Was not the whole necessary to complete the charm? To have drained half the Elixir of Immortality is but to be half-immortal – my For-ever is thus truncated and null.

But again, who shall number the years of the half of eternity? I often try to imagine by what rule the infinite may be divided. Sometimes I fancy age advancing upon me. One grey hair I have found. Fool! Do I lament? Yes, the fear of age and death often creeps coldly into my heart; and the more I live, the more I dread death, even while I abhor life. Such an enigma is man – born to perish – when he wars, as I do, against the established laws of his nature.

But for this anomaly of feeling surely I might die: the medicine of the alchymist would not be proof against fire, sword and the strangling waters. I have gazed upon the blue depths of many a placid lake, and the tumultuous rushing of many a mighty river, and have said, 'peace inhabits those waters'; yet I have turned my steps away, to live yet another day. I have asked myself, whether suicide would be a crime in one to whom thus only the portals of the other world could be opened. I have done all, except presenting myself as a soldier or duellist, an object of destruction to my – no, *not* my fellow mortals, and therefore I have shrunk away. They are not my fellows. The inextinguishable power of life in my frame, and their ephemeral existence, places us wide as the poles asunder. I could not raise a hand against the meanest or the most powerful among them.

Thus have I lived on for many a year – alone, and weary of myself – desirous of death, yet never dying – a mortal immortal. Neither ambition nor avarice can enter my mind, and the ardent love that gnaws at my heart, never to be returned – never to find an equal on which to expend itself – lives there only to torment me.

This very day I conceived a design by which I may end all – without self-slaughter, without making another man a Cain – an expedition, which mortal frame can never survive, even endued with the youth and strength that inhabits mine. Thus I shall put my immortality to the test, and rest for ever – or return, the wonder and benefactor of the human species.

Before I go, a miserable vanity has caused me to pen these pages. I would not die, and leave no name behind. Three centuries have passed since I quaffed the fatal beverage; another year shall not elapse before, encountering gigantic dangers – warring with the powers of frost in their home – beset by famine, toil, and tempest – I yield this body, too tenacious a cage for a soul which thirsts for freedom, to the destructive elements of air and water; or, if I survive, my name shall be recorded as one of the most famous among the sons of men; and, my task achieved, I shall adopt more resolute means, and, by scattering and annihilating the atoms that compose my frame, set at liberty the life imprisoned within, and so cruelly prevented from soaring from this dim earth to a sphere more congenial to its immortal essence.

Harriet Prescott Spofford

THE MOONSTONE MASS

Harriet Elizabeth Prescott (1835–1921), as she was before her marriage in 1865, was one of those many gifted New England writers who produced a wealth of regional and supernatural fiction. Prescott showed much literary promise in her youth, but early illness and frailty in her parents meant that she had to work long hours to support the family – she was the eldest of five surviving children – and her work suffered accordingly. There were moments of glory. 'The Amber Gods' (1860) was regarded as 'one of the most powerful stories in the English language' in its day, and it became the title story of her first collection, published in 1863, which remains her best-known book. But she published much else besides, including this story, which Jessica Salmonson called 'the greatest of all her weird tales' when she compiled a selection of the best in The Moonstone Mass and Others *(2000).*

It is a weird tale, but I also classify it as a scientific romance, as it is a story of exploration into unknown territory, which is fundamental to most science fiction. The story was published in 1868 when there was considerable interest in opening up the North-West Passage through the Arctic Ocean across northern Canada between the Atlantic and the Pacific. The ill-fated expedition led by John Franklin in 1845 had been back in the news in 1854 when the explorer John Rae learned of their fate, and it was Rae who identified the last link in the maze of channels through the islands that would become the North-West Passage – although it was not until 1906 that Roald Amundsen actually made the journey successfully by sea. Harriet Spofford was therefore still free to speculate just what might await explorers in the Frozen North.

The Moonstone Mass

THERE WAS A certain weakness possessed by my ancestors, though in nowise peculiar to them, and of which, in common with other more or less undesirable traits, I have come into the inheritance.

It was the fear of dying in poverty. That, too, in the face of a goodly share of pelf stored in stocks, and lands, and copper-bottomed clippers, or what stood for copper-bottomed clippers, or rather sailed for them, in the clumsy commerce of their times.

There was one old fellow in particular – his portrait is hanging over the hall stove today, leaning forward, somewhat blistered by the profuse heat and wasted fuel there, and as if as long as such an outrageous expenditure of caloric was going on he meant to have the full benefit of it – who is said to have frequently shed tears over the probable price of his dinner, and on the next day to have sent home a silver dish to eat it from at a hundred times the cost. I find the inconsistencies of this individual constantly cropping out in myself; and although I could by no possibility be called a niggard, yet I confess that even now my prodigalities make me shiver.

Some years ago I was the proprietor of the old family estate, unencumbered by anything except timber, that is worth its weight in gold; yet, as you might say, alone in the world, save for an unloved relative; and with a sufficiently comfortable income, as I have since discovered, to meet all reasonable wants. I had, moreover, promised me in marriage the hand of a woman without a peer, and which, I believe now, might have been mine on any day when I saw fit to claim it.

That I loved Eleanor tenderly and truly you cannot doubt; that I desired to bring her home, to see her flitting here and there in my dark old house, illuminating it with her youth and beauty, sitting at the head of my table that sparkled with its gold and silver heirlooms, making my days and nights like one delightful dream, was just as true.

And yet I hesitated. I looked over my bankbook – I cast up my accounts. I have enough for one, I said; I am not sure that it is enough for two. Eleanor, daintily nurtured, requires as dainty care for all time to come; moreover, it is not two alone to be considered, for should children come, there is their education, their maintenance, their future provision and portion to be found. All this would impoverish us, and unless we ended by becoming mere dependants, we had, to my excited vision, only the cold charity of the world and the work-house to which to look forward. I do not believe that Eleanor thought me right in so much of the matter as I saw fit to explain, but in maiden pride her lips perforce were sealed. She laughed, though, when I confessed my work-house fear, and said that for her part she was thankful there was such a refuge at all, standing as it did on its knoll in the midst of green fields, and shaded by broad-limbed oaks – she had always envied the old women sitting there by their evening fireside, and mumbling over their small affairs to one another. But all her words seemed merely idle badinage – so I delayed. I said – when this ship sails in, when that dividend is declared, when I see how this speculation turns out. The days were long that added up the count of years, the nights were dreary; but I believed that I was actuated by principle, and took pride to myself for my strength and self-denial.

Moreover, old Paul, my great-uncle on my mother's side, and the millionaire of the family, was a bitter misogynist, and regarded women and marriage and household cares as the three remediless mistakes of an overruling Providence. He knew of my engagement to Eleanor, but so long as it remained in that stage he had nothing to say. Let me once marry, and my share of his million would be best represented by a cipher. However, he was not a man to adore, and he could not live for ever.

Still, with all my own effort, I amassed wealth but slowly, according to my standard. My various ventures had various luck, and one day my old Uncle Paul, always intensely interested in the subject, both scientifically and from a commercial point of view, too old and feeble to go himself, but fain to send a proxy, and desirous of money in the family, made me an offer of that portion of his wealth on my return which would be mine on his demise, funded safely subject to my order, provided I made one of those who sought the discovery of the North-West Passage.

I went to town, canvassed the matter with the experts – I had always an adventurous streak, as old Paul well knew – and having given many hours to the pursuit of the smaller sciences, had a turn for danger and discovery as well. And when the *Albatross* sailed – in spite of Eleanor's shivering remonstrance and prayers and tears, in spite of the grave looks of my friends – I was one of those that clustered on her deck, prepared for either fate. They – my companions – it is true, were led by nobler lights; but as for me, it was much as I told Eleanor – my affairs were so regulated that they would go on uninterruptedly in my absence; I should be no worse off for going, and if I returned, letting alone the renown of the thing, my Uncle Paul's donation was to be appropriated; everything then was assured, and we stood possessed of lucky lives. If I had any keen or eager desire of search, any purpose to aid the growth of the world or to penetrate the secrets of its formation, as indeed I think I must have had, I did not at that time know any thing about it. But I was to learn that death and stillness have no kingdom on this globe, and that even in the extremest bitterness of cold and ice perpetual interchange and motion is taking place. So we went, all sails set on favourable winds, bounding over blue sea, skirting frowning coasts, and ever pushing our way up into the dark mystery of the North.

I shall not delay here to tell of Danish posts and the hospitality of summer settlements in their long afternoon of Arctic daylight; nor will I weary you with any description of the succulence of the radishes that grew under the panes of glass in the Governor's scrap of moss and soil, scarcely of more size than a lady's parlour fernery, and which seemed to our dry mouths full of all the earth's cool juices – but advance, as we ourselves hastened to do, while that chill and crystalline sun shone, up into the ice-cased dens and caverns of the Pole. By the time that the long, blue twilight fell, when the rough and rasping cold sheathed all the atmosphere, and the great stars pricked themselves out on the heavens like spears' points, the *Albatross* was hauled up for winter quarters, banked and boarded, heaved high on fields of ice; and all her inmates, during the wintry dark, led the life that prepared them for further exploits in higher latitudes the coming year, learning the dialects of the Esquimaux, the tricks of the seal and walrus, making long explorations with the dogs and Glipnu, their master, breaking ourselves in for business that had no play about it.

Then, at last, the August suns set us free again; inlets of tumultuous water traversed the great ice-floes; the *Albatross*, refitted, ruffled all her plumage and spread her wings once more for the North – for the secret that sat there domineering all its substance.

It was a year since we had heard from home; but who staid to think of that while our keel spurned into foam the sheets of steely seas, and day by day brought us nearer to the hidden things we sought? For myself I confess that, now so close to the end as it seemed, curiosity and research absorbed every other faculty. Eleanor might be mouldering back to the parent earth – I could not stay to meditate on such a possibility; my Uncle Paul's donation might enrich itself with gold-dust instead of the gathered dust of idle days – it was nothing to me. I had but one thought, one ambition, one desire in those days – the discovery of the clear seas and open passage. I endured all our hardships as if they had been luxuries: I made light of scurvy, banqueted off train-oil, and met that cold for which there is no language framed, and which might be a new element; or which, rather, had seemed in that long night like the vast void of ether beyond the uttermost star, where was neither air nor light nor heat, but only bitter negation and emptiness. I was hardly conscious of my body; I was only a concentrated search in myself.

The recent explorers had announced here, in the neighbourhood of where our third summer at last found us, the existence of an immense space of clear water. One even declared that he had seen it.

My Uncle Paul had pronounced the declaration false, and the sight an impossibility. The North he believed to be the breeder of icebergs, an ever-welling fountain of cold; the great glaciers there forever form, forever fall; the ice-packs line the gorges from year to year unchanging; peaks of volcanic rock drop their frozen mantles like a scale only to display the fresher one beneath. The whole region, said he, is Plutonic, blasted by a primordial convulsion of the great forces of creation; and though it may be a few miles nearer to the central fires of the earth, allowing that there are such things, yet that would not in itself detract from the frigid power of its sunless solitudes, the more especially when it is remembered that the spinning of the earth, while in its first plastic material, which gave it greater circumference and thinness of shell at its equator, must have thickened the shell correspondingly at the poles; and the character of all the waste and wilderness there only signifies the impenetrable wall between its surface and centre, through which wall no heat could enter or escape. The great rivers, like the White and the Mackenzie, emptying to the north of the continents, so far from being enough in themselves to form any body of ever fresh and flowing water, can only pierce the opposing ice-fields in narrow streams and bays and inlets as they seek the Atlantic and the Pacific seas. And as for the theory of the currents of water heated in the tropics and carried by the rotary motion of the planet to the Pole, where they rise and melt the ice-floes into this great supposititious sea, it is simply an absurdity on the face of it, he argued, when you remember that warm water being in its nature specifically lighter than cold it would have risen to the surface long before it reached there. No, thought my Uncle Paul, who took nothing for granted; 'It is, as I said, an absurdity on the face of it; my nephew shall prove it, and I stake half the earnings of my life upon it.'

To tell the truth, I thought much the same as he did, and now that such a mere trifle of distance intervened between me and the proof, I was full of a feverish impatience that almost amounted to insanity.

We had proceeded but a few days, coasting the crushing capes of rock that everywhere seemed to run out in a diablerie of tusks and horns to drive us from the region that they warded, now cruising through a runlet of blue water just wide enough for our keel, with silver reaches of frost stretching away into a ghastly horizon, now plunging upon tossing seas, the sun wheeling round and round, and never sinking from the strange, weird sky above us, when again to our look-out a glimmer in the low horizon told its awful tale – a sort of smoky lustre like that which might ascend from an army of spirits – the fierce and fatal spirits tented on the terrible field of the ice-floe.

We were alone, our single little ship speeding ever upwards in the midst of that untravelled desolation. We spoke seldom to one another, oppressed with the sense of our situation. It was a loneliness that seemed more than a death in life, a solitude that was supernatural. Here and now it was clear water; ten hours later and we were caught in the teeth of the cold, wedged in the ice that had advanced upon us and surrounded us, fettered by another winter in latitudes where human life had never before been supported.

We found, before the hands of the dial had taught us the lapse of a week, that this would be something not to be endured. The sun sank lower every day behind the crags and silvery horns; the heavens grew to wear a hue of violet, almost black, and yet unbearably dazzling; as the notes of our voices fell upon the atmosphere they assumed a metallic tone, as if the air itself had become frozen from the beginning of the world and they tinkled against it; our sufferings had mounted in their intensity till they were too great to be resisted.

It was decided at length – when the one long day had given place to its answering night, and in the jet-black heavens the stars, like knobs of silver, sparkled so large and close upon us that we might have grasped them in our hands – that I should take a sledge with Glipnu and his dogs, and see if there were any path to the westward by which, if the *Albatross* were forsaken, those of her crew that remained might follow it, and find an escape to safety. Our path was on a frozen sea; if we discovered land we did not know that the foot of man had ever trodden it; we could hope to find no cache of snow-buried food – neither fish nor game lived in this desert of ice that was so devoid of life in any shape as to seem dead itself. But, well provisioned, furred to the eyes, and essaying to nurse some hopefulness of heart, we set out on our way through this Valley of Death, relieving one another, and travelling day and night.

Still night and day to the west rose the black coast, one interminable height; to the east extended the sheets of unbroken ice; sometimes a huge glacier hung pendulous from the precipice; once we saw, by the starlight, a white, foaming, rushing river arrested and transformed to ice in its flight down that steep. A south wind began to blow behind us; we travelled on the ice; three days, perhaps, as days are measured among men, had passed, when we found that we made double progress, for the ice travelled, too; the whole field, carried by some northward-bearing current, was afloat; it began to be crossed and cut by a thousand crevasses, the cakes, an acre each, tilted up and down, and made wide waves with their ponderous plashing in the black body of the sea; we could hear them grinding distantly in the clear dark against the coast, against each other. There was no retreat – there was no advance; we were on the ice, and the ice was breaking up.

Suddenly we rounded a tongue of the primeval rock, and recoiled before a narrow gulf – one sharp shadow, as deep as despair, as full of anguish fears. It was just wide enough for the sledge to span. Glipnu made the dogs leap; we could be no worse off if they drowned. They touched the opposite block; it careened; it went under, the sledge went with it; I was left alone where I had stood. Two dogs broke loose, and scrambled up beside me; Glipnu and the others I never saw again. I sank upon the ice; the dogs crouched beside me; sometimes I think they saved my brain from total ruin, for without them I could not have withstood the enormity of that loneliness, a loneliness that it was impossible should be broken – floating on and on with that vast journeying company of spectral ice. I had food enough to support life for several days to come, in the pouch at my belt; the dogs and I shared it – for, last as long as it would, when it should be gone there was only death before us – no reprieve –

sooner or later that; as well sooner as later – the living terrors of this icy hell were all about us, and death could be no worse.

Still the south wind blew, the rapid current carried us, the dark skies grew deep and darker, the lanes and avenues between the stars were crowded with forebodings – for the air seemed full of a new power, a strange and invisible influence, as if a king of unknown terrors here held his awful state. Sometimes the dogs stood up and growled and bristled their shaggy hides; I, prostrate on the ice, in all my frame was stung with a universal tingle. I was no longer myself. At this moment my blood seemed to sing and bubble in my veins; I grew giddy with a sort of delirious and inexplicable ecstasy; with another moment unutterable horror seized me; I was plunged and weighed down with a black and suffocating load, while evil things seemed to flap their wings in my face, to breathe in my mouth, to draw my soul out of my body and carry it careering through the frozen realm of that murky heaven, to restore it with a shock of agony.

Once as I lay there, still floating, floating northward, out of the dim dark rim of the water-world, a lance of piercing light shot up the zenith; it divided the heavens like a knife; they opened out in one blaze, and the fire fell sheetingly down before my face – cold fire, curdingly cold – light robbed of heat, and set free in a preternatural anarchy of the elements; its fringes swung to and fro before my face, pricked it with flaming spiculae, dissolving in a thousand colours that spread everywhere over the low field, flashing, flickering, creeping, reflecting, gathering again in one long serpentine line of glory that wavered in slow convolutions across the cuts and crevasses of the ice, wreathed ever nearer, and, lifting its head at last, became nothing in the darkness but two great eyes like glowing coals, with which it stared me to a stound, till I threw myself face down to hide me in the ice; and the whining, bristling dogs cowered backwards, and were dead.

I should have supposed myself to be in the region of the magnetic pole of the sphere, if I did not know that I had long since left it behind me. My pocket-compass had become entirely useless, and every scrap of metal that I had about me had become a lodestone.

The very ice, as if it were congealed from water that held large quantities of iron in solution; iron escaping from whatever solid land there was beneath or around the Plutonic rock that such a region could have alone veined and seamed with metal. The very ice appeared to have a magnetic quality; it held me so that I changed my position upon it with difficulty, and, as if it established a battery by the aid of the singular atmosphere above it, frequently sent thrills quivering through and through me till my flesh seemed about to resolve into all the jarring atoms of its original constitution; and again soothed me, with a velvet touch, into a state which, if it were not sleep, was at least haunted by visions that I dare not believe to have been realities, and from which I always awoke with a start to find myself still floating, floating.

My watch had long since ceased to beat. I felt an odd persuasion that I had died when that stood still, and only this slavery of the magnet, of the cold, this power that locked everything in invisible fetters and let nothing loose again, held my soul still in the bonds of my body. Another idea, also, took possession of me, for my mind was open to whatever visitant chose to enter, since utter despair of safety or release had left it vacant of a hope or fear. These enormous days and nights, swinging in their arc six months long, were the pendulum that dealt time in another measure than that dealt by the sunlight of lower zones; they told the time of interminable years, the years of vast generations far beyond the span that covered the age of the primeval men of Scripture – they measured time on this gigantic and enduring scale for what wonderful and mighty beings, old as the everlasting hills, as destitute as they of mortal sympathy, cold and inscrutable, handling the two-edged javelins of frost and magnetism, and served by all the unknown polar agencies. I fancied that I saw their far-reaching cohorts, marshalling and manoeuvring at times in the field of an horizon that was boundless, the glitter of their spears and casques, the sheen of their white banners; and again, sitting in fearful circle with their phantasmagoria, they shut and hemmed me in and watched me writhe like a worm before them.

I had a fancy that the perpetual play of magnetic impulses here gradually disintegrated the expanse of ice, as sunbeams might have done. If it succeeded in unseating me from my cold station I should drown, and there would be an end of me; it would be all one; for though I clung to life I did not cling to suffering. Something of the wild beast seemed to spring up in my nature; that ignorance of any moment but the present. I felt a certain kinship to the bear in her comfortable snowiness whom I had left in the parallels far below this unreal tract of horrors. I remembered traditions of such metempsychoses; the thought gave me a pang that none of these fierce and subtle elements had known how to give before. But all the time my groaning, cracking ice was moving with me, splitting now through all its leagues of length along the darkness, with an explosion like a cannon's shot, that echoed again and again in every gap and chasm of its depth, and seemed to be caught up and repeated by a thousand airy sprites, and snatched on from one to another till it fell dead through the frozen thickness of the air.

It was at about this time that I noticed another species of motion than that which had hitherto governed it seizing this journeying ice. It bent and bent, as a glacier does in its viscous flow between mountains; it crowded, and loosened, and rent apart, and at last it broke in every direction, and every fragment was crushed and jammed together again; and the whole mass was following, as I divined, the curve of some enormous whirlpool that swept it from beneath. It might have been a day and night, it might have been an hour, that we travelled on this vast curve – I had no more means of knowing than if I had veritably done with time. We were one expanse of shadow; not a star above us, only a sky of impenetrable gloom received the shimmering that now and again the circling ice cast off. It was a strange slow motion, yet with such a steadiness and strength about it that it had the effect of swiftness. It was long since any water, or the suspicion of any, had been visible; we might have been grinding through some gigantic hollow for all I could have told; snow had never fallen here; the mass moved you knew as if you felt the prodigious hand that grasped and impelled it from beneath. Whither was it tending, in the eddy of what huge stream that went,

with the smoke of its fall hovering on the brink, to plunge a tremendous cataract over the limits of the earth into the unknown abyss of
space? Far in advance there was a faint glimmering, a sort of powdery
light glancing here and there. As we approached it – the ice and I –
it grew fainter, and was, by-and-by, lost in a vast twilight that surrounded us on all sides; at the same time it became evident that we
had passed under a roof, an immense and vaulted roof. As crowding, stretching, rending, we passed on, uncanny gleams were playing
distantly above us and around us, now and then overlaying all
things with a sheeted illumination as deathly as a grave-light, now
and then shooting up in spires of blood-red radiance that disclosed
the terrible aurora. I was in a cavern of ice, as wide and as high as
the heavens; these flashes of glory, alternated with equal flashes of
darkness, as you might say, taught me to perceive. Perhaps tremendous tide after tide had hollowed it with all its fantastic recesses; or
had that Titanic race of the interminable years built it as a palace
for their monarch, a temple for their deity, with its domes that
sprung far up immeasurable heights and hung palely shining like
mock heavens of hazy stars, its aisles that stretched away down
colonnades of crystal columns into unguessed darkness, its high-
heaved arches, its pierced and open sides? Now an aurora burned
up like a blue light, and went skimming under all the vaults far off
into far and farther hollows, revealing, as it went, still loftier heights
and colder answering radiances. Then these great arches glowed
like blocks of beryl. Wondrous tracery of delicate vines and leaves,
greener than the greenest moss, wandered over them, wreathed the
great pillars, and spread round them in capitals of flowers: roses
crimson as a carbuncle; hyacinths like bedded cubes of amethyst;
violets bluer than sapphires – all as if the flowers had been turned
to flame, yet all so cruelly cold, as if the power that wrought such
wonders could simulate a sparkle beyond even the lustre of light, but
could not give it heat, that principle of life, that fountain of first
being. Yonder a stalactite of clustered ruby – that kept the aurora
and glinted faintly, and more faintly, till the thing came again, when
it grasped a whole body-full of splendour – hung downwards and

dropped a thread-like stem and a blossom of palest pink, like a transfigured Linnaea, to meet the snow-drop in its sheath of green that shot up from a spire of aquamarine below. Here living rainbows flew from buttress to buttress and frolicked in the domes – the only things that dared to live and sport where beauty was frozen into horror. It seemed as if that shifting death-light of the aurora photographed all these things upon my memory, for I noted none of them at the time, I only wondered idly whither we were tending as we drove in deeper and deeper under that ice-roof, and curved more and more, circling upon our course while the silent flashes sped on overhead. Now we were in the dark again crashing onwards; now a cold blue radiance burst from every icicle, from every crevice, and I saw that the whole enormous mass of our motion bent and swept around a single point – a dark yet glittering form that sat as if upon the apex of the world. Was it one of those mightier than the Anakim, more than the sons of God, to whom all the currents of this frozen world converged? Sooth I know not – for presently I imagined that my vision made only an exaggeration of some brown Esquimau sealed up and left in his snow-house to die. A thin sheathing of ice appeared to clothe him and give the glister to his duskiness. Insensible as I had thought myself to any further fear, I cowered beneath the stare of those dead and icy eyes. Slowly we rounded, and ever rounded; the inside, on which my place was, moving less slowly than the outer circle of the sheeted mass in its viscid flow; and as we moved, by some fate my eye was caught by the substance on which this figure sat. It was no figure at all now, but a bare jag of rock rising in the centre of this solid whirlpool, and carrying on its summit something which held a light that not one of these icy freaks, pranking in the dress of gems and flowers, had found it possible to assume. It was a thing so real, so genuine, my breath became suspended; my heart ceased to beat; my brain, that had been a lump of ice, seemed to move in its skull; hope, that had deserted me, suddenly sprung up like a second life within me; the old passion was not dead, if I was. It rose stronger than life or death or than myself. If I could but snatch that mass of moonstone, that inestimable wealth! It was nothing deceptive, I declared to myself. What more natural home could it have than this region, thrown up here by the old Plutonic powers of the planet, as the same substance in smaller shape was thrown up on the peaks of the Mount St Gothard, when the Alpine aiguilles first sprang into the day? There it rested, limpid with its milky pearl, casting out flakes of flame and azure, of red and leaf-green light, and holding yet a sparkle of silver in the reflections and refractions of its inner axis – the splendid Turk's-eye of the lapidaries, the cousin of the water-opal and the girasole, the precious essence of feldspar. Could I break it, I would find clusters of great hemitrope crystals. Could I obtain it, I should have a jewel in that mass of moonstone such as the world never saw! The throne of Jemschid could not cast a shadow beside it.

Then the bitterness of my fate overwhelmed me. Here, with this treasure of a kingdom, this jewel that could not be priced, this wealth beyond an Emperor's – and here only to die! My stolid apathy vanished, old thoughts dominated once more, old habits, old desires. I thought of Eleanor then in her warm, sunny home, the blossoms that bloomed around her, the birds that sang, the cheerful evening fires, the longing thoughts for one who never came, who never was to come. But I would! I cried, where human voice had never cried before. I would return! I would take this treasure with me! I would not be defrauded! Should not I, a man, conquer this inanimate blind matter? I reached out my hands to seize it. Slowly it receded – slowly, and less slowly, or was the motion of the ice still carrying me onwards? Had we encircled this apex? And were we driving out into the open and uncovered North, and so down the seas and out to the open main of black water again? If so – if I could live through it – I must have this thing!

I rose, and as well as I could, with my cramped and stiffened limbs, I moved to go back for it. It was useless; the current that carried us was growing invincible, the gaping gulfs of the outer seas were sucking us towards them. I fell; I scrambled to my feet; I would still have gone back, but, as I attempted it, the ice whereon I was inclined ever so slightly, tipped more boldly, gave way, and rose in a billow, broke, and piled over on another mass beneath. Then the cavern was behind us, and I comprehended that this ice-stream, having doubled its central point, now in its outward movement encountered the still incoming body, and was to pile above and pass over it, the whole expanse bending, cracking, breaking, crowding, and compressing, till its rearing tumult made bergs more mountainous than the off-shot glaciers of the Greenland continent, that should ride safely down to crumble in the surging seas below. As block after block of the rent ice rose in the air, lighted by the blue and bristling aurora-points, toppled and mounted higher, it seemed to me that now indeed I was battling with those elemental agencies in the dreadful fight I had desired – one man against the might of matter. I sprang from that block to another; I gained my balance on a third, climbing, shouldering, leaping, struggling, holding with my hands, catching with my feet, crawling, stumbling, tottering, rising higher and higher with the mountain ever making progress; a power unknown to my foes coming to my aid, a blessed rushing warmth that glowed on all the surface of my skin, that set the blood to racing in my veins, that made my heart beat with newer hope, sink with newer despair, rise buoyant with new determination. Except when the shaft of light pierced the shivering sky I could not see or guess the height that I had gained. I was vaguely aware of chasms that were bottomless, of precipices that opened on them, of pinnacles rising round me in aerial spires, when suddenly the shelf, on which I must have stood, yielded, as if it were pushed by great hands, swept down a steep incline like an avalanche, stopped halfway, but sent me flying on, sliding, glancing, like a shooting-star, down, down the slippery side, breathless, dizzy, smitten with blistering pain by awful winds that whistled by me, far out upon the level ice below that tilted up and down again with the great resonant plash of open water and, con-scious for a moment that I lay at last upon a fragment that the mass behind urged on, I knew and I remembered nothing more.

Faces were bending over me when I opened my eyes again, rough, uncouth, and bearded faces, but no monsters of the Pole.

Whalemen, rather, smelling richly of train-oil, but I could recall nothing in all my life one fraction so beautiful as they; the angels on whom I hope to open my eyes when Death has really taken me will scarcely seem sights more blest than did those rude whalers of the North Pacific Sea. The North Pacific Sea – for it was there that I was found, explain it how you may – whether the *Albatross* had pierced farther to the west than her sailing-master knew, and had lost her reckoning with a disordered compass-needle under new stars – or whether I had really been the sport of the demoniac beings of the ice, tossed by them from zone to zone in a dozen hours. The whalers, real creatures enough, had discovered me on a block of ice, they said; nor could I, in their opinion, have been many days undergoing my dreadful experience, for there was still food in my wallet when they opened it They would never believe a word of my story, and, so far from regarding me as one who had proved the North-West Passage in my own person, they considered me a mere idle maniac, as uncomfortable a thing to have on shipboard as a ghost or a dead body, wrecked and unable to account for myself, and gladly transferred me to a homeward-bound Russian man-of-war, whose officers afforded me more polite but quite as decided scepticism.

I have never to this day found any one who believed my story when I told it – so you can take it for what it is worth. Even my Uncle Paul flouted it, and absolutely refused to surrender the sum on whose expectation I had taken ship; while my old ancestor, who hung peeling over the hall fire, dropped from his frame in disgust at the idea of one of his hard-cash descendants turning romancer. But all I know is that the *Albatross* never sailed into port again, and that if I open my knife today and lay it on the table it will wheel about till the tip of its blade points full at the North Star.

I have never found anyone to believe me, did I say? Yes, there is one – Eleanor never doubted a word of my narration, never asked me if cold and suffering had not shaken my reason. But then, after the first recital, she has never been willing to hear another word about it, and if I ever allude to my lost treasure or the possibility of instituting a search for it, she asks me if I need more lessons to be content with the treasure that I have, and gathers up her work and gently leaves the room. So that, now I speak of it so seldom, if I had not told the thing to you it might come to pass that I should forget altogether the existence of my mass of moonstone. My mass of moonshine, old Paul calls it. I let him have his say; he can not have that nor anything else much longer; but when all is done I recall Galileo and I mutter to myself, '*Per si muove* – it *was* a mass of moonstone! With these eyes I saw it, with these hands I touched it, with this heart I longed for it, with this will I mean to have it yet!'

Alice W. Fuller

A WIFE MANUFACTURED TO ORDER

*The idea of synthetic humans – androids rather than robots – has become
a staple of science fiction but developed quite late. Most early science
fiction considered mechanical robots rather than ones almost indistin-
guishable from people. There was the Greek legend of Pygmalion, who
made a statue of a woman so beautiful that he fell in love with it and
begged Aphrodite to bring it to life, which the goddess did. One might
think of the creature in Mary Shelley's* Frankenstein *as a synthetic
human, but that was made out of human tissue rather than anything
synthetic. Then there was Olympia in E.T.A. Hoffmann's 'The
Sandman' (1816), which is certainly mistaken for a woman despite
seeming rather mechanical, and it is easily revealed as a clockwork
automaton. The earliest story I know of to depict a synthetic android was*
L'Eve Future *by Villiers de L'Isle Adam. Although it was published in
full in 1886 it was not translated into English until 1922, yet the
following story, which appeared in 1895, may well have been inspired by
Adam's novel as they share several ideas, most significantly the creation of
an artificial wife out of wax. I'm pretty sure this is the first ever story of
an android written in English. Although it is narrated by a man, it
strikes me as clearly reflecting the views of a woman.*

*Nothing seems to be known of Alice W. Fuller, and I cannot be sure
which, if any, of the four with that name who appear in the 1900 US
Census might be her. I have a sneaking suspicion she may be the 26-year-
old teacher living in Hartford, Connecticut, but I cannot substantiate
that; nor am I aware of anything else she wrote.*

A Wife Manufactured to Order

AS I WAS going down G Street in the city of W———, a strange sign attracted my attention. I stopped, looked, fairly rubbed my eyes to see if they were rightly focused; yes, there it was plainly lettered in gilt: 'Wives made to order! Satisfaction guaranteed or money refunded.'

Well! well! Does some lunatic live here, I wonder? By Jove! I will investigate. I had inherited (I suppose from my mother) a bit of curiosity, and the truth of the matter was this: now nearing the age of forty, I thought it might be advisable to settle down in a home of my own; but, alas,! to settle down to a life of strife and turmoil, that would not be pleasant; and that I should have to do, I knew very well, if I should marry any of my numerous lady acquaintances – especially Florence Ward, the one I most admired. She unfortunately had strong-minded ways, and inclinations to be investigating women's rights, politics, theosophy, and all that sort of thing. Bah! I could never endure it. I should be miserable, and the outcome would be a separation; I knew it. To be dictated to, perhaps found fault with – no, no, it would never do; better be a bachelor and at least live in peace. But – what does this sign mean? I'll find out for myself.

A ring of the bell brought a little white-haired, wiry sort of a man to the door. 'Walk in, walk in, sir,' he said.

I asked for an explanation of the strange sign over the door.

'Just step right in here and be seated, sir. My master is engaged at present, sir, with a great politician who had to separate from his wife; was so fractious, sir, got so many strange notions in her head; in fact, she wanted to hold the reins herself. You may have seen it – the papers have been full of it. Why, law bless you, sir, the poor man couldn't say his soul was his own, and he is here now making arrangements with master to make him a quieter sort of wife, someone to do the honours of the home without feelin' neglected if he happens to be a little courteous to some of his young lady friends. You see, master makes 'em to order, makes 'em to think just as you do, just as you want 'em to; then you've got a happy home, something to live for. Beautiful – golly! I've seen some of the beautifulest women turned out, 'most make your mouth water to look at.' And so the old man rattled on until I was quite bewildered.

I interrupted him by asking if I could see his master.

'Oh, certainly, sir; you just make yourself comfortable and I will let you know when he is through.'

I sat for some time like one in a dream, wondering if this could be so, and with many wonderful modern inventions in mind I began to think it possible. And then there was a vision of a happy home, a wife beautiful as a dream, gentle and loving, without a thought for anyone but me; one who would never reproach me if I didn't happen to get home just at what she thought was the proper time; one who would not ask me to go to church when she knew it was against my wishes; one who would never find fault with me if I wished to go to a base-ball game on Sunday, or bother me to take her to the theatre or opera. A man, you know, can't give much time to such things without interfering greatly with his comfort. Oh! could all this be realized? But just then my reverie was broken by the old man, who was saying: 'Just step this way. Master, let me introduce you to Mr Charles Fitzsimmons.'

Short, thick-set, florid complexion, pale blue eyes with a sinister twinkle, was the description of Mr Sharper, whom I confronted. Reaching out his hand, which was cold and clammy and reminded me very much of a piece of cold boiled pork, he said:

'Now, young man, what can I do for you? Want a life-companion, a pleasant one? Man of means, no doubt, and can enjoy yourself; a little fun now and then with the boys and no harm at all – none in the least. When a man comes home tired, doesn't like to be dictated to; want someone always to meet you with a smile, some one that doesn't expect you to be fondlin' and pettin' 'em all the time. I understand it – I know just how it is. Law bless my soul, I've made more'n one man happy, and I've only been in the business a short time, too. Now, sir, I can get you up any style you want – *wax*, but can't be detected.'

'Do you mean to say you manufacture a woman out of wax, who will talk?'

'That's just what I do; you give me the subjects you most enjoy talking upon, and tell me what kind of a looking wife you want, and leave the rest to me, and you will never regret it. I will furnish as many "phones" as you wish; most men don't care for such a variety for a wife – too much talk, you know'; and he chuckled and laughed like a big baby.

'What are your prices, may I ask?'

'Well, it's owing a good deal to how they are got up – from five hundred to a thousand dollars.'

'Well,' I said, 'I think that rather high.'

'Dear man alive, a pleasant companion for life for a few hundred dollars! Most men don't grumble at all for the sake of having their own way and a pleasant home, and you see she ain't always asking for money.' (Sure enough, I hadn't thought of that.)

'Very well, I will decide upon the matter and let you know.'

'All right, young man; you'll come back. They all do, them as knows about it.'

I went to my room at the hotel and thought it all out, thought of the pleasant evenings I could have with someone whose thoughts were like my own, someone who would not vex me by differing in opinion. I wondered what Florence would say. I really believed she cared for me, but she knew how I disliked so many of the topics she persisted in talking upon. What mattered it to me what Emerson said, or Edward Bellamy wrote, or Henry George, or Pentecost? What did I care about Hume or Huxley or Stuart Mill, any of those sciences, Christian Science or Divine Science or mind cure? – bah! it was all nonsense. The topics of the day were enough, and if I attended closely to my business I needed recreation, not such things as she would prescribe. Still Florence was interesting to talk to, and I rather liked her at times when she talked every-day talk; but I could not marry her, and it was her own fault. She knew my sentiments, and if she would persist in going on as she did I couldn't help it.

Yes, I decided I would have a home of my own, and a wife made to order at once. Before leaving the city I made all necessary arrangements, hurried home, rented a house, and went to see old Susan Tyler, whom I engaged as housekeeper; she was deaf and had an impediment in her speech, but she was a fine housekeeper. All my preparations made, the ideal home! Oh! how my heart beat as I looked around! – what happiness to do as I liked, a beautiful, uncomplaining wife ready to grant every wish and meet me with a smile! What would the boys say when, out a little late at night, I should be so perfectly at ease? I could just see jealousy on their faces, and I laughed outright for joy. Tomorrow I was going for my bride. Side-looks and innuendos were thrust at me from all quarters, but I was too happy to demur or explain. When I reached the city I could scarcely wait for the appointed time.

Alighting from the carriage the door was opened, and I was ushered into the presence of the most beautiful creature I had ever beheld. The hands extended towards mine, the lips opened, and a low, sweet voice said, 'Dear Charles, how glad I am you have come!' I stood spellbound, and only a chuckle from Mr Sharper brought me to my senses.

'Kiss your affianced, why don't you?' he said, and chuckled again.

I felt as though I wanted to knock him down for speaking so in that beautiful creature's presence. And then a little soft rippling laugh, and she moved towards me. Oh, could I get that beast to leave the room! Why did he stand there chuckling in that manner?

'Sir,' I said, 'you will oblige me by leaving the room for a few moments.'

With that he chuckled still louder and muttered, 'Bless me, I really believe he thinks her alive.' Then to me: 'To be sure, to be sure, but you only have a short time before going to the minister's, and I must show you how to adjust her. When you get home' – and he chuckled again – 'you can be just as sentimental as you please, but just now we will attend to business. Here is a box of tubes made to talk as you wished them. They are adjusted so. Place the one you wish in your sleeve. You can carelessly touch her right here if there is any one around. Here is a spring in each hand and the tips of her fingers. I will give you a book of instructions, and you will soon learn to arrange her with very little effort, just to suit yourself, and I am sure you will be very happy. Now, sir, the time is up; you can go to the minister's.'

As I put her wraps around her and drew her arm through mine she murmured so sweetly, 'Thank you, dear.' How glad I was to get out of the presence of that vile man who was constantly pulling or pushing her; I could scarcely keep my hands off from him, and my serene Margurette – for I decided to call her that – would only smile and say, 'Thank you!' 'Oh, how lovely!' 'Ah, indeed!' I was almost vexed with her to think she did not resent it. I wanted her all to myself where I could have the smiles, and thought I should be thankful when we were in our own home.

During our journey I could not help noticing the admiring glances from my fellow travellers, but my beautiful wife did not return any of their looks. In fact, I overheard a couple of young dudes say, 'Just wait till that old codger's back is turned, and we shall see whether she will have no smiles for any but him.' I had half a notion to adjust her to give them some cutting reply and then go into the smoker awhile, for I was sure they would try to get into conversation with her; but pshaw! I hadn't ordered any tubes of that kind. I believed I'd send and get one in case of an emergency. No, I wouldn't have such in the house; I wanted an amiable wife, and when we were once at home it would not be necessary. I wouldn't *have* to go with her anywhere unless I wanted to. Only think of that! – never feel that my wife would ask me to go with her and I have to refuse, then ten to one have her cry and make a fuss about it. I knew how it was, for I had seen too much of that sort of thing in the homes of my friends.

Business ran smoothly; everything was perfect harmony; my home was heaven on earth. I smoked when I wished to, I went to my base-ball games, I stayed out as long as I pleased, played cards when I wished, drank champagne or whatever I fancied, in fact had as good a time as I did before marriage. My male friends congratulated me upon my good fortune, and I was considered the luckiest man anywhere around. No one knew how I had made the good luck for myself.

There are some things in life I could never understand. One of them is that, when everything seems so prosperous, calamity is so often in the wake. And that was the case with me. After so many prosperous years a financial crash came. I tried to ward it off; I was up early and late. Margurette never complained, but was always sweet and smiling, with the same endearing words. Sometimes as the years went by I felt as though I would not object to her differing with me a little, for variety's sake; still, it was best. When I would say, 'Margurette, do you really think so?' and I would speak so cross to her often – I don't know but that I did so more than was necessary; still, a man must have some place where he can be himself, and if he can't have that privilege at home, what's the use of having a home? But she was never out of patience, and my wife would only say, 'Yes, darling,' so low and sweet. I remember once I said, when I was worried more than usual, 'I am damned tired of this sort of thing,' and she laughed so sweetly and called me her 'own precious boy'.

But the crash came, and there was no use trying to stay it any longer. I came home sick and tired. It was nine o'clock at night, with a cold, drizzling rain falling. Susan had gone to bed sick, and forgotten to light a fire in the grate. I went into the library, where Margurette always waited for me. No lights; I stumbled over a chair. I accidentally touched Margurette. She put up her lips to kiss me and laughingly said, 'Precious darling, tired tonight?' Great God! I came very near striking her.

'Margurette, don't call me darling; talk to me; talk to me about something – anything sensible. Don't you know I am a ruined man? Everything I have got has been swept away from me.'

'There, precious, I love you;' and she laughed again.

'Did you not hear what I said?' I screamed.

But she only laughed the more and said, 'Oh, how lovely!'

I rushed from the house. I could not endure it longer; I was like one mad. My first thought was: Where can I go, to whom can I go for sympathy? I cannot stand this strain much longer, and to show weakness to men I could never do that. I will go to Florence, I said. I will see what she says. Strange I should think of her just then!

I asked the servant who admitted me for Miss Florence.

'She is indisposed and cannot see anyone tonight.'

'But,' I said, writing on a card hastily, 'take this to her.'

Only a few moments elapsed and she came in, holding out her hand in an assuring and friendly way. 'I am surprised to see you tonight, Mr Fitzsimmons.'

'Oh, Florence!' I cried, 'I am in trouble. I believe I shall lose my mind if I cannot have someone to go to; and you, dear Florence, you will know my needs; you can counsel, you can understand me.'

'Sir!' Florence said, 'are you mad, that you come here to insult me?'

'But I love you. I know it. I love the traits that I once thought I despised.'

'Stop where you are! I did not receive you to hear such language. You forget yourself and me; you forget that you are a married man – shame upon you for humiliating me so!'

'Florence, Florence, I am not married; it is all a lie, a deception.'

'Have you lost your reason, Mr Fitzsimmons? Sit down, pray, and let me call my father. You are ill.'

'Stop,' I cried, 'I do not need your father. I need you. Listen to me. I imagined I could never be happy with a wife who differed in opinion from me. In fact, I had almost decided to remain single all the rest of my days, until I came across a man who manufactured wives to order. Wait, Florence, until I have finished – do not look at me so. I am indeed sane. My wife was manufactured to my own ideas, a perfect human being as I supposed.'

'Mr Fitzsimmons, let me call my father.' And Florence started towards the door. She was so pale that she frightened me, but I clutched her frantically.

'Listen,' I said; 'will you go with me? I will prove that all I have told you is true.'

My earnestness seemed to reassure her. She stopped as if carefully thinking, then asked me to repeat what I had already told her. Finally she said yes, she would go.

We were soon in the presence of my beautiful Margurette, whom I literally hated – I could not endure her face. 'Now, Florence, see,' I cried; and I had my wife talk the namby-pamby lingo I once thought so sweet. 'Oh! how I hate her!' and I glared at her like a madman. 'Florence, save me. I am a ruined man. Everything has been swept away – the last today. I am a pauper, an egotist, a bigot, a selfish –'

'Stop!' cried Florence. 'You wrong yourself; you are a man in your prime. What if your money has gone, you have your health and your faculties, I guess' (and there was a merry twinkle in her eyes); 'the whole world is before you, and, best of all, no one to interfere with you or argue on disagreeable topics.'

'Oh, Florence! I am punished enough for my selfishness. Oh, God!' and I threw myself on the couch, 'were I not a pauper, too, there might be some hope for happiness yet.'

'You are not a pauper,' said Florence; 'you are the master of your fate, and if you are not happy it is your own fault.'

'Florence, I can never be happy without you. I know now it is too late.'

'Too late – never say that. But could you be happy with me, "a woman wedded to an idea", "strong-minded"? Why, Charles, I am liable to investigate all sorts of scientific subjects and reforms. And then supposing I should talk about it sometimes; if it was not for that I might think of the matter. As far as money is concerned, that would have little to do with my actions. Still, Charles, upon the whole I should be afraid to marry the "divorced" husband of so amiable a wife as your present one is. I, with my faults and imperfections! The contrast would be too great.'

'Florence, Florence,' I said, 'say no more. All I ask is, can you overlook my folly and take me for better, for worse? I have learned my lesson. I see now it is only a petty and narrow type of man who would wish to live only with his own personal echo. I want a woman, one who retains her individuality, a thinking woman. Will you be mine?'

'I will consider the matter favourably,' said Florence; 'but we shall have to wait a year, for opinion's sake, as I suppose there are not many who know how you had your late wife manufactured to order.'

And we both laughed.

Mary E. Braddon

GOOD LADY DUCAYNE

Mary Elizabeth Braddon (1835–1915) was, with Mrs Henry Wood, the bestselling novelist at the end of the nineteenth century. She had a long and very prolific career in what was known as the sensational school of fiction, which were novels involving characters and plots frequently beyond the normal propriety of Victorian Britain. Her first big success was Lady Audley's Secret *(1862), and other major works include* Aurora Floyd *(1863),* John Marchmont's Legacy *(1863) and* Joshua Haggard's Daughter *(1876). Her private life was every bit as sensational as her fiction. She lived with her publisher, John Maxwell, from 1860, even though he was still married and had five children. His wife was in an asylum and did not die until 1874. It was only then that Braddon and Maxwell could marry, which meant declaring that their previous relationship, which they had passed off as being a married couple, had been false. It did not seem to dent her popularity with her readers, however, and her books continued to sell or be in demand at the 'Circulating Libraries' in huge quantities.*

Mary Braddon might not seem an obvious person to include here, but in several of her novels and stories she portrays characters interested in the potential of science. Her story 'The Shadow in the Corner' (1879) – which was included in a companion volume to this one, The Darker Sex – *has a protagonist struggling to balance his scientific viewpoint with a supernatural event. In 'From a Doctor's Diary' (1887) a young man fascinated by science proclaims, 'There is knowledge to be yet revealed to us, which will almost appear miraculous.' The following tale is sometimes classed as a vampire story, yet is based on very sound science. Without revealing the ending, I might mention that the technique used in the story had been around since 1818, although it was not until 1901, five years after this work appeared, that the process was made safer by the discovery of blood groups.*

Good Lady Ducayne

I

BELLA ROLLESTON HAD made up her mind that her only chance of earning her bread and helping her mother to an occasional crust was by going out into the great unknown world as companion to a lady. She was willing to go to any lady rich enough to pay her a salary and so eccentric as to wish for a hired companion. Five shillings told off reluctantly from one of those sovereigns which were so rare with the mother and daughter, and which melted away so quickly, five solid shillings, had been handed to a smartly dressed lady in an office in Harbeck Street, W., in the hope that this very Superior Person would find a situation and a salary for Miss Rolleston.

The Superior Person glanced at the two half-crowns as they lay on the table where Bella's hand had placed them, to make sure they were neither of them florins, before she wrote a description of Bella's qualifications and requirements in a formidable-looking ledger.

'Age?' she asked curtly.

'Eighteen, last July.'

'Any accomplishments?'

'No; I am not at all accomplished. If I were I should want to be a governess – a companion seems the lowest stage.'

'We have some highly accomplished ladies on our books as companions, or chaperon companions.'

'Oh, I know!' babbled Bella, loquacious in her youthful candour. 'But that is quite a different thing. Mother hasn't been able to afford a piano since I was twelve years old, so I'm afraid I've forgotten how to play. And I have had to help mother with her needlework, so there hasn't been much time to study.'

'Please don't waste time upon explaining what you can't do, but kindly tell me anything you can do,' said the Superior Person, crush-ingly, with her pen poised between delicate fingers waiting to write. 'Can you read aloud for two or three hours at a stretch? Are you active and handy, an early riser, a good walker, sweet-tempered, and obliging?'

'I can say yes to all those questions except about the sweetness. I· think I have a pretty good temper, and I should be anxious to oblige anybody who paid for my services. I should want them to feel that I was really earning my salary.'

'The kind of ladies who come to me would not care for a talka-tive companion,' said the Person, severely, having finished writing in her book. 'My connection lies chiefly among the aristocracy, and in that class considerable deference is expected.'

'Oh, of course,' said Bella; 'but it's quite different when I'm talk-ing to you. I want to tell you all about myself once and for ever.'

'I am glad it is to be only once!' said the Person, with the edges of her lips.

The Person was of uncertain age, tightly laced in a black silk gown. She had a powdery complexion and a handsome clump of somebody else's hair on the top of her head. It may be that Bella's girlish freshness and vivacity had an irritating effect upon nerves weakened by an eight-hours day in that over-heated second floor in Harbeck Street. To Bella, the official apartment, with its Brussels carpet, velvet curtains and velvet chairs, and French clock, ticking loud on the marble chimney-piece, suggested the luxury of a palace, as compared with another second floor in Walworth where Mrs Rolleston and her daughter had managed to exist for the last six years.

'Do you think you have anything on your books that would suit me?' faltered Bella, after a pause.

'Oh dear, no; I have nothing in view at present,' answered the Person, who had swept Bella's half-crowns into a drawer absent-mindedly with the tips of her fingers. 'You see, you are so very unformed – so much too young to be companion to a lady of position. It is a pity you have not enough education for a nursery governess; that would be more in your line.'

'And do you think it will be very long before you can get me a situation?' asked Bella, doubtfully.

'I really cannot say. Have you any particular reason for being so impatient – not a love affair, I hope?'

'A love affair!' cried Bella, with flaming cheeks. 'What utter nonsense. I want a situation because mother is poor, and I hate being a burden to her. I want a salary that I can share with her.'

'There won't be much margin for sharing in the salary you are likely to get at your age – and with your – very – unformed manners,' said the Person, who found Bella's peony cheeks, bright eyes, and unbridled vivacity more and more oppressive.

'Perhaps if you'd be kind enough to give me back the fee I could take it to an agency where the connection isn't quite so aristocratic,' said Bella, who – as she told her mother in her recital of the interview – was determined not to be sat upon.

'You will find no agency that can do more for you than mine,' replied the Person, whose harpy fingers never relinquished coin. 'You will have to wait for your opportunity. Yours is an exceptional case: but I will bear you in mind, and if anything suitable offers I will write to you. I cannot say more than that.'

The half-contemptuous bend of the stately head, weighted with borrowed hair, indicated the end of the interview. Bella went back to Walworth – tramped sturdily every inch of the way in the September afternoon – and 'took off' the Superior Person for the amusement of her mother and the landlady, who lingered in the shabby litle sitting-room after bringing in the tea-tray to applaud Miss Rolleston's 'taking off'.

'Dear, dear, what a mimic she is!' said the landlady. 'You ought to have let her go on the stage, mum. She might have made her fortune as a hactress.'

II

Bella waited and hoped, and listened for the postman's knocks which brought such store of letters for the parlours and the first floor, and so few for that humble second floor, where mother and daughter sat sewing with hand and with wheel and treadle for the greater part of the day.

Mrs Rolleston was a lady by birth and education; but it had been her bad fortune to marry a scoundrel; for the last half-dozen years she had been that worst of widows, a wife whose husband had deserted her. Happily, she was courageous, industrious, and a clever needle-woman; and she had been able just to earn a living for herself and her only child, by making mantles and cloaks for a West-end house. It was not a luxurious living. Cheap lodgings in a shabby street off the Walworth Road, scanty dinners, homely food, well-worn raiment had been the portion of mother and daughter; but they loved each other so dearly, and Nature had made them both so light-hearted, that they had contrived somehow to be happy. But now this idea of going out into the world as companion to some fine lady had rooted itself into Bella's mind, and although she idolized her mother, and although the parting of mother and daughter must needs tear two loving hearts into shreds, the girl longed for enterprise and change and excitement, as the pages of old longed to be knights, and to start for the Holy Land to break a lance with the infidel.

She grew tired of racing downstairs every time the postman knocked, only to be told 'Nothing for you, miss' by the smudgy-faced drudge who picked up the letters from the passage floor.

'Nothing for you, miss,' grinned the lodging-house drudge, till at last Bella took heart of grace and walked up to Harbeck Street, and asked the Superior Person how it was that no situation had been found for her.

'You are too young,' said the Person, 'and you want a salary.'

'Of course I do,' answered Bella; 'don't other people want salaries?'

'Young ladies of your age generally want a comfortable home.'

'I don't,' snapped Bella; 'I want to help mother.'

'You can call again this day week,' said the Person; 'or, if I hear of anything in the meantime, I will write to you.'

No letter came from the Person, and in exactly a week Bella put on her neatest hat, the one that had been seldomest caught in the rain, and trudged off to Harbeck Street.

It was a dull October afternoon, and there was a greyness in the air which might turn to fog before night. The Walworth Road shops gleamed brightly through that grey atmosphere, and though to a young lady reared in Mayfair or Belgravia such shop-windows would have been unworthy of a glance, they were a snare and temptation for Bella. There were so many things that she longed for, and would never be able to buy.

Harbeck Street is apt to be empty at this dead season of the year, a long, long street, an endless perspective of eminently respectable houses. The Person's office was at the further end, and Bella looked down that long, grey vista almost despairingly, more tired than usual with the trudge from Walworth. As she looked, a carriage passed her, an old-fashioned yellow chariot, on C-springs, drawn by a pair of high grey horses, with the stateliest of coachmen driving them, and a tall footman sitting by his side.

'It looks like the fairy god-mother's coach,' thought Bella. 'I shouldn't wonder if it began by being a pumpkin.'

It was a surprise when she reached the Person's door to find the yellow chariot standing before it, and the tall footman waiting near the doorstep. She was almost afraid to go in and meet the owner of that splendid carriage. She had caught only a glimpse of its occu-pant as the chariot rolled by, a plumed bonnet, a patch of ermine.

The Person's smart page ushered her upstairs and knocked at the official door. 'Miss Rolleston,' he announced, apologetically, while Bella waited outside.

'Show her in,' said the Person, quickly; and then Bella heard her murmuring something in a low voice to her client.

Bella went in fresh, blooming, a living image of youth and hope, and before she looked at the Person her gaze was riveted by the owner of the chariot.

Never had she seen anyone as old as the old lady sitting by the Person's fire: a little old figure, wrapped from chin to feet in an ermine mantle; a withered old face under a plumed bonnet – a face so wasted by age that it seemed only a pair of eyes and a peaked chin. The nose was peaked, too, but between the sharply pointed chin and the great, shining eyes the small, aquiline nose was hardly visible. 'This is Miss Rolleston, Lady Ducayne.'

Claw-like fingers, flashing with jewels, lifted a double eyeglass to Lady Ducayne's shining black eyes, and through the glasses Bella saw those unnaturally bright eyes magnified to a gigantic size, and glaring at her awfully.

'Miss Torpinter has told me all about you,' said the old voice that belonged to the eyes. 'Have you good health? Are you strong and active, able to eat well, sleep well, walk well, able to enjoy all that there is good in life?'

'I have never known what it is to be ill, or idle,' answered Bella.

'Then I think you will do for me.'

'Of course, in the event of references being perfectly satisfactory,' put in the Person.

'I don't want references. The young woman looks frank and innocent. I'll take her on trust.'

'So like you, dear Lady Ducayne,' murmured Miss Torpinter.

'I want a strong young woman whose health will give me no trouble.'

'You have been so unfortunate in that respect,' cooed the Person, whose voice and manner were subdued to a melting sweetness by the old woman's presence.

'Yes, I've been rather unlucky,' grunted Lady Ducayne.

'But I am sure Miss Rolleston will not disappoint you, though certainly after your unpleasant experience with Miss Tomson, who looked the picture of health – and Miss Blandy, who said she had never seen a doctor since she was vaccinated –'

'Lies, no doubt,' muttered Lady Ducayne, and then turning to Bella, she asked, curtly, 'You don't mind spending the winter in Italy, I suppose?'

In Italy! The very word was magical. Bella's fair young face flushed crimson.

'It has been the dream of my life to see Italy,' she gasped.

From Walworth to Italy! How far, how impossible such a journey had seemed to that romantic dreamer.

'Well, your dream will be realized. Get yourself ready to leave Charing Cross by the train deluxe this day week at eleven. Be sure you are at the station a quarter before the hour. My people will look after you and your luggage.'

Lady Ducayne rose from her chair, assisted by her crutch-stick, and Miss Torpinter escorted her to the door.

'And with regard to salary?' questioned the Person on the way.

'Salary, oh, the same as usual – and if the young woman wants a quarter's pay in advance you can write to me for a cheque,' Lady Ducayne answered, carelessly.

Miss Torpinter went all the way downstairs with her client, and waited to see her seated in the yellow chariot. When she came upstairs again she was slightly out of breath, and she had resumed that superior manner which Bella had found so crushing.

'You may think yourself uncommonly lucky, Miss Rolleston,' she said. 'I have dozens of young ladies on my books whom I might have recommended for this situation – but I remembered having told you to call this afternoon – and I thought I would give you a chance.

'Old Lady Ducayne is one of the best people on my books. She gives her companion a hundred a year, and pays all travelling expenses. You will live in the lap of luxury.'

'A hundred a year! How too lovely! Shall I have to dress very grandly? Does Lady Ducayne keep much company?'

'At her age! No, she lives in seclusion – in her own apartments – her French maid, her footman, her medical attendant, her courier.'

'Why did those other companions leave her?' asked Bella.

'Their health broke down!'

'Poor things, and so they had to leave?'

'Yes, they had to leave. I suppose you would like a quarter's salary in advance?'

'Oh, yes, please. I shall have things to buy.'

'Very well, I will write for Lady Ducayne's cheque, and I will send you the balance – after deducting my commission for the year.'

'To be sure, I had forgotten the commission.'

'You don't suppose I keep this office for pleasure.'

'Of course not,' murmured Bella, remembering the five shillings entrance fee; but nobody could expect a hundred a year and a winter in Italy for five shillings.

III

From Miss Rolleston, at Cap Ferrino, to Mrs Rolleston, in Beresford Street, Walworth.

How I wish you could see this place, dearest; the blue sky, the olive woods, the orange and lemon orchards between the cliffs and the sea – sheltering in the hollow of the great hills – and with summer waves dancing up to the narrow ridge of pebbles and weeds which is the Italian idea of a beach! Oh, how I wish you could see it all, mother dear, and bask in this sunshine, that makes it so difficult to believe the date at the head of this paper. November! The air is like an English June – the sun is so hot that I can't walk a few yards without an umbrella. And to think of you at Walworth while I am here! I could cry at the thought that perhaps you will never see this lovely coast, this wonderful sea, these summer flowers that bloom in winter. There is a hedge of pink geraniums under my window, mother – a thick, rank hedge, as if the flowers grew wild – and there are Dijon roses climbing over arches and palisades all along the terrace; a rose-garden full of bloom in November! Just picture it all! You could never imagine the luxury of this hotel.

It is nearly new, and has been built and decorated regardless of expense. Our rooms are upholstered in pale blue satin, which shows up Lady Ducayne's parchment complexion; but as she sits all day in a corner of the balcony basking in the sun, except when she is in her carriage, and all the evening in her armchair close to the fire, and never sees anyone but her own people, her complexion matters very little.

She has the handsomest suite of rooms in the hotel. My bed-room is inside hers, the sweetest room – all blue satin and white lace – white enamelled furniture, looking-glasses on every wall, till I know my pert little profile as I never knew it before. The room was really meant for Lady Ducayne's dressing-room, but she ordered one of the blue satin couches to be arranged as a bed for me – the prettiest little bed, which I can wheel near the window on sunny mornings, as it is on castors and easily moved about. I feel as if Lady Ducayne were a funny old grandmother who had suddenly appeared in my life, very, very rich and very, very kind.

She is not at all exacting. I read aloud to her a good deal, and she dozes and nods while I read.

Sometimes I hear her moaning in her sleep – as if she had troublesome dreams. When she is tired of my reading she orders Francine, her maid, to read a French novel to her, and I hear her chuckle and groan now and then, as if she were more interested in those books than in Dickens or Scott. My French is not good enough to follow Francine, who reads very quickly. I have a great deal of liberty, for Lady Ducayne often tells me to run away and amuse myself; I roam about the hills for hours. Everything is so lovely. I lose myself in olive woods, always climbing up and up towards the pine woods above – and above the pines there are the snow mountains that just show their white peaks above the dark hills. Oh, you poor dear, how can I ever make you understand what this place is like – you, whose poor, tired eyes have only the opposite side of Beresford Street? Sometimes I go no farther than the terrace in front of the hotel, which is a favourite lounging-place with everybody. The gardens lie below, and the tennis courts where I sometimes play with a very nice girl, the only person in the hotel with whom I have made friends. She is a year older than I, and has come to Cap Ferrino with her brother, a doctor – or a medical student, who is going to be a doctor. He passed his M.B. exam at Edinburgh just before they left home, Lotta told me. He came to Italy entirely on his sister's account. She had a troublesome chest attack last summer and was ordered to winter abroad. They are orphans, quite alone in the world, and so fond of each other. It is very nice for me to have such a friend as Lotta. She is so thoroughly respectable. I can't help using that word, for some of the girls in this hotel go on in a way that I know you would shudder at. Lotta was brought up by an aunt, deep down in the country, and knows hardly anything about life. Her brother won't allow her to read a novel, French or English, that he has not read and approved.

'He treats me like a child,' she told me, 'but I don't mind, for it's nice to know somebody loves me, and cares about what I do, and even about my thoughts.'

Perhaps this is what makes some girls so eager to marry – the want of someone strong and brave and honest and true to care for them and order them about. I want no one, mother darling, for I have you, and you are all the world to me. No husband could ever come between us two. If I ever were to marry he would have only the second place in my heart. But I don't suppose I ever shall marry, or even know what it is like to have an offer of marriage. No young man can afford to marry a penniless girl nowadays. Life is too expensive.

Mr Stafford, Lotta's brother, is very clever, and very kind. He thinks it is rather hard for me to have to live with such an old woman as Lady Ducayne, but then he does not know how poor we are – you and I – and what a wonderful life this seems to me in this lovely place. I feel a selfish wretch for enjoying all my luxuries, while you, who want them so much more than I, have none of them – hardly know what they are like – do you, dearest? – for my scamp of a father began to go to the dogs soon after you were married, and since then life has been all trouble and care and struggle for you.

This letter was written when Bella had been less than a month at Cap Ferrino, before the novelty had worn off the landscape, and before the pleasure of luxurious surroundings had begun to cloy. She wrote to her mother every week, such long letters as girls who have lived in closest companionship with a mother alone can write; letters that are like a diary of heart and mind. She wrote gaily always; but when the new year began Mrs Rolleston thought she detected a note of melancholy under all those lively details about the place and the people.

My poor girl is getting homesick, she thought. Her heart is in Beresford Street.

It might be that she missed her new friend and companion, Lotta Stafford, who had gone with her brother for a little tour to Genoa and Spezzia, and as far as Pisa. They were to return before February; but in the meantime Bella might naturally feel very solitary among all those strangers, whose manners and doings she described so well.

The mother's instinct had been true. Bella was not so happy as she had been in that first flush of wonder and delight which followed the change from Walworth to the Riviera. Somehow, she knew not how, lassitude had crept upon her. She no longer loved to climb the hills, no longer flourished her orange stick in sheer gladness of heart as her light feet skipped over the rough ground and the coarse grass on the mountain side. The odour of rosemary and thyme, the fresh breath of the sea no longer filled her with rapture. She thought of Beresford Street and her mother's face with a sick longing. They were so far – so far away! And then she thought of Lady Ducayne, sitting by the heaped-up olive logs in the over-heated salon – thought of that wizened nut-cracker profile, and those gleaming eyes, with an invincible horror.

Visitors at the hotel had told her that the air of Cap Ferrino was relaxing – better suited to age than to youth, to sickness than to health. No doubt it was so. She was not so well as she had been at Walworth; but she told herself that she was suffering only from the pain of separation from the dear companion of her girlhood, the mother who had been nurse, sister, friend, flatterer, all things in this world to her. She had shed many tears over that parting, had spent many a melancholy hour on the marble terrace with yearning eyes looking westward, and with her heart's desire a thousand miles away.

She was sitting in her favourite spot, an angle at the eastern end of the terrace, a quiet little nook sheltered by orange trees, when she heard a couple of Riviera habitués talking in the garden below. They were sitting on a bench against the terrace wall.

She had no idea of listening to their talk, till the sound of Lady Ducayne's name attracted her, and then she listened without any thought of wrong-doing. They were talking no secrets – just casually discussing an hotel acquaintance.

They were two elderly people whom Bella only knew by sight. An English clergyman who had wintered abroad for half his lifetime; a stout, comfortable, well-to-do spinster whose chronic bronchitis obliged her to migrate annually.

'I have met her about Italy for the last ten years,' said the lady; 'but have never found out her real age.'

'I put her down at a hundred – not a year less,' replied the parson. 'Her reminiscences all go back to the Regency. She was evidently then in her zenith; and I have heard her say things that showed she was in Parisian society when the First Empire was at its best – before Josephine was divorced.'

'She doesn't talk much now.'

'No; there's not much life left in her. She is wise in keeping herself secluded. I only wonder that wicked old quack, her Italian doctor, didn't finish her off years ago.'

'I should think it must be the other way, and that he keeps her alive.'

'My dear Miss Manders, do you think foreign quackery ever kept anybody alive?'

'Well, there she is – and she never goes anywhere without him. He certainly has an unpleasant countenance.'

'Unpleasant,' echoed the parson, 'I don't believe the foul fiend himself can beat him in ugliness. I pity that poor young woman who has to live between old Lady Ducayne and Dr Parravicini.'

'But the old lady is very good to her companions.'

'No doubt. She is very free with her cash; the servants call her good Lady Ducayne. She is a withered old female Croesus, and knows she'll never be able to get through her money, and doesn't relish the idea of other people enjoying it when she's in her coffin. People who live to be as old as she is become slavishly attached to life. I daresay she's generous to those poor girls – but she can't make them happy. They die in her service.'

'Don't say they, Mr Carton; I know that one poor girl died at Mentone last spring.'

'Yes, and another poor girl died in Rome three years ago. I was there at the time. Good Lady Ducayne left her there in an English family. The girl had every comfort. The old woman was very liberal to her – but she died. I tell you, Miss Manders, it is not good for any young woman to live with two such horrors as Lady Ducayne and Parravicini.' They talked of other things – but Bella hardly heard them. She sat motionless, and a cold wind seemed to come down upon her from the mountains and to creep up to her from the sea, till she shivered as she sat there in the sunshine, in the shelter of the orange trees in the midst of all that beauty and brightness.

Yes, they were uncanny, certainly, the pair of them – she so like an aristocratic witch in her withered old age; he of no particular age, with a face that was more like a waxen mask than any human countenance Bella had ever seen. What did it matter? Old age is venerable, and worthy of all reverence; and Lady Ducayne had been very kind to her. Dr Parravicini was a harmless, inoffensive student, who seldom looked up from the book he was reading. He had his private sitting-room, where he made experiments in chemistry and natural science – perhaps in alchemy.

What could it matter to Bella? He had always been polite to her, in his far-off way. She could not be more happily placed than she was – in this palatial hotel, with this rich old lady.

No doubt she missed the young English girl who had been so friendly, and it might be that she missed the girl's brother, for Mr Stafford had talked to her a good deal – had interested himself in the books she was reading, and her manner of amusing herself when she was not on duty.

'You must come to our little salon when you are "off"', as the hospital nurses call it, and we can have some music. No doubt you play and sing?' upon which Bella had to own with a blush of shame that she had forgotten how to play the piano ages ago.

'Mother and I used to sing duets sometimes between the lights, without accompaniment,' she said, and the tears came into her eyes as she thought of the humble room, the half-hour's respite from work, the sewing-machine standing where a piano ought to have been, and her mother's plaintive voice, so sweet, so true, so dear.

Sometimes she found herself wondering whether she would ever see that beloved mother again. Strange forebodings came into her mind. She was angry with herself for giving way to melancholy thoughts.

One day she questioned Lady Ducayne's French maid about those two companions who had died within three years.

'They were poor, feeble creatures,' Francine told her. 'They looked fresh and bright enough when they came to Miladi; but they ate too much and they were lazy. They died of luxury and idleness. Miladi was too kind to them. They had nothing to do; and so they took to fancying things; fancying the air didn't suit them, that they couldn't sleep.'

'I sleep well enough, but I have had a strange dream several times since I have been in Italy.'

'Ah, you had better not begin to think about dreams, or you will be like those other girls. They were dreamers – and they dreamed themselves into the cemetery.'

The dream troubled her a little, not because it was a ghastly or frightening dream but on account of sensations which she had never felt before in sleep – a whirring of wheels that went round in her brain, a great noise like a whirlwind, but rhythmical like the ticking of a gigantic clock: and then in the midst of this uproar as of winds and waves she seemed to sink into a gulf of unconsciousness, out of sleep into far deeper sleep – total extinction. And then, after that blank interval, there had come the sound of voices, and then again the whirr of wheels, louder and louder – and again the blank – and then she knew no more till morning, when she awoke, feeling languid and oppressed.

She told Dr Parravicini of her dream one day, on the only occasion when she wanted his professional advice. She had suffered rather severely from the mosquitoes before Christmas – and had been almost frightened at finding a wound upon her arm which she could only attribute to the venomous sting of one of these torturers. Parravicini put on his glasses, and scrutinized the angry mark on the round, white arm, as Bella stood before him and Lady Ducayne with her sleeve rolled up above her elbow.

'Yes, that's rather more than a joke,' he said, 'he has caught you on the top of a vein. What a vampire! But there's no harm done, signorina, nothing that a little dressing of mine won't heal.

'You must always show me any bite of this nature. It might be dangerous if neglected. These creatures feed on poison and dissem-inate it.'

'And to think that such tiny creatures can bite like this,' said Bella; 'my arm looks as if it had been cut by a knife.'

'If I were to show you a mosquito's sting under my microscope you wouldn't be surprised at that,' replied Parravicini.

Bella had to put up with the mosquito bites, even when they came on the top of a vein, and produced that ugly wound. The wound recurred now and then at longish intervals, and Bella found Dr Parravicini's dressing a speedy cure. If he were the quack his enemies called him, he had at least a light hand and a delicate touch in performing this small operation.

Bella Rolleston to Mrs Rolleston – April 14th.
Ever Dearest, – Behold the cheque for my second quarter's salary – five and twenty pounds.

There is no one to pinch off a whole tenner for a year's com-mission as there was last time, so it is all for you, mother, dear. I have plenty of pocket-money in hand from the cash I brought away with me, when you insisted on my keeping more than I wanted. It isn't possible to spend money here – except on occasional tips to servants, or sous to beggars and children – unless one had lots to spend, for everything one would like to buy – tortoise-shell, coral, lace – is so ridiculously dear that only a millionaire ought to look at it. Italy is a dream of beauty: but for shopping, give me Newington Causeway.

You ask me so earnestly if I am quite well that I fear my letters must have been very dull lately. Yes, dear, I am well – but I am not quite so strong as I was when I used to trudge to the West-end to buy half a pound of tea – just for a constitutional walk – or to Dulwich to look at the pictures. Italy is relaxing; and I feel what the people here call "slack". But I fancy I can see your dear face looking worried as you read this. And, indeed, I am not ill. I am only a little tired of this lovely scene – as I suppose one might get tired of looking at one of Turner's pictures if it hung on a wall that was always opposite one. I think of you every hour in every day – think of you and our homely little room – our dear little shabby parlour, with the arm-chairs from the wreck of your old home, and Dick singing in his cage over the sewing-machine. Dear, shrill, maddening Dick, who, we flattered ourselves, was so passionately fond of us. Do tell me in your next that he is well.

My friend Lotta and her brother never came back after all. They went from Pisa to Rome. Happy mortals! And they are to be on the Italian lakes in May; which lake was not decided when Lotta last wrote to me. She has been a charming correspondent, and has confided all her little flirtations to me. We are all to go to Bellaggio next week – by Genoa and Milan. Isn't that lovely? Lady Ducayne travels by the easiest stages – except when she is bottled up in the train de luxe. We shall stop two days at Genoa and one at Milan. What a bore I shall be to you with my talk about Italy when I come home.

Love and love – and ever more love from your adoring, Bella.

IV

Herbert Stafford and his sister had often talked of the pretty English girl with her fresh complexion, which made such a pleasant touch of rosy colour among all those sallow faces at the Grand Hotel. The young doctor thought of her with a compassionate tenderness – her utter loneliness in that great hotel where there were so many people, her bondage to that old, old woman, where everybody else was free to think of nothing but enjoying life. It was a hard fate; and the poor child was evidently devoted to her mother, and felt the pain of separation – only two of them, and very poor, and all the world to each other, he thought.

Lotta told him one morning that they were to meet again at Bellaggio. 'The old thing and her court are to be there before we are,' she said. 'I shall be charmed to have Bella again. She is so bright and gay – in spite of an occasional touch of homesickness. I never took to a girl on a short acquaintance as I did to her.'

'I like her best when she is homesick,' said Herbert, 'for then I am sure she has a heart.'

'What have you to do with hearts, except for dissection? Don't forget that Bella is an absolute pauper. She told me in confidence that her mother makes mantles for a West-end shop. You can hardly have a lower depth than that.'

'I shouldn't think any less of her if her mother made match-boxes.'

'Not in the abstract – of course not. Match-boxes are honest labour. But you couldn't marry a girl whose mother makes mantles.'

'We haven't come to the consideration of that question yet,' answered Herbert, who liked to provoke his sister.

In two years' hospital practice he had seen too much of the grim realities of life to retain any prejudices about rank. Cancer, phthisis, gangrene, leave a man with little respect for the outward differences which vary the husk of humanity. The kernel is always the same – fearfully and wonderfully made – a subject for pity and terror.

Mr Stafford and his sister arrived at Bellaggio in a fair May evening. The sun was going down as the steamer approached the pier; and all that glory of purple bloom which curtains every wall at this season of the year flushed and deepened in the glowing light. A group of ladies were standing on the pier watching the arrivals, and among them Herbert saw a pale face that startled him out of his wonted composure.

'There she is,' murmured Lotta, at his elbow, 'but how dreadfully changed. She looks a wreck.'

They were shaking hands with her a few minutes later, and a flush had lighted up her poor pinched face in the pleasure of meeting.

'I thought you might come this evening,' she said. 'We have been here a week.'

She did not add that she had been there every evening to watch the boat in, and a good many times during the day. The *Grand Bretagne* was close by, and it had been easy for her to creep to the pier when the boat bell rang. She felt a joy in meeting these people again; a sense of being with friends; a confidence which Lady Ducayne's goodness had never inspired in her.

'Oh, you poor darling, how awfully ill you must have been, exclaimed Lotta, as the two girls embraced.

Bella tried to answer, but her voice was choked with tears.

'What has been the matter, dear? That horrid influenza, I suppose?'

'No, no, I have not been ill – I have only felt a little weaker than I used to be. I don't think the air of Cap Ferrino quite agreed with me.'

'It must have disagreed with you abominably. I never saw such a change in anyone. Do let Herbert doctor you. He is fully qualified, you know. He prescribed for ever so many influenza patients at the Londres. They were glad to get advice from an English doctor in a friendly way.'

'I am sure he must be very clever!' faltered Bella, 'but there is really nothing the matter. I am not ill, and if I were ill, Lady Ducayne's physician –'

'That dreadful man with the yellow face? I would as soon one of the Borgias prescribed for me. I hope you haven't been taking any of his medicines.'

'No, dear, I have taken nothing. I have never complained of being ill.'

This was said while they were all three walking to the hotel. The Staffords' rooms had been secured in advance, pretty ground-floor rooms, opening into the garden. Lady Ducayne's statelier apartments were on the floor above.

'I believe these rooms are just under ours,' said Bella.

'Then it will be all the easier for you to run down to us,' replied

Lotta, which was not really the case, as the grand staircase was in the centre of the hotel.

'Oh, I shall find it easy enough,' said Bella. 'I'm afraid you'll have too much of my society. Lady Ducayne sleeps away half the day in this warm weather, so I have a good deal of idle time; and I get awfully moped thinking of mother and home.'

Her voice broke upon the last word. She could not have thought of that poor lodging which went by the name of home more tenderly had it been the most beautiful that art and wealth ever created. She moped and pined in this lovely garden, with the sunlit lake and the romantic hills spreading out their beauty before her. She was homesick and she had dreams: or, rather, an occasional recurrence of that one bad dream with all its strange sensations – it was more like a hallucination than dreaming – the whirring of wheels; the sinking into an abyss; the struggling back to consciousness. She had the dream shortly before she left Cap Ferrino, but not since she had come to Bellaggio, and she began to hope the air in this lake district suited her better, and that those strange sensations would never return.

Mr Stafford wrote a prescription and had it made up at the chemist's near the hotel. It was a powerful tonic, and after two bottles, and a row or two on the lake, and some rambling over the hills and in the meadows where the spring flowers made earth seem paradise, Bella's spirits and looks improved as if by magic.

'It is a wonderful tonic,' she said, but perhaps in her heart of hearts she knew that the doctor's kind voice and the friendly hand that helped her in and out of the boat, and the watchful care that went with her by land and lake, had something to do with her cure.

'I hope you don't forget that her mother makes mantles,' Lotta said, warningly.

'Or match-boxes: it is just the same thing, so far as I am concerned.'

'You mean that in no circumstances could you think of marrying her?'

'I mean that if ever I love a woman well enough to think of

marrying her, riches or rank will count for nothing with me. But I fear – I fear your poor friend may not live to be any man's wife.'

'Do you think her so very ill?'

He sighed, and left the question unanswered.

One day, while they were gathering wild hyacinths in an upland meadow, Bella told Mr Stafford about her bad dream.

'It is curious only because it is hardly like a dream,' she said. 'I daresay you could find some common-sense reason for it. The position of my head on my pillow, or the atmosphere, or something.'

And then she described her sensations; how in the midst of sleep there came a sudden sense of suffocation; and then those whirring wheels, so loud, so terrible; and then a blank, and then a coming back to waking consciousness.

'Have you ever had chloroform given you – by a dentist, for instance?'

'Never – Dr Parravicini asked me that question one day.'

'Lately?'

'No, long ago, when we were in the train de luxe.'

'Has Dr Parravicini prescribed for you since you began to feel weak and ill?'

'Oh, he has given me a tonic from time to time, but I hate medicine, and took very little of the stuff. And then I am not ill, only weaker than I used to be. I was ridiculously strong and well when I lived at Walworth, and used to take long walks every day. Mother made me take those tramps to Dulwich or Norwood, for fear I should suffer from too much sewing-machine; sometimes – but very seldom – she went with me. She was generally toiling at home while I was enjoying fresh air and exercise. And she was very careful about our food – that, however plain it was, it should be always nourishing and ample. I owe it to her care that I grew up such a great, strong creature.'

'You don't look great or strong now, you poor dear,' said Lotta.

'I'm afraid Italy doesn't agree with me.'

'Perhaps it is not Italy, but being cooped up with Lady Ducayne that has made you ill.'

'But I am never cooped up. Lady Ducayne is absurdly kind, and lets me roam about or sit in the balcony all day if I like. I have read more novels since I have been with her than in all the rest of my life.'

'Then she is very different from the average old lady, who is usually a slave-driver,' said Stafford. 'I wonder why she carries a companion about with her if she has so little need of society.'

'Oh, I am only part of her state. She is inordinately rich – and the salary she gives me doesn't count. Apropos of Dr Parravicini, I know he is a clever doctor, for he cures my horrid mosquito bites.'

'A little ammonia would do that, in the early stage of the mischief. But there are no mosquitoes to trouble you now.'

'Oh, yes, there are, I had a bite just before we left Cap Ferrino.'

She pushed up her loose lawn sleeve, and exhibited a scar, which he scrutinized intently, with a surprised and puzzled look.

'This is no mosquito bite,' he said.

'Oh, yes it is – unless there are snakes or adders at Cap Ferrino.'

'It is not a bite at all. You are trifling with me. Miss Rolleston – you have allowed that wretched Italian quack to bleed you. They killed the greatest man in modern Europe that way, remember. How very foolish of you.'

'I was never bled in my life, Mr Stafford.'

'Nonsense! Let me look at your other arm. Are there any more mosquito bites?'

'Yes; Dr Parravicini says I have a bad skin for healing, and that the poison acts more virulently with me than with most people.'

Stafford examined both her arms in the broad sunlight, scars new and old.

'You have been very badly bitten, Miss Rolleston,' he said, 'and if ever I find the mosquito I shall make him smart. But, now tell me, my dear girl, on your word of honour, tell me as you would tell a friend who is sincerely anxious for your health and happiness – as you would tell your mother if she were here to question you – have you no knowledge of any cause for these scars except mosquito bites – no suspicion even?'

'No, indeed! No, upon my honour! I have never seen a mosquito biting my arm. One never does see the horrid little fiends. But I have heard them trumpeting under the curtains, and I know that I have often had one of the pestilent wretches buzzing about me.'

Later in the day Bella and her friends were sitting at tea in the garden, while Lady Ducayne took her afternoon drive with her doctor.

'How long do you mean to stop with Lady Ducayne, Miss Rolleston?' Herbert Stafford asked, after a thoughtful silence, breaking suddenly upon the trivial talk of the two girls.

'As long as she will go on paying me twenty-five pounds a quarter.'

'Even if you feel your health breaking down in her service?'

'It is not the service that has injured my health. You can see that I have really nothing to do – to read aloud for an hour or so once or twice a week; to write a letter once in a way to a London tradesman. I shall never have such an easy time with anybody else. And nobody else would give me a hundred a year.'

'Then you mean to go on till you break down; to die at your post?'

'Like the other two companions? No! If ever I feel seriously ill – really ill – I shall put myself in a train and go back to Walworth without stopping.'

'What about the other two companions?'

'They both died. It was very unlucky for Lady Ducayne. That's why she engaged me; she chose me because I was ruddy and robust. She must feel rather disgusted at my having grown white and weak. By the bye, when I told her about the good your tonic had done me, she said she would like to see you and have a little talk with you about her own case.'

'And I should like to see Lady Ducayne. When did she say this?'

'The day before yesterday.'

'Will you ask her if she will see me this evening?'

'With pleasure. I wonder what you will think of her. She looks rather terrible to a stranger; but Dr Parravicini says she was once a famous beauty.'

It was nearly ten o'clock when Mr Stafford was summoned by message from Lady Ducayne, whose courier came to conduct him to her ladyship's salon. Bella was reading aloud when the visitor was admitted; and he noticed the languor in the low, sweet tones, the evident effort.

'Shut up the book,' said the querulous old voice. 'You are beginning to drawl like Miss Blandy.'

Stafford saw a small, bent figure crouching over the piled-up olive logs; a shrunken old figure in a gorgeous garment of black and crimson brocade, a skinny throat emerging from a mass of old Venetian lace, clasped with diamonds that flashed like fire-flies as the trembling old head turned towards him.

The eyes that looked at him out of the face were almost as bright as the diamonds – the only living feature in that narrow parchment mask. He had seen terrible faces in the hospital – faces on which disease had set dreadful marks – but he had never seen a face that impressed him so painfully as this withered countenance, with its indescribable horror of death outlived, a face that should have been hidden under a coffin-lid years and years ago.

The Italian physician was standing on the other side of the fireplace, smoking a cigarette, and looking down at the little old woman brooding over the hearth as if he were proud of her.

'Good evening, Mr Stafford; you can go to your room, Bella, and write your everlasting letter to your mother at Walworth,' said Lady Ducayne. 'I believe she writes a page about every wild flower she discovers in the woods and meadows. I don't know what else she can find to write about,' she added, as Bella quietly withdrew to the pretty little bedroom opening out of Lady Ducayne's spacious apartment. Here, as at Cap Ferrino, she slept in a room adjoining the old lady's.

'You are a medical man, I understand, Mr Stafford.'

'I am a qualified practitioner, but I have not begun to practise.'

'You have begun upon my companion, she tells me.'

'I have prescribed for her, certainly, and I am happy to find my prescription has done her good; but I look upon that improvement as temporary. Her case will require more drastic treatment.

'Never mind her case. There is nothing the matter with the girl – absolutely nothing – except girlish nonsense; too much liberty and not enough work.'

'I understand that two of your ladyship's previous companions died of the same disease,' said Stafford, looking first at Lady Ducayne, who gave her tremulous old head an impatient jerk, and then at Parravicini, whose yellow complexion had paled a little under Stafford's scrutiny.

'Don't bother me about my companions, sir,' said Lady Ducayne. 'I sent for you to consult you about myself – not about a parcel of anaemic girls. You are young, and medicine is a progressive science, the newspapers tell me. Where have you studied?'

'In Edinburgh – and in Paris.'

'Two good schools. And you know all the new-fangled theories, the modern discoveries – that remind one of the medieval witchcraft, of Albertus Magnus, and George Ripley; you have studied hypnotism – electricity?'

'And the transfusion of blood,' said Stafford, very slowly, looking at Parravicini.

'Have you made any discovery that teaches you to prolong human life – any elixir – any mode of treatment? I want my life prolonged, young man. That man there has been my physician for thirty years. He does all he can to keep me alive – after his lights. He studies all the new theories of all the scientists – but he is old; he gets older every day – his brain-power is going – he is bigoted – prejudiced – can't receive new ideas – can't grapple with new systems. He will let me die if I am not on my guard against him.'

'You are of an unbelievable ingratitude, Ecclenza,' said Parravicini.

'Oh, you needn't complain. I have paid you thousands to keep me alive. Every year of my life has swollen your hoards; you know there is nothing to come to you when I am gone. My whole fortune is left to endow a home for indigent women of quality who have reached their ninetieth year. Come, Mr Stafford, I am a rich woman. Give me a few years more in the sunshine, a few years more above ground, and I will give you the price of a fashionable London practice – I will set you up at the West-end.'

'How old are you, Lady Ducayne?'

'I was born the day Louis XVI was guillotined.'

'Then I think you have had your share of the sunshine and the pleasures of the earth, and that you should spend your few remaining days in repenting your sins and trying to make atonement for the young lives that have been sacrificed to your love of life.'

'What do you mean by that, sir?'

'Oh, Lady Ducayne, need I put your wickedness and your physician's still greater wickedness in plain words? The poor girl who is now in your employment has been reduced from robust health to a condition of absolute danger by Dr Parravicini's experimental surgery; and I have no doubt those other two young women who broke down in your service were treated by him in the same manner. I could take upon myself to demonstrate – by most convincing evidence, to a jury of medical men – that Dr Parravicini has been bleeding Miss Rolleston, after putting her under chloroform, at intervals, ever since she has been in your service. The deterioration in the girl's health speaks for itself; the lancet marks upon the girl's arms are unmistakable; and her description of a series of sensations, which she calls a dream, points unmistakably to the administration of chloroform while she was sleeping. A practice so nefarious, so murderous, must, if exposed, result in a sentence only less severe than the punishment of murder.'

'I laugh,' said Parravicini, with an airy motion of his skinny fingers; 'I laugh at once at your theories and at your threats. I, Parravicini Leopold, have no fear that the law can question anything I have done.'

'Take the girl away, and let me hear no more of her,' cried Lady Ducayne, in the thin, old voice, which so poorly matched the energy and fire of the wicked old brain that guided its utterances. 'Let her go back to her mother – I want no more girls to die in my service. There are girls enough and to spare in the world, God knows.'

'If you ever engage another companion – or take another English girl into your service, Lady Ducayne – I will make all England ring with the story of your wickedness.'

'I want no more girls. I don't believe in his experiments. They have been full of danger for me as well as for the girl – an air bubble, and I should be gone. I'll have no more of his dangerous quackery. I'll find some new man – a better man than you, sir, a discoverer like Pasteur, or Virchow, a genius – to keep me alive. Take your girl away, young man. Marry her if you like.

'I'll write her a cheque for a thousand pounds, and let her go and live on beef and beer, and get strong and plump again. I'll have no more such experiments. Do you hear, Parravicini?' she screamed, vindictively, the yellow, wrinkled face distorted with fury, the eyes glaring at him.

The Staffords carried Bella Rolleston off to Varese next day. She very loath to leave Lady Ducayne, whose liberal salary afforded such help for the dear mother. Herbert Stafford insisted, however, treating Bella as coolly as if he had been the family physician and she had been given over wholly to his care.

'Do you suppose your mother would let you stop here to die?' he asked. 'If Mrs Rolleston knew how ill you are, she would come post-haste to fetch you.

'I shall never be well again till I get back to Walworth,' answered Bella, who was low-spirited and inclined to tears this morning, a reaction after her good spirits of yesterday.

'We'll try a week or two at Varese first,' said Stafford. 'When you can walk half-way up Monte Generoso without palpitation of the heart, you shall go back to Walworth.'

'Poor mother, how glad she will be to see me, and how sorry that I've lost such a good place.'

This conversation took place on the boat when they were leaving Bellaggio. Lotta had gone to her friend's room at seven o'clock that morning, long before Lady Ducayne's withered eyelids had opened to the daylight, before even Francine, the French maid, was astir, and had helped to pack a Gladstone bag with essentials, and hustled Bella downstairs and out of doors before she could make any strenuous resistance.

'It's all right,' Lotta assured her. 'Herbert had a good talk with Lady Ducayne last night and it was settled for you to leave this morning. She doesn't like invalids, you see.'

'No,' sighed Bella, 'she doesn't like invalids. It was very unlucky that I should break down, just like Miss Tomson and Miss Blandy.'

'At any rate, you are not dead, like them,' answered Lotta, 'and my brother says you are not going to die.'

It seemed rather a dreadful thing to be dismissed in that off-hand way, without a word of farewell from her employer.

'I wonder what Miss Torpinter will say when I go to her for another situation,' Bella speculated, ruefully, while she and her friends were breakfasting on board the steamer.

'Perhaps you may never want another situation,' said Stafford.

'You mean that I may never be well enough to be useful to any-body?'

'No, I don't mean anything of the kind.'

It was after dinner at Varese, when Bella had been induced to take a whole glass of Chianti, and quite sparkled after that unaccustomed stimulant, that Mr Stafford produced a letter from his pocket.

'I forgot to give you Lady Ducayne's letter of adieu,' he said.

'What, did she write to me? I am so glad – I hated to leave her in such a cool way; for after all she was very kind to me, and if I didn't like her it was only because she was too dreadfully old.'

She tore open the envelope. The letter was short and to the point.

'Goodbye, child. Go and marry your doctor. I enclose a farewell gift for your trousseau. – Adeline Ducayne.'

'A hundred pounds, a whole year's salary – no – why, it's for a – a cheque for a thousand!' cried Bella. 'What a generous old soul! She really is the dearest old thing.'

'She just missed being very dear to you, Bella,' said Stafford.

He had dropped into the use of her Christian name while they were on board the boat. It seemed natural now that she was to be in his charge till they all three went back to England.

'I shall take upon myself the privileges of an elder brother till we land at Dover,' he said; 'after that – well, it must be as you please.'

The question of their future relations must have been satisfactorily settled before they crossed the Channel, for Bella's next letter to her mother communicated three startling facts.

First, that the enclosed cheque for £1,000 was to be invested in debenture stock in Mrs Rolleston's name, and was to be her very own, income and principal, for the rest of her life.

Next, that Bella was going home to Walworth immediately.

And last, that she was going to be married to Mr Herbert Stafford in the following autumn.

'And I am sure you will adore him, mother, as much as I do,' wrote Bella. 'It is all good Lady Ducayne's doing. I never could have married if I had not secured that little nest-egg for you.

'Herbert says we shall be able to add to it as the years go by, and that wherever we live there shall be always a room in our house for you. The word "mother-in-law" has no terrors for him.'

Mary Wilkins Freeman
THE HALL BEDROOM

Mary Wilkins Freeman (1852–1930) was one of the best of the New England regional writers who also produced a number of ghost and unusual stories. Some were collected as The Wind in the Rose Bush *(1903) with the majority in* Collected Ghost Stories *(1974). The following story, which was first published in 1903, was not included in either of those volumes, even though some may regard it as supernatural. It is certainly an unusual tale and very advanced for its time. The idea that there might be a world beyond our own and one that we might slip into in dreams had, of course, been around for a long time and was linked to the world of 'faerie', which somehow existed in a different time-scale to our own. But the idea of a mathematical proof for a fourth or fifth dimension beyond the three we know (a point, a square and a cube) had only been set down by Charles H. Hinton in a series of essays collected as* Scientific Romances *(1884). Earlier, Johann Zöllner had introduced mathematical concepts in* Transcendental Physics *(1865) in order to justify the idea of an astral plane, which was key to the belief of spiritualists and later theosophists. Mary Freeman must have been aware of the thinking in either of these books, perhaps through the literary circles she maintained, which included Mark Twain, Henry James and William Dean Howells. Few writers had used the concept of the mathematical fourth or fifth dimension in fiction prior to Mary Freeman and none in quite the way she did.*

The Hall Bedroom

MY NAME IS Mrs Elizabeth Jennings. I am a highly respectable woman. I may style myself a gentlewoman, for in my youth I enjoyed advantages. I was well brought up, and I graduated at a young ladies' seminary. I also married well. My husband was that most genteel of all merchants, an apothecary. His shop was on the corner of the main street in Rockton, the town where I was born, and where I lived until the death of my husband. My parents had died when I had been married a short time, so I was left quite alone in the world. I was not competent to carry on the apothecary business by myself, for I had no knowledge of drugs, and had a mortal terror of giving poisons instead of medicines. Therefore I was obliged to sell at a considerable sacrifice, and the proceeds, some five thousand dollars, were all I had in the world. The income was not enough to support me in any kind of comfort, and I saw that I must in some way earn money. I thought at first of teaching, but I was no longer young, and methods had changed since my school days. What I was able to teach, nobody wished to know. I could think of only one thing to do: take boarders. But the same objection to that business as to teaching held good in Rockton. Nobody wished to board. My husband had rented a house with a number of bedrooms, and I advertised, but nobody applied. Finally my cash was running very low, and I became desperate. I packed up my furniture, rented a large house in this town and moved here. It was a venture attended with many risks. In the first place the rent was exorbitant, in the next I was entirely unknown. However, I am a person of considerable ingenuity, and have inventive power, and much enterprise when the occasion presses. I advertised in a very original manner, although that actually took my last penny, that is, the last penny of my ready money, and I was forced to draw on my principal to purchase my first supplies, a thing which I had resolved never on any account to do. But the great risk met with a reward, for I had several applicants within two days after my advertisement appeared in the paper. Within two weeks my boarding-house was well established, I became very successful, and my success would have been uninterrupted had it not been for the mysterious and bewildering occurrences which I am about to relate. I am now forced to leave the house and rent another. Some of my old boarders accompany me, some, with the most unreasonable nervousness, refuse to be longer associated in any way, however indirectly, with the terrible and uncanny happenings which I have to relate. It remains to be seen whether my ill luck in this house will follow me into another, and whether my whole prosperity in life will be for ever shadowed by the Mystery of the Hall Bedroom. Instead of telling the strange story myself in my own words, I shall present the journal of Mr George H. Wheatcroft. I shall show you the portions beginning on January 18 of the present year, the date when he took up his residence with me. Here it is:

JANUARY 18, 1883. Here I am established in my new boarding-house. I have, as befits my humble means, the hall bedroom, even the hall bedroom on the third floor. I have heard all my life of hall bedrooms, I have seen hall bedrooms, I have been in them, but never until now, when I am actually established in one, did I comprehend what, at once, an ignominious and sternly uncompromising thing a hall bedroom is. It proves the ignominy of the dweller therein. No man at thirty-six (my age) would be domiciled in a hall bedroom, unless he were himself ignominious, at least comparatively speaking. I am proved by this means incontrovertibly to have been left far behind in the race. I see no reason why I should not live in this hall bedroom for the rest of my life, that is, if I have money enough to pay the landlady, and that seems probable, since my small funds are invested as safely as if I were an orphan-ward in charge of a pillar of a sanctuary. After the valuables have been stolen, I have most carefully locked the stable door. I have experienced the revulsion which comes sooner or later to the adventurous soul who experiences nothing but defeat and so-called ill luck. I have swung to the opposite extreme. I have lost in everything – I have lost in love, I have lost in money, I have lost in the struggle for preferment, I have lost in health and strength. I am now settled down in a hall bedroom to live upon my small income, and regain my health by mild potations of the mineral waters here, if possible; if not, to live here without my health – for mine is not a necessarily fatal malady – until Providence shall take me out of my hall bedroom. There is no one place more than another where I care to live. There is not sufficient motive to take me away, even if the mineral waters do not benefit me. So I am here and to stay in the hall bedroom. The landlady is civil, and even kind, as kind as a woman who has to keep her poor womanly eye upon the main chance can be. The struggle for money always injures the fine grain of a woman; she is too fine a thing to do it; she does not by nature belong with the gold grubbers, and it therefore lowers her; she steps from heights to claw and scrape and dig. But she cannot help it oftentimes, poor thing, and her deterioration thereby is to be condoned. The landlady is all she can be, taking her strain of adverse circumstances into consideration, and the table is good, even conscientiously so. It looks to me as if she were foolish enough to strive to give the boarders their money's worth, with the due regard for the main chance which is inevitable. However, that is of minor importance to me, since my diet is restricted.

It is curious what an annoyance a restriction in diet can be, even to a man who has considered himself somewhat indifferent to gastronomic delights. There was today a pudding for dinner, which I could not taste without penalty, but which I longed for. It was only because it looked unlike any other pudding that I had ever seen, and assumed a mental and spiritual significance. It seemed to me, whimsically no doubt, as if tasting it might give me a new sensation, and consequently a new outlook. Trivial things may lead to large results: why should I not get a new outlook by means of a pudding? Life here stretches before me most monotonously, and I feel like clutching at alleviations, though paradoxically, since I have settled down with the utmost acquiescence. Still one can not immediately overcome and change radically all one's nature. Now I look at myself critically and search for the keynote to my whole self, and my actions; I have always been conscious of a reaching out, an overweening desire for the new, the untried, for the broadness of further horizons, the seas beyond seas, the thought beyond thought. This characteristic has been the primary cause of all my misfortunes. I have the soul of an explorer, and in nine out of ten cases this leads to destruction. If I had possessed capital and sufficient push, I should have been one of the searchers after the North Pole. I have been an eager student of astronomy. I have studied botany with avidity, and have dreamed of new flora in unexplored parts of the world, and the same with animal life and geology. I longed for riches in order to discover the power and sense of possession of the rich. I longed for love in order to discover the possibilities of the emotions. I longed for all that the mind of man could conceive as desirable for man, not so much for purely selfish ends, as from an insatiable thirst for knowledge of a universal trend. But I have limitations, I do not quite understand of what nature – for what mortal ever did quite understand his own limitations, since a knowledge of them would preclude their existence? – but they have prevented my progress to any extent. Therefore behold me in my hall bedroom, settled at last into a groove of fate so deep that I have lost the sight of even my horizons. Just at present, as I write here, my horizon on the left, that is my physical horizon, is a wall covered with cheap paper. The paper is an indeterminate pattern in white and gilt. There are a few photographs of my own hung about, and on the large wall space beside the bed there is a large oil painting which belongs to my landlady. It has a massive tarnished gold frame, and, curiously enough, the painting itself is rather good. I have no idea who the artist could have been. It is of the conventional landscape type in vogue some fifty years since, the type so fondly reproduced in chromos – the winding river with the little boat occupied by a pair of lovers, the cottage nestled among trees on the right shore, the gentle slope of the hills and the church spire in the background – but still it is well done. It gives me the impression of an artist without the slightest originality of design, but much of technique. But for some inexplicable reason the picture frets me. I find myself gazing at it when I do not wish to do so. It seems to compel my attention like some intent face in the room. I shall ask Mrs Jennings to have it removed. I will hang in its place some photographs which I have in a trunk.

JANUARY 26. I do not write regularly in my journal. I never did. I see no reason why I should. I see no reason why anyone should have the slightest sense of duty in such a matter. Some days I have nothing which interests me sufficiently to write out, some days I feel either too ill or too indolent. For four days I have not written, from a mixture of all three reasons. Now, today I both feel like it and I have something to write. Also I am distinctly better than I have been. Perhaps the waters are benefiting me, or the change of air. Or possibly it is something else more subtle. Possibly my mind has seized upon something new, a discovery which causes it to react upon my failing body and serves as a stimulant. All I know is, I feel distinctly better, and am conscious of an acute interest in doing so, which is of late strange to me. I have been rather indifferent, and sometimes have wondered if that were not the cause rather than the result of my state of health. I have been so continually balked that I have settled into a state of inertia. I lean rather comfortably against my obstacles. After all, the worst of the pain always lies in the struggle. Give up and it is rather pleasant than otherwise. If one did not kick, the pricks would not in the least matter. However, for some reason, for the last few days, I seem to have awakened from my state of quiescence. It means future trouble for me, no doubt, but in the meantime I am not sorry. It began with the picture – the large oil painting. I went to Mrs Jennings about it yesterday, and she, to my surprise – for I thought it a matter that could be easily arranged – objected to having it removed. Her reasons were two; both simple, both sufficient, especially since I, after all, had no very strong desire either way. It seems that the picture does not belong to her. It hung here when she rented the house. She says if it is removed a very large and unsightly discoloration of the wall-paper will be exposed, and she does not like to ask for new paper. The owner, an old man, is travelling abroad, the agent is curt, and she has only been in the house a very short time. Then it would mean a sad upheaval of my room, which would disturb me. She also says that there is no place in the house where she can store the picture, and there is not a vacant space in another room for one so large. So I let the picture remain. It really, when I came to think of it, was very immaterial after all. But I got my photographs out of my trunk, and I hung them around the large picture. The wall is almost completely covered. I hung them yesterday afternoon, and last night I repeated a strange experience which I have had in some degree every night since I have been here, but was not sure whether it deserved the name of experience, but was not rather one of those dreams in which one dreams one is awake. But last night it came again, and now I know. There is something very singular about this room. I am very much interested. I will write down for future reference the events of last night. Concerning those of the preceding nights since I have slept in this room, I will simply say that they have been of a similar nature, but, as it were, only the preliminary stages, the prologue to what happened last night.

I am not depending upon the mineral waters here as the one remedy for my malady, which is sometimes of an acute nature, and indeed constantly threatens me with considerable suffering unless by medicine I can keep it in check. I will say that the medicine which I employ is not of the class commonly known as drugs. It is impossible that it can be held responsible for what I am about to transcribe. My mind last night and every night since I have slept in this room was in an absolutely normal state. I take this medicine, prescribed by the specialist in whose charge I was before coming here, regularly every four hours while awake. As I am never a good sleeper, it follows that I am enabled with no inconvenience to take any medicine during the night with the same regularity as during the day. It is my habit, therefore, to place my bottle and spoon where I can put my hand upon them easily without lighting the gas. Since I have been in this room, I have placed the bottle of medicine upon my dresser at the side of the room opposite the bed. I have done this rather than place it nearer, as once I jostled the bottle and spilled most of the contents, and it is not easy for me to replace it, as it is expensive. Therefore I placed it in security on the dresser, and, indeed, that is but three or four steps from my bed, the room being so small. Last night I wakened as usual, and I knew, since I had fallen asleep about eleven, that it must be in the neighbourhood of three. I wake with almost clock-like regularity and it is never necessary for me to consult my watch.

I had slept unusually well and without dreams, and I awoke fully at once, with a feeling of refreshment to which I am not accustomed. I immediately got out of bed and began stepping across the room in the direction of my dresser, on which I had set my medicine-bottle and spoon.

To my utter amazement, the steps which had hitherto sufficed to take me across my room did not suffice to do so. I advanced several paces, and my outstretched hands touched nothing. I stopped and went on again. I was sure that I was moving in a straight direction, and even if I had not been I knew it was impossible to advance in any direction in my tiny apartment without coming into collision either with a wall or a piece of furniture. I continued to walk falteringly, as I have seen people on the stage: a step, then a long falter, then a sliding step. I kept my hands extended; they touched nothing. I stopped again. I had not the least sentiment of fear or consternation. It was rather the very stupefaction of surprise. 'How is this?' seemed thundering in my ears. 'What is this?'

The room was perfectly dark. There was nowhere any glimmer, as is usually the case, even in a so-called dark room, from the walls, picture-frames, looking-glass or white objects. It was absolute gloom. The house stood in a quiet part of the town. There were many trees about; the electric street lights were extinguished at midnight; there was no moon and the sky was cloudy. I could not distinguish my one window, which I thought strange, even on such a dark night. Finally I changed my plan of motion and turned, as nearly as I could estimate, at right angles. Now, I thought, I must reach soon, if, I kept on, my writing-table underneath the window; or, if I am going in the opposite direction, the hall door. I reached neither. I am telling the unvarnished truth when I say that I began to count my steps and carefully measure my paces after that, and I traversed a space clear of furniture at least twenty feet by thirty – a very large apartment. And as I walked I was conscious that my naked feet were pressing something which gave rise to sensations the like of which I had never experienced before. As nearly as I can express it, it was as if my feet pressed something as elastic as air or water, which was in this case unyielding to my weight. It gave me a curious sensation of buoyancy and stimulation. At the same time this surface, if surface be the right name, which I trod, felt cool to my feet with the coolness of vapour or fluidity, seeming to overlap the soles.

Finally I stood still; my surprise was at last merging into a measure of consternation. 'Where am I?' I thought. 'What am I going to do?' Stories that I had heard of travellers being taken from their beds and conveyed into strange and dangerous places, Middle Age stories of the Inquisition flashed through my brain. I knew all the time that for a man who had gone to bed in a commonplace hall bedroom in a very commonplace little town such surmises were highly ridiculous, but it is hard for the human mind to grasp anything but a human explanation of phenomena. Almost anything seemed then, and seems now, more rational than an explanation bordering upon the supernatural, as we understand the supernatural. At last I called, though rather softly, 'What does this mean?' I said quite aloud, 'Where am I? Who is here? Who is doing this? I tell you I will have no such nonsense. Speak, if there is anybody here.' But all was dead silence. Then suddenly a light flashed through the open transom of my door. Somebody had heard me – a man who rooms next door, a decent kind of man, also here for his health. He turned on the gas in the hall and called to me. 'What's the matter?' he asked, in an agitated, trembling voice. He is a nervous fellow.

Directly, when the light flashed through my transom, I saw that I was in my familiar hall bedroom. I could see everything quite distinctly – my tumbled bed, my writing-table, my dresser, my chair, my little wash-stand, my clothes hanging on a row of pegs, the old picture on the wall. The picture gleamed out with singular distinctness in the light from the transom. The river seemed actually to run and ripple, and the boat to be gliding with the current. I gazed fascinated at it, as I replied to the anxious voice:

'Nothing is the matter with me,' said I. 'Why?'

'I thought I heard you speak,' said the man outside. 'I thought maybe you were sick.'

'No,' I called back. 'I am all right. I am trying to find my medicine in the dark, that's all. I can see now you have lighted the gas.'

'Nothing is the matter?'

'No; sorry I disturbed you. Good-night.'

'Good-night.' Then I heard the man's door shut after a minute's pause. He was evidently not quite satisfied. I took a pull at my medicine-bottle, and got into bed. He had left the hall-gas burning. I did not go to sleep again for some time. Just before I did so, some one, probably Mrs Jennings, came out in the hall and extinguished the gas. This morning when I awoke everything was as usual in my room. I wonder if I shall have any such experience tonight.

JANUARY 27. I shall write in my journal every day until this draws to some definite issue. Last night my strange experience deepened, as something tells me it will continue to do. I retired quite early, at half past ten. I took the precaution, on retiring, to place beside my bed, on a chair, a box of safety matches, that I might not be in the dilemma of the night before. I took my medicine on retiring; that made me due to wake at half past two. I had not fallen asleep directly, but had had certainly three hours of sound, dreamless slumber when I awoke. I lay a few minutes hesitating whether or not to strike a safety match and light my way to the dresser, whereon stood my medicine-bottle. I hesitated, not because I had the least sensation of fear, but because of the same shrinking from a nerve shock that leads one at times to dread the plunge into an icy bath. It seemed much easier to me to strike that match and cross my hall bedroom to my dresser, take my dose, then return quietly to my bed, than to risk the chance of floundering about in some unknown limbo either of fancy or reality.

At last, however, the spirit of adventure, which has always been such a ruling one for me, conquered. I rose. I took the box of safety matches in my hand, and started on, as I conceived, the straight course for my dresser, about five feet across from my bed. As before, I travelled and travelled and did not reach it. I advanced with groping hands extended, setting one foot cautiously before the other, but I touched nothing except the indefinite, unnameable surface which my feet pressed.

All of a sudden, though, I became aware of something. One of my senses was saluted, nay, more than that, hailed, with imperiousness, and that was, strangely enough, my sense of smell, but in a hitherto unknown fashion. It seemed as if the odour reached my mentality first. I reversed the usual process, which is, as I understand it, like this: the odour when encountered strikes first the olfactory nerve, which transmits the intelligence to the brain. It is as if, to put it rudely, my nose met a rose, and then the nerve belonging to the sense said to my brain, 'Here is a rose.' This time my brain said, 'Here is a rose,' and my sense then recognized it. I say rose, but it was not a rose, that is, not the fragrance of any rose which I had ever known. It was undoubtedly a flower odour, and rose came perhaps the nearest to it. My mind realized it first with what seemed a leap of rapture. 'What is this delight?' I asked myself. And then the ravishing fragrance smote my sense. I breathed it in and it seemed to feed my thoughts, satisfying some hitherto unknown hunger. Then I took a step further and another fragrance appeared, which I liken to lilies for lack of something better, and then came violets, then mignonette. I can not describe the experience, but it was a sheer delight, a rapture of sublimated sense. I groped further and further, and always into new waves of fragrance. I seemed to be wading breast-high through flower-beds of Paradise, but all the time I touched nothing with my groping hands. At last a sudden giddiness as of surfeit overcame me. I realized that I might be in some unknown peril. I was distinctly afraid. I struck one of my safety matches, and I was in my hall bedroom, midway between my bed and my dresser. I took my dose of medicine and went to bed, and after a while fell asleep and did not wake till morning.

JANUARY 28. Last night I did not take my usual dose of medicine. In these days of new remedies and mysterious results upon certain organizations, it occurred to me to wonder if possibly the drug might have, after all, something to do with my strange experience.

I did not take my medicine. I put the bottle as usual on my dresser, since I feared if I interrupted further the customary sequence of affairs I might fail to wake. I placed my box of matches on the chair beside the bed. I fell asleep about quarter past eleven o'clock, and I waked when the clock was striking two – a little earlier than my wont. I did not hesitate this time. I rose at once, took my box of matches and proceeded as formerly. I walked what seemed a great space without coming into collision with anything. I kept sniffing for the wonderful fragrances of the night before, but they did not recur. Instead, I was suddenly aware that I was tasting something, some morsel of sweetness hitherto unknown, and, as in the case of the odour, the usual order seemed reversed, and it was as if I tasted it first in my mental consciousness. Then the sweetness rolled under my tongue. I thought involuntarily of 'Sweeter than honey or the honeycomb' of the Scripture. I thought of the Old Testament manna.

An ineffable content as of satisfied hunger seized me. I stepped further, and a new savour was upon my palate. And so on. It was never cloying, though of such sharp sweetness that it fairly stung. It was the merging of a material sense into a spiritual one. I said to myself, 'I have lived my life and always have I gone hungry until now.' I could feel my brain act swiftly under the influence of this heavenly food as under a stimulant. Then suddenly I repeated the experience of the night before. I grew dizzy, and an indefinite fear and shrinking were upon me. I struck my safety match and was back in my hall bedroom. I returned to bed, and soon fell asleep. I did not take my medicine. I am resolved not to do so longer. I am feeling much better.

JANUARY 29. Last night to bed as usual, matches in place; fell asleep about eleven and waked at half-past one. I heard the half-hour strike; I am waking earlier and earlier every night. I had not taken my medicine, though it was on the dresser as usual. I again took my match-box in hand and started to cross the room, and, as always, traversed strange spaces, but this night, as seems fated to be the case every night, my experience was different. Last night I neither smelled nor tasted, but I heard – my Lord, I heard! The first sound of which I was conscious was one like the constantly gathering and receding murmur of a river, and it seemed to come from the wall behind my bed where the old picture hangs. Nothing in nature except a river gives that impression of at once advance and retreat. I could not mistake it. On, ever on, came the swelling murmur of the waves, past and ever past they died in the distance. Then I heard above the murmur of the river a song in an unknown tongue which I recognized as being unknown, yet which I understood; but the understanding was in my brain, with no words of interpretation. The song had to do with me, but with me in unknown futures for which I had no images of comparison in the past; yet a sort of ecstasy as of a prophecy of bliss filled my whole consciousness. The song never ceased, but as I moved on I came into new sound-waves. There was the pealing of bells which might have been made of crystal, and might have summoned to the gates of heaven. There was music of strange instruments, great harmonies pierced now and then by small whispers as of love, and it all filled me with a certainty of a future of bliss.

At last I seemed the centre of a mighty orchestra which constantly deepened and increased until I seemed to feel myself being lifted gently but mightily upon the waves of sound as upon the waves of a sea. Then again the terror and the impulse to flee to my own familiar scenes was upon me. I struck my match and was back in my hall bedroom. I do not see how I sleep at all after such wonders, but sleep I do. I slept dreamlessly until daylight this morning.

JANUARY 30. I heard yesterday something with regard to my hall bedroom which affected me strangely. I cannot for the life of me say whether it intimidated me, filled me with the horror of the abnormal, or rather roused to a greater degree my spirit of adventure and discovery. I was down at the Cure, and was sitting on the veranda sipping idly my mineral water, when somebody spoke my name. 'Mr Wheatcroft?' said the voice politely, interrogatively, somewhat apologetically, as if to provide for a possible mistake in my identity. I turned and saw a gentleman whom I recognized at once. I seldom forget names or faces. He was a Mr Addison whom I had seen considerable of three years ago at a little summer hotel in the mountains. It was one of those passing acquaintances which signify little one way or the other. If never renewed, you have no regret; if renewed, you accept the renewal with no hesitation. It is in every way negative. But just now, in my feeble, friendless state, the sight of a face which beams with pleased remembrance is rather grateful. I felt distinctly glad to see the man. He sat down beside me. He also had a glass of the water. His health, while not as bad as mine, leaves much to be desired.

Addison had often been in this town before. He had in fact lived here at one time. He had remained at the Cure three years, taking the waters daily. He therefore knows about all there is to be known about the town, which is not very large. He asked me where I was staying, and when I told him the street, rather excitedly inquired the number. When I told him the number, which is 240, he gave a manifest start, and after one sharp glance at me sipped his water in silence for a moment. He had so evidently betrayed some ulterior knowledge with regard to my residence that I questioned him.

'What do you know about 240 Pleasant Street?' said I.

'Oh, nothing,' he replied, evasively, sipping his water.

After a little while, however, he inquired, in what he evidently tried to render a casual tone, what room I occupied. 'I once lived a few weeks at 240 Pleasant Street myself,' he said. 'That house always was a boarding-house, I guess.'

'It had stood vacant for a term of years before the present occupant rented it, I believe,' I remarked. Then I answered his question. 'I have the hall bedroom on the third floor,' said I. 'The quarters are pretty straitened, but comfortable enough as hall bedrooms go.'

But Mr Addison had showed such unmistakable consternation at my reply that then I persisted in my questioning as to the cause, and at last he yielded and told me what he knew. He had hesitated, both because he shrank from displaying what I might consider an unmanly superstition, and because he did not wish to influence me beyond what the facts of the case warranted. 'Well, I will tell you, Wheatcroft,' he said. 'Briefly all I know is this: When last I heard of 240 Pleasant Street it was not rented because of foul play which was supposed to have taken place there, though nothing was ever proved. There were two disappearances, and – in each case – of an occupant of the hall bedroom which you now have. The first disappearance was of a very beautiful girl who had come here for her health and was said to be the victim of a profound melancholy, induced by a love disappointment. She obtained board at 240 and occupied the hall bedroom about two weeks; then one morning she was gone, having seemingly vanished into thin air. Her relatives were communicated with; she had not many, nor friends either, poor girl, and a thorough search was made, but the last I knew she had never come to light. There were two or three arrests, but nothing ever came of them. Well, that was before my day here, but the second disappearance took place when I was in the house – a fine young fellow who had overworked in college. He had to pay his own way. He had taken cold, had the grip, and that and the overwork about finished him, and he came on here for a month's rest and recuperation. He had been in that room about two weeks, a little less, when one morning he wasn't there. Then there was a great hullabaloo. It seems that he had let fall some hints to the effect that there was something queer about the room, but, of course, the police did not think much of that. They made arrests right and left, but they never found him, and the arrested were discharged, though some of them are probably under a cloud of suspicion to this day. Then the boarding-house was shut up. Six years ago nobody would have boarded there, much less occupied that hall bedroom, but now I suppose new people have come in and the story has died out. I dare say your landlady will not thank me for reviving it.'

I assured him that it would make no possible difference to me. He looked at me sharply, and asked bluntly if I had seen anything wrong or unusual about the room. I replied, guarding myself from falsehood with a quibble, that I had seen nothing in the least unusual about the room, as indeed I had not, and have not now, but that may come. I feel that that will come in due time. Last night I neither saw, nor heard, nor smelled, nor tasted, but I felt. Last night, having started again on my exploration of, God knows what, I had not advanced a step before I touched something. My first sensation was one of disappointment. 'It is the dresser, and I am at the end of it now,' I thought. But I soon discovered that it was not the old painted dresser which I touched, but something carved, as nearly as I could discover with my unskilled finger-tips, with winged things. There were certainly long keen curves of wings which seemed to overlay an arabesque of fine leaf and flower work. I do not know what the object was that I touched. It may have been a chest. I may seem to be exaggerating when I say that it somehow failed or exceeded in some mysterious respect of being the shape of anything I had ever touched. I do not know what the material was. It was as smooth as ivory, but it did not feel like ivory; there was a singular warmth about it, as if it had stood long in hot sunlight. I continued, and I encountered other objects I am inclined to think were pieces of furniture of fashions and possibly of uses unknown to me, and about them all was the strange mystery as to shape. At last I came to what was evidently an open window of large area. I distinctly felt a soft, warm wind, yet with a crystal freshness, blow on my face. It was not the window of my hall bedroom, that I know. Looking out, I could see nothing. I only felt the wind blowing on my face.

Then suddenly, without any warning, my groping hands to the right and left touched living beings, beings in the likeness of men and women, palpable creatures in palpable attire. I could feel the soft silken texture of their garments which swept around me, seeming to half infold me in clinging meshes like cobwebs. I was in a crowd of these people, whatever they were, and whoever they were, but, curiously enough, without seeing one of them I had a strong sense of recognition as I passed among them. Now and then a hand that I knew closed softly over mine; once an arm passed around me. Then I began to feel myself gently swept on and impelled by this softly moving throng; their floating garments seemed to fairly wind me about, and again a swift terror overcame me. I struck my match, and was back in my hall bedroom. I wonder if I had not better keep my gas burning tonight? I wonder if it be possible that this is going too far? I wonder what became of those other people, the man and the woman who occupied this room? I wonder if I had better not stop where I am?

JANUARY 31. Last night I saw – I saw more than I can describe, more than is lawful to describe. Something which nature has rightly hidden has been revealed to me, but it is not for me to disclose too much of her secret. This much I will say, that doors and windows open into an out-of-doors to which the outdoors which we know is but a vestibule. And there is a river; there is something strange with respect to that picture. There is a river upon which one could sail away. It was flowing silently, for tonight I could only see. I saw that I was right in thinking I recognized some of the people whom I encountered the night before, though some were strange to me. It is true that the girl who disappeared from the hall bedroom was very beautiful. Everything which I saw last night was very beautiful to my one sense that could grasp it. I wonder what it would all be if all my senses together were to grasp it? I wonder if I had better not keep my gas burning tonight? I wonder –

*

This finishes the journal which Mr Wheatcroft left in his hall bedroom. The morning after the last entry he was gone. His friend, Mr Addison, came here, and a search was made. They even tore down the wall behind the picture, and they did find something rather queer for a house that had been used for boarders, where you would think no room would be let run to waste. They found another room, a long, narrow one, the length of the hall bedroom, but narrower, hardly more than a closet. There was no window, nor door, and all there was in it was a sheet of paper covered with figures, as if somebody had been doing sums.

They made a lot of talk about those figures, and they tried to make out that the fifth dimension, whatever that is, was proved, but they said afterwards they didn't prove anything. They tried to make out then that somebody had murdered poor Mr Wheatcroft and hid the body, and they arrested poor Mr Addison, but they couldn't make out anything against him. They proved he was in the Cure all that night and couldn't have done it. They don't know what became of Mr Wheatcroft, and now they say two more disappeared from that same room before I rented the house.

The agent came and promised to put the new room they discovered into the hall bedroom and have everything new-papered and painted. He took away the picture; folks hinted there was something queer about that, I don't know what. It looked innocent enough, and I guess he burned it up. He said if I would stay he would arrange it with the owner, who everybody says is a very queer man, so I should not have to pay much, if any, rent. But I told him I couldn't stay if he was to give me the rent. That I wasn't afraid of anything myself, though I must say I wouldn't want to put anybody in that hall bedroom without telling him all about it; but my boarders would leave, and I knew I couldn't get any more. I told him I would rather have had a regular ghost than what seemed to be a way of going out of the house to nowhere and never coming back again. I moved, and, as I said before, it remains to be seen whether my ill luck follows me to this house or not. Anyway, it has no hall bedroom.

G.M. Barrows

THE CURIOUS EXPERIENCE OF THOMAS DUNBAR

The name of Francis Stevens is almost legendary among devotees of early scientific romance as being the first woman writer to contribute such fiction regularly to the pulp magazines. Despite the masculine spelling of her first name there were those who believed it was an alias that masked the identity of a woman, and so it proved to be. It was years before Francis Stevens was identified and even longer before her details were pieced together. It was discovered that she was Gertrude Mary Barrows Bennett (1883–1948) – the Bennett being added after her marriage – a secretary and clerk living in Philadelphia at the time she was writing and looking after her widowed invalid mother and young daughter. Bennett's husband had drowned in an accident a few years earlier, and she turned to writing for additional income. After her mother's death she continued to write for a while but then returned to secretarial work. Just what it was in her background that caused her to write such remarkable stories is not known. She had, for a while, worked as a secretary for a professor at the University of Pennsylvania, typing students' papers, so she may have picked up some ideas there. She moved to California in 1926 and remarried, becoming estranged from her daughter, and wrote no more.

The name Francis Stevens appeared on seven serials and five short stories from 1917 to 1923 and then vanished. The fact that nothing else appeared added to the mystery. Moreover, her best remembered serial, 'The Heads of Cerberus', which appeared in one of the rarest pulp magazines, The Thrill Book, *during 1919, was the first novel to develop the idea of other dimensions and consider variant time streams and alternate worlds. The serial was eventually published in hardcover in 1952 but only in a limited edition. It has only been since the 1970s that most of her work has been available again. This includes the novels* The Citadel of Fear *and* Claimed *and a story collection* The Nightmare *(2004).*

The following is missing from that collection. In a short note that Bennett wrote to accompany the start of Claimed *in* The Argosy *in 1920, she said she had written her first story when she was seventeen and that, although she thought it was wonderful, she was still surprised when the first magazine she submitted it to,* The Argosy, *bought and published it. She did not identify the story, but avid collectors eventually tracked it down in the March 1904 edition where it had appeared under her maiden name, G.M. Barrows.*

The Curious Experience of Thomas Dunbar

I CAME BACK into conscious existence with a sighing in my ears like the deep breathing of a great monster; it was everywhere, pervading space, filling my mind to the exclusion of thought.

Just a sound – regular, even soothing in its nature – but it seemed to bear some weird significance to my clouded brain. That was thought trying to force its way in.

Then waves and waves of whispering that washed all thought away – till I grasped again at some confused and wandering idea.

It was the definite sensation of a cool, firm hand laid on my brow that lifted me up at last through that surging ocean of sighs. As a diver from the depths I came up – up – and emerged suddenly, it seemed, into the world.

I opened my eyes wide and looked straight up into the face of a man. A man – but everything was swimming before my eyes, and at first his face seemed no more than part of a lingering dream.

And fantastic visions of the Orient! What a face! It was wrinkled as finely as the palm of a woman's hand, and in as many directions.

It was yellow in hue, and round like a baby's. And the eyes were narrow, and black, and they slanted, shining like a squirrel's.

I thought that of them at first; but sometimes when you just happened to look at him, they seemed to have widened and to be possessed of strange depths and hues.

In height he was not more than four feet five, and, of all contrasts, this little, wizened curiosity with the countenance of a Chinese god was clad in the very careful and appropriate afternoon attire of a very careful and appropriate American gentleman!

The long sighing was still in my ears, but no longer at war with thought. I lay in a neat white bedstead in a plainly furnished room.

I lifted my hand (it took an astonishing effort to do it), rubbed my eyes, and stared at the man who sat beside me.

His expression was kind, and in spite of its ugliness there was something in the strange face which encouraged me to friendliness.

'What – what's the matter with me?' I asked, and I was surprised to note the question was a mere whisper.

'Nothing now, except that you are very weak.'

His voice was full, strong, and of a peculiar resonant quality. He spoke perfect English, with a kind of clear-cut dip to the words.

'You had an accident – an automobile went over you – but you're all right now, and don't need to think about it'

'What is it – that whispering noise? Are we near the sea?'

He smiled and shook his head. His smile merely accentuated the wrinkles – it could not multiply them.

'You are very near my laboratory – that is all. Here, drink this, and then you must rest.'

I obeyed him meekly, like a child, weak of mind and body.

I wondered a little why I was with him instead of at a hospital or with friends, but I soon dropped off. I was really quite weak just then.

Yet before I slept I did ask one more question.

'Would you tell me – if you don't mind – your name?'

'Lawrence.'

'Lawrence what?' I whispered, 'Just – ?'

'Yes,' he smiled (and his face ran into a very tempest of wrinkles), 'just Lawrence. No more.'

Then I slept.

And I did little but sleep, and wake, and eat, and sleep again, for some five days. And during this time I learned marvellously little of my host and his manner of life.

Most questions he evaded cleverly, but he told me that it was his auto which had nearly ruined my earthly tenement; Lawrence had himself taken me from the scene of the accident without waiting for an ambulance, telling the police and bystanders that I was an acquaintance. He had carried me to his own house, because, he said, he felt somewhat responsible for my injuries and wanted to give me a better chance for my life than the doctors would allow me.

He seemed to be possessed of a great scorn for all doctors. I knew long after that he had studied the profession very thoroughly, and in many countries, and truly held the right to the title he contemptuously denied himself.

At the time I considered only that he had cured me up in wonderfully short order, considering the extent of the injuries I had received, and that I had suffered not at all. Therefore I was grateful.

Also he told me, on I forget what occasion, that his mother was a Japanese woman of very ancient descent, his father a scholarly and rather wealthy American. And for some eccentric reason of his own, his dwarfed son had chosen to eschew the family patronym and use merely his Christian name.

During the time I lay in bed I saw no servants; Lawrence did all things necessary. And never, day or night, did the humming and sighing of the machines cease.

Lawrence spoke vaguely of great dynamos, but on this subject, as on most others, he was very reticent. Frequently I saw him in the dress of a mechanic, for he would come in to see me at all hours of the day, and I imagine must have inconvenienced himself considerably for my welfare.

I had no particular friends to worry about my whereabouts, and so I lay quiet and at peace with the world for those five days in inert contentment.

Then an hour came – it was in the morning, and Lawrence had left me to go to his laboratory – when I became suddenly savagely impatient of the dull round. Weak though I was, I determined to dress and get out into the open air – out into the world.

Mind you, during those five days I had seen no face save that of my dwarfed host, heard no voice but his. And so my impatience overcame my good judgment and his counsels, and I declared to myself that I was well enough to join once more in the rush of life.

Slowly, and with trembling limbs that belied that assertion, I got into my clothes. Very slowly – though in foolish terror lest Lawrence should catch me putting aside his mandates – I hurried my toilet as best I could.

At last I stood, clothed and in my right mind, as I told myself, though I had already begun to regret my sudden resolve.

I opened the door and looked into the bare, narrow hall. No one in sight, up or down.

I made my way, supporting myself, truth to tell, by the wall, towards a door at the far end, which stood slightly ajar.

I had almost reached it when I heard a terrible screaming. It was harsh, rough, tense with some awful agony, and to my startled senses pre-eminently human.

I stopped, shaking from head to foot with the shock. Then I flung myself on the door, from behind which the noises seemed to issue. It was not locked, and I plunged almost headlong into a great room, shadowy with whirring machinery under great arc lights.

Before a long table, loaded with retorts and the paraphernalia of the laboratory, stood Lawrence. His back was towards me, but he had turned his head angrily at my sudden entrance, and his queer, narrow eyes were blazing with annoyance.

In the room were two or three other men, evidently common mechanics, and none save Lawrence had more than glanced around. The screaming had ceased.

'Well?' his voice was little better than a snarl.

'That – that noise!' I gasped, already wondering if I had not made a fool of myself. 'What was it?'

'Eh? Oh, that was nothing – the machinery – why are you –'

He was interrupted by a crash and splash from the far end of the place, followed by an exclamation of terror and horror, and a nice collection of French and English oaths from the men.

Lawrence had been holding in his hand while he spoke to me what looked like a peculiar piece of metal. It was cylindrical in shape, and little shades of colour played over its surface continually.

Now he thrust this into my hands with a muttered injunction to be careful of it, and rushed off to the scene of the catastrophe. I followed him, at my best pace, with the thing in my hand.

At the end of the room were two immense vats of enamelled iron, their edges flush with the floor, half filled with some livid, seething acid mixture, through which little currents writhed and wriggled.

The farther side of the largest vat sloped up at an angle of about thirty degrees, a smooth, slimy slide of zinc about ten feet from top to bottom and extending the full length of the vat.

The surface of this slide was covered to about half an inch in thickness with some kind of yellowish paste, whose ultimate destination was the mixture in the vat.

Above towered an engine of many wheels and pistons, and this operated two great pestles or stamps, slant-faced to fit the slide; these, running from one end of the zinc to the other, worked the paste with a grinding motion, as an artist mixes his paints with a palette knife.

The grinding motion was quite swift, but the lateral movement was comparatively slow. I should say that it must have taken about four minutes for the two stamps to pass from one end of the fifteen-foot vat to the other.

In the vat floated a plank. On the surface of the slide, almost in the middle, sprawled a man, his arms spread out on either side, not daring to move an inch on the slippery paste, for the slightest motion meant a slip downwards into the hissing acid.

Worst of all, there seemed to be no means of getting across to him. The great engine occupied one side entirely to the wall – on the other the second vat barred passage.

Beyond the vats the room extended some little distance, and there was a door there, open, through which one could see a fenced yard piled high with ashes and cinders.

And the great stamps, twenty cubic feet of solid metal in each, were making their inevitable way towards the man. When they reached him – well, their smooth surface would afford him no finger hold, even if their rapid movement allowed him to clutch them. They must push him down – they might stun him first, but most certainly they would push him down.

I need hardly say that I did not take in the full significance of all this at the time – it was only afterwards that I fully understood the details.

Even as Lawrence ran he shouted: 'Stop that engine! Quick, men!'

I saw two stalwart workmen spring at the levers of the stamp machine – saw them twisting at the wheel – heard another crash, and a deep groan from all! The guiding mechanism had slipped a cog, or broken a rod, or something.

In my excitement, shaking so from weakness that I could hardly stand, I had half fallen against a piece of machinery that seemed to be at a standstill. Unconsciously my fingers grasped at a sort of handle.

I heard a whirring noise, felt something like a tremendous shock, and a burning pain. I let go of the handle in a hurry, just as Lawrence wheeled on me with the cry, 'For God's sake, you fool –'

But I could give no heed either to what I had done or to him. My eyes were still fixed on the unfortunate man on the slide.

The stamps were not more than five feet from his body now, and their low rattle and swish sounded in my ears loud as the tread of an army.

'A rope!' cried Lawrence in despair.

And then, in my horror, and in the sheer impossibility of standing by quiescent and seeing a fellow being done to death in this manner, I did a mad thing.

Wild with resentment, as if it were a living thing I could have fought, I flung myself on the great, swiftly revolving flywheel of the engine, seized its rim in my fingers, and braced back with all the force in my arms and shoulders.

By all precedent and reason my hands should have been crushed to a jelly in the maze of machinery, but to my intense astonishment the wheel stopped under my grasp with no very great effort on my part.

For a moment I held it so (it seemed to me to pull with no more force than is in the arms of a child), and then there was a loud report somewhere within the intestines of the monster. I saw a guiding rod as thick as my wrist double up and twist like a wire cable, things generally went to smash inside the engine, and the stamps stopped – not three inches from the man's head!

And even as they ceased to grind, men came running in at the door on the farther side of the vats – they had to go clean round the workshop to reach it – and were at the top of the slide with a rope which they let down.

In a moment the fellow was drawn to safely out of the reach of as horrible a death as a man can die – death in a bath consisting largely of sulphuric acid.

I stood as one in a stupor, still grasping the eccentric, dazed by the suddenness of it all – hardly able to believe that the danger was over.

A touch on my shoulder roused me, and I turned to look down into the narrow eyes of Lawrence. He was gazing at me with something very like awe in his expression.

'Well,' I said, smiling shakily, 'I'm afraid I've spoiled your engine.'

'Spoiled the engine!' he said slowly, but emphatically. 'What kind of a man are you, Mr Dunbar? Do you know that that is a three-hundred horsepower Danbury stamp? That the force required to stop that wheel in the way you did would run a locomotive – pick up the whole mass of that engine itself as easily as I would a pound weight?'

'It stopped very easily,' I muttered.

For some ridiculous reason I felt a little ashamed – as if such an exhibition of strength were really a trifle indecent. And I couldn't understand.

Of course, I thought, he exaggerated the power used, but though I am naturally quite strong, still I could, before my accident, boast of nothing abnormal – and was I not just up from a sick bed, only a moment ago barely able to stand or walk without support?

I found that I was nervously clenching and unclenching my hands, and became suddenly conscious that they felt as if they had been burned – the minute I began to think about it the pain became really excruciating.

I glanced at them. They were in a terrible condition – especially my right. They looked as if they had been clasped about a piece of red-hot iron.

'What is it?' asked Lawrence quickly. He bent over my hands, peering at them with his little black eyes.

Then he looked up quickly, and I saw the dawning of a curious expression in his wrinkled face – a strange excitement, a pale flash of triumph, I could have sworn.

Then, 'Where is it?' he cried imperatively, his voice sharp and strenuous. 'What have you done with it?'

He dropped my hands and fell quickly to his knees on the floor, his head bent, and began searching – feeling about in the shadows of the engines.

'Here – you there!' he cried to one of the men. 'A light here! God! If it should be lost now – after all these years – all these years!'

'What?' said I stupidly.

'The new element,' he cried impatiently. 'Stellarite, I call it. Oh' – glancing up quickly – 'of course you don't know. That little piece of metal I gave you to hold – the iridescent cylinder – don't you remember?'

He spoke irritably, as if it was almost impossible for him to restrain himself to civil language.

'Oh, yes – that.' I looked around vaguely. 'Why, yes, I had it in my hand – of course. I must have dropped it when I grabbed the fly-wheel. It's on the floor somewhere probably; but, if you don't mind, could I have something for my hands? They hurt pretty badly.'

Indeed, the air was fall of black, swimming dots before my eyes, and iridescent cylinders had very little interest for me just then.

He almost snapped at me.

'Wait! If it's lost – but it couldn't be! Ah, the light at last. Now we can see something.'

Still he was hunting, and now the men were helping him. I looked on dully.

Then an unreasonable anger seized me at their neglect – their indifference to my very real agony. I leaned forward, and, in spite of the added pain the raw flesh of my hand gave me, I took hold of Lawrence's collar and started to shake him.

He felt curiously light – rather like a piece of cork, in fact. I picked him up from the ground as you would a kitten and held him at arm's length.

Then suddenly I realized that what I was doing was somewhat unusual, and let go of his collar. He lit on his feet like a cat.

I expected anger, but he only said impatiently, 'Don't do that – help me hunt, can't you?' quite as if it were an ordinary incident.

The queerness of it all came over me in full force; I felt as if I were in a dream.

I stooped down and helped him search. But it was no use. The little cylinder of stellarite seemed to have disappeared.

Suddenly Lawrence rose to his feet, his face, whose multitudinous wrinkles had a moment before been twitching with mingled triumph and despair, wiped clean of emotion, like a blank slate from which all significance has been erased.

'Come, Mr Dunbar,' he said quietly, 'it is quite time those hands of yours were seen to. You, Johnson, Duquirke, go on hunting. But I'm afraid it's no use, boys. That vat of acid is too near.'

'You think –'

'I'm afraid it rolled in,' he said.

I was silent, dimly conscious that I stood, as it were, just inside the ring of some great catastrophe whose influence, barely reaching me, had this little wrinkled man in the grip of its vortex.

I followed him to a small office, opening off the laboratory; fitted up much like a doctor's, it was, with its cabinet of shining instruments. He explained its convenience while he bound up my hands with all the skilled gentleness of an experienced surgeon.

'Accidents are always on view in such a place as mine out there,' he observed, with a nod of his head toward the laboratory.

'I wish you'd tell me what I've done,' I said at last when the thing was over.

I felt no weakness, nor any desire for rest, which was odd, seeing the excitement I had been through and my recent illness.

'Two things, then, to be brief,' he replied, smiling rather sadly, I thought. 'You've accidentally stumbled on a magnificent fact, and you've at the same time destroyed, I fear, all results that might have flowed from that fact.'

I stared at him, puzzled.

'You lifted me just now like a feather,' he said abruptly. 'You think, possibly, that I don't weigh much – I'm not a giant. Duquirke,' he called, 'come here a minute, will you, please?'

Duquirke appeared, a very mountain of a man, all muscle, too. I am up to the six-foot mark myself, and fairly broad in the shoulders, but this fellow could better me by three good inches in any direction.

'You can't use your hands, of course,' said Lawrence to me; 'but just stoop down and stretch out your arm, will you? Now, Duquirke, just seat yourself on his arm. That's it. Oh, don't be afraid – he can hold you all right. Ah, I thought so!'

We had both obeyed him, I in some doubt, the Canadian with stolid indifference. But what was my amazement to find that this great big man weighed really comparatively nothing.

I rose, still with my arm outstretched, with perfect ease, and there the fellow sat, perched precariously, his mouth open, his eyes fixed on his master in almost a dog-like appeal.

'What are you all made of?' I gasped. 'Cork?'

I let my arm drop, really expecting to see the man fall light as a feather – instead of which he tumbled with a crash that shook the house, and lay for a minute, swearing violently.

Then he got to his feet in a hurry and backed out of the door, his eyes on me to the last, his tongue, really unconsciously I believe, letting go a string of such language as would have done credit to a canal-boat driver.

'What is the matter with you all,' I cried, 'or' – my voice sank with the thought – 'with me?'

'Sit down,' said Lawrence. 'Don't lose your head.'

His eyes had widened, and the strange colours I had sometimes caught a glimpse of were blazing in their depths. His wrinkled face was almost beautiful in its animation – lighted as by a fire from within.

'There's nothing at all astonishing or miraculous about any of it – it's the simple working of a law. Now listen. When we heard La Due fall (the fool had tried to walk across a plank laid over that death trap to save going round the shop – he was well repaid by the fright), I handed you the cylinder of stellarite. I did not lay it on my work-table, because that is made of aluminium, and this cylinder must not come into contact with any other metal, for the simple reason that stellarite has such an affiliation for all other metals that for it to touch one of them means absorption into it. All its separate molecules interpenetrate, or assimilate, molecules, and stellarite ceases to have its "individual being". So I gave it to you, because I wanted my hands free, and ran down to the vats with you at my heels. I confess I would never have been so careless if I had not allowed myself to become unduly excited by a mere matter of life and death.'

He paused regretfully.

'However, to continue; you for some reason seized hold of the lever of a dynamo of very great voltage and started the armature revolving, at the same time stepping on to the plate at its base. Now, in the ordinary course of things you would probably be at this moment lying on that couch over there – dead!'

I looked at the couch with sudden interest.

'But you are not.'

I murmured that such was indeed the case.

'No – instead of that thunderbolt burning the life out of you, like that' – he snapped his fingers melodramatically – 'it passed directly through your body into the cylinder of stellarite, which, completing the circuit, sent the current back through your chest, but possessed of a new quality.'

'And that quality?'

'Ah, there you have me! What that quality was I fear it is now too late for the world ever to know. Well, you dropped the lever, and, I think, the cylinder, too, when I shouted. A moment after, you seized the fly-wheel of the stamp machine, stopped it as if it had been the balance of a watch – and, well, incidentally you saved La Due's life.'

He ceased, the light faded out of his wrinkled face, his eyes darkened and narrowed. His head sank forward on to his chest

'But to think of it – years – years of effort thrown away just at the moment of conquest!'

'I don't understand,' I said, seeming to catch little glimpses of his full meaning, as through a torn veil. 'Do you intend to say –'

'I intend to say,' he snapped, with a sudden return of irritability, 'that in that minute when you held the stellarite and the lever of the dynamo you absorbed enough of the life principle to vivify a herd of elephants. Why, what is strength, man? Is a muscle strong in itself? Can a mere muscle lift so much as a pin? It's the life principle, I tell you – and I had it under my hand!'

'But this stellarite,' I protested. 'You can make more, surely?'

'Make!' he scoffed. 'It's an element, I say! And it was, so far as I know, all there was in all the world!'

'Maybe it will be found yet,' I argued. 'Or – if it went into the acid vat, would it have been absorbed by the metal – or what?'

'No – at the touch of that bath it would evaporate into thin air – an odourless, colourless gas. I have but one hope – that it rolled against some of the iron machinery and was absorbed. In that case I may be able to place it by the increased bulk of the assimilating metal. Well, I can but go to work again, test every particle of machinery in the vicinity of the vats – and work – and work. If I had but known before that it was electricity and animal magnetism that were needed to complete the combination – but now it means years of patience at best.'

He shook his head dismally.

'And I?' I mused, rather to myself than to him.

'Oh – you!' he smiled, his face ran into that tempest of wrinkles. 'You can pose as Samson, if you like! Your strength is really almost limitless!'

Roquia Sakhawat Hossein

THE SULTANA'S DREAM

When researching for this anthology I was delighted to discover this story because it shows that the writing of scientific and utopian fiction by women was not confined to Britain and the United States. Roquia Sakhawat Hossein (1880–1932) was an Indian Muslim from Rangpur (now part of Bangladesh) who became the wife of the Deputy Magistrate of Bhagalpur in eastern India. She had received an excellent education, if little love, from her father, and both she and her sister became writers. The following story appeared in English in 1905 in The Indian Ladies' Magazine, *published in Madras. After her husband's death in 1909, Roquia moved to Calcutta and opened a girls' school in his name, which still operates today. Roquia was a fervent proponent of women's rights and equality in India and in 1916 founded the Islamic Women's Association in Calcutta.*

The Sultana's Dream

ONE EVENING I was lounging in an easy chair in my bedroom and thinking lazily of the condition of Indian womanhood. I am not sure whether I dozed off or not. But, as far as I remember, I was wide awake. I saw the moonlit sky sparkling with thousands of diamond-like stars, very distinctly.

All on a sudden a lady stood before me; how she came in, I do not know. I took her for my friend, Sister Sara.

'Good morning,' said Sister Sara. I smiled inwardly as I knew it was not morning, but starry night. However, I replied to her, saying, 'How do you do?'

'I am all right, thank you. Will you please come out and have a look at our garden?'

I looked again at the moon through the open window, and thought there was no harm in going out at that time. The men-servants outside were fast asleep just then, and I could have a pleasant walk with Sister Sara.

I used to have my walks with Sister Sara when we were at Darjeeling. Many a time did we walk hand in hand and talk light-heartedly in the botanical gardens there. I fancied Sister Sara had probably come to take me to some such garden, and I readily accepted her offer and went out with her.

When walking I found to my surprise that it was a fine morning. The town was fully awake and the streets alive with bustling crowds. I was feeling very shy, thinking I was walking in the street in broad daylight, but there was not a single man visible.

Some of the passers-by made jokes at me. Though I could not understand their language, yet I felt sure they were joking. I asked my friend, 'What do they say?'

'The women say that you look very mannish.'

'Mannish?' said I, 'What do they mean by that?'

'They mean that you are shy and timid like men.'

'Shy and timid like men?' It was really a joke. I became very nervous when I found that my companion was not Sister Sara but a stranger. Oh, what a fool had I been to mistake this lady for my dear old friend, Sister Sara.

She felt my fingers tremble in her hand, as we were walking hand in hand.

'What is the matter, dear?' she said affectionately.

'I feel somewhat awkward,' I said in a rather apologizing tone, 'as being a purdahnishin woman I am not accustomed to walking about unveiled.'

'You need not be afraid of coming across a man here. This is Ladyland, free from sin and harm. Virtue herself reigns here.'

By and by I was enjoying the scenery. Really it was very grand. I mistook a patch of green grass for a velvet cushion. Feeling as if I were walking on a soft carpet, I looked down and found the path covered with moss and flowers.

'How nice it is,' said I.

'Do you like it?' asked Sister Sara. (I continued calling her 'Sister Sara', and she kept calling me by my name).

'Yes, very much; but I do not like to tread on the tender and sweet flowers.'

'Never mind, dear Sultana; your treading will not harm them; they are street flowers.'

'The whole place looks like a garden,' said I admiringly. 'You have arranged every plant so skilfully.'

'Your Calcutta could become a nicer garden than this if only your countrymen wanted to make it so.'

'They would think it useless to give so much attention to horti-culture while they have so many other things to do.'

'They could not find a better excuse,' said she with smile.

I became very curious to know where the men were. I met more than a hundred women while walking there, but not a single man.

'Where are the men?' I asked her.

'In their proper places, where they ought to be.'

'Pray let me know what you mean by "their proper places".'

'Oh, I see my mistake, you cannot know our customs, as you were never here before. We shut our men indoors.'

'Just as we are kept in the zenana?'

'Exactly so.'

'How funny,' I burst into a laugh. Sister Sara laughed, too.

'But dear Sultana, how unfair it is to shut in the harmless women and let loose the men.'

'Why? It is not safe for us to come out of the zenana, as we are naturally weak.'

'Yes, it is not safe so long as there are men about the streets, nor is it so when a wild animal enters a marketplace.'

'Of course not.'

'Suppose, some lunatics escape from the asylum and begin to do all sorts of mischief to men, horses and other creatures; in that case what will your countrymen do?'

'They will try to capture them and put them back into their asylum.'

'Thank you! And you do not think it wise to keep sane people inside an asylum and let loose the insane?'

'Of course not!' said I, laughing lightly.

'As a matter of fact, in your country this very thing is done! Men, who do, or at least are capable of doing, no end of mischief, are let loose and the innocent women shut up in the zenana! How can you trust those untrained men out of doors?'

'We have no hand or voice in the management of our social affairs. In India man is lord and master, he has taken to himself all powers and privileges and shut up the women in the zenana.'

'Why do you allow yourselves to be shut up?'

'Because it cannot be helped as they are stronger than women.'

'A lion is stronger than a man, but it does not enable him to dominate the human race. You have neglected the duty you owe to yourselves and you have lost your natural rights by shutting your eyes to your own interests.'

'But, my dear Sister Sara, if we do everything by ourselves, what will the men do then?'

'They should not do anything, excuse me; they are fit for nothing. Only catch them and put them into the zenana.'

'But would it be very easy to catch and put them inside the four walls?' said I. 'And even if this were done, would all their business – political and commercial – also go with them into the zenana?'

Sister Sara made no reply. She only smiled sweetly. Perhaps she thought it useless to argue with one who was no better than a frog in a well.

By this time we reached Sister Sara's house. It was situated in a beautiful heart-shaped garden. It was a bungalow with a corrugated iron roof. It was cooler and nicer than any of our rich buildings. I cannot describe how neat and how nicely furnished and how tastefully decorated it was.

We sat side by side. She brought out of the parlour a piece of embroidery work and began putting on a fresh design.

'Do you know knitting and needlework?'

'Yes; we have nothing else to do in our zenana.'

'But we do not trust our zenana members with embroidery!' she said laughing, 'as a man has not patience enough to pass thread through a needle hole even!'

'Have you done all this work yourself?' I asked her pointing to the various pieces of embroidered teapoy cloths.

'Yes.'

'How can you find time to do all these? You have to do the office work as well, have you not?'

'Yes. I do not stick to the laboratory all day long. I finish my work in two hours.'

'In two hours! How do you manage? In our land the officers – magistrates, for instance – work seven hours daily.'

'I have seen some of them doing their work. Do you think they work all the seven hours?'

'Certainly they do!'

'No, dear Sultana, they do not. They dawdle away their time in smoking. Some smoke two or three choroots during the office time. They talk much about their work, but do little. Suppose one choroot takes half an hour to burn off, and a man smokes twelve choroots daily; then you see, he wastes six hours every day in sheer smoking.'

We talked on various subjects, and I learned that they were not subject to any kind of epidemic disease, nor did they suffer from mosquito bites as we do. I was very much astonished to hear that in Ladyland no one died in youth except by rare accident.

'Will you care to see our kitchen?' she asked me.

'With pleasure,' said I, and we went to see it. Of course the men had been asked to clear off when I was going there. The kitchen was situated in a beautiful vegetable garden. Every creeper, every tomato plant was itself an ornament. I found no smoke, nor any chimney either in the kitchen – it was clean and bright; the windows were decorated with flower gardens. There was no sign of coal or fire.

'How do you cook?' I asked.

'With solar heat,' she said, at the same time showing me the pipe through which passed the concentrated sunlight and heat. And she cooked something then and there to show me the process.

'How did you manage to gather and store up the sun-heat?' I asked her in amazement.

'Let me tell you a little of our past history then. Thirty years ago, when our present Queen was thirteen years old, she inherited the throne. She was Queen in name only, the Prime Minister really ruling the country.

'Our good Queen liked science very much. She circulated an order that all the women in her country should be educated. Accordingly, a number of girls' schools were founded and supported by the government. Education was spread far and wide among women. And early marriage also was stopped. No woman was to be allowed to marry before she was twenty-one. I must tell you that before this change we had been kept in strict purdah.'

'How the tables are turned,' I interposed with a laugh.

'But the seclusion is the same,' she said. 'In a few years we had separate universities, where no men were admitted.'

'In the capital, where our Queen lives, there are two universities. One of these invented a wonderful balloon, to which they attached a number of pipes. By means of this captive balloon, which they managed to keep afloat above the cloud-land, they could draw as much water from the atmosphere as they pleased. As the water was incessantly being drawn by the university people no cloud gathered and the ingenious Lady Principal stopped rain and storms thereby.'

'Really! Now I understand why there is no mud here!' said I. But I could not understand how it was possible to accumulate water in the pipes. She explained to me how it was done, but I was unable to understand her, as my scientific knowledge was very limited. However, she went on, 'When the other university came to know of this, they became exceedingly jealous and tried to do something more extraordinary still. They invented an instrument by which they could collect as much sun-heat as they wanted. And they kept the heat stored up to be distributed among others as required.

'While the women were engaged in scientific research, the men of this country were busy increasing their military power. When they came to know that the female universities were able to draw water from the atmosphere and collect heat from the sun, they only laughed at the members of the universities and called the whole thing "a sentimental nightmare"!'

'Your achievements are very wonderful indeed! But, tell me, how you managed to put the men of your country into the zenana. Did you entrap them first?'

'No.'

'It is not likely that they would surrender their free and open-air life of their own accord and confine themselves within the four walls of the zenana! They must have been overpowered.'

'Yes, they have been!'

'By whom? By some lady-warriors, I suppose?'

'No, not by arms.'

'It cannot be so. Men's arms are stronger than women's. Then?'

'By brain.'

'Even their brains are bigger and heavier than women's. Are they not?'

'Yes, but what of that? An elephant also has got a bigger and heavier brain than a man has. Yet man can enchain elephants and employ them, according to their own wishes.'

'Well said, but tell me, please, how it all actually happened. I am dying to know it!'

'Women's brains are somewhat quicker than men's. Ten years ago, when the military officers called our scientific discoveries "a sentimental nightmare", some of the young ladies wanted to say something in reply to those remarks. But both the Lady Principals restrained them and said they should reply not by word but by deed, if ever they got the opportunity. And they had not long to wait for that opportunity.'

'How marvellous!' I heartily clapped my hands. 'And now the proud gentlemen are dreaming sentimental dreams themselves.'

'Soon afterwards, certain persons came from a neighbouring country and took shelter in ours. They were in trouble having committed some political offence. The king, who cared more for power than for good government, asked our kind-hearted Queen to hand them over to his officers. She refused, as it was against her principle to turn out refugees. For this refusal the king declared war against our country.

'Our military officers sprang to their feet at once and marched out to meet the enemy. The enemy, however, was too strong for them. Our soldiers fought bravely, no doubt. But in spite of all their bravery the foreign army advanced step by step to invade our country.

'Nearly all the men had gone out to fight; even a boy of sixteen was not left home. Most of our warriors were killed, the rest driven back, and the enemy came within twenty-five miles of the capital.

'A meeting of a number of wise ladies was held at the Queen's palace to advise as to what should be done to save the land. Some proposed to fight like soldiers; others objected and said that women were not trained to fight with swords and guns, nor were they accustomed to fighting with any weapons. A third party regretfully remarked that they were hopelessly weak of body.

'"If you cannot save your country for lack of physical strength," said the Queen, "try to do so by brain power."

'There was a dead silence for a few minutes. Her Royal Highness said again, "I must commit suicide if the land and my honour are lost."

'Then the Lady Principal of the second university (who had collected sun-heat), who had been silently thinking during the consultation, remarked that they were all but lost, and there was little hope left for them. There was, however, one plan which she would like to try, and this would be her first and last efforts; if she failed in this, there would be nothing left but to commit suicide. All present solemnly vowed that they would never allow themselves to be enslaved, no matter what happened.

'The Queen thanked them heartily, and asked the Lady Principal to try her plan. The Lady Principal rose again and said, "Before we go out, the men must enter the zenanas. I make this prayer for the sake of purdah."

'"Yes, of course," replied Her Royal Highness.

'On the following day the Queen called upon all men to retire into zenanas for the sake of honour and liberty. Wounded and tired as they were, they took that order rather for a boon! They bowed low and entered the zenanas without uttering a single word of protest. They were sure that there was no hope for this country at all.

'Then the Lady Principal with her two thousand students marched to the battle field, and arriving there directed all the rays of the concentrated sunlight and heat towards the enemy.

'The heat and light were too much for them to bear. They all ran away panic-stricken, not knowing in their bewilderment how to counteract that scorching heat. When they fled away leaving their guns and other ammunitions of war, they were burned down by means of the same sun-heat. Since then no one has tried to invade our country any more.'

'And since then your countrymen never tried to come out of the zenana?'

'Yes, they wanted to be free. Some of the police commissioners and district magistrates sent word to the Queen to the effect that the military officers certainly deserved to be imprisoned for their failure; but they never neglected their duty and therefore they should not be punished and they prayed to be restored to their respective offices.

'Her Royal Highness sent them a circular letter intimating to them that if their services should ever be needed they would be sent for, and that in the meanwhile they should remain where they were. Now that they are accustomed to the purdah system and have ceased to grumble at their seclusion, we call the system "Mardana" instead of "zenana".'

'But how do you manage,' I asked Sister Sara, 'to do without the police or magistrates in case of theft or murder?'

'Since the "Mardana" system has been established, there has been no more crime or sin; therefore we do not require a policeman to find out a culprit, nor do we want a magistrate to try a criminal case.'

'That is very good, indeed. I suppose if there was any dishonest person, you could very easily chastise her. As you gained a decisive victory without shedding a single drop of blood, you could drive off crime and criminals, too, without much difficulty!'

'Now, dear Sultana, will you sit here or come to my parlour?' she asked me.

'Your kitchen is not inferior to a queen's boudoir!' I replied with a pleasant smile, 'but we must leave it now; for the gentlemen may be cursing me for keeping them away from their duties in the kitchen so long.' We both laughed heartily.

'How my friends at home will be amused and amazed when I go back and tell them that in the far-off Ladyland, ladies rule over the country and control all social matters, while gentlemen are kept in the Mardanas to mind babies, to cook and to do all sorts of domestic work; and that cooking is so easy a thing that it is simply a pleasure to cook!'

'Yes, tell them about all that you see here.'

'Please let me know, how you carry on land cultivation and how you plough the land and do other hard manual work.'

'Our fields are tilled by means of electricity, which supplies motive power for other hard work as well, and we employ it for our aerial conveyances, too. We have no railroad nor any paved streets here.'

'Therefore neither street nor railway accidents occur here,' said I. 'Do you not ever suffer from want of rainwater?' I asked.

'Never since the "water balloon" has been set up. You see the big balloon and pipes attached thereto. By their aid we can draw as much rainwater as we require. Nor do we ever suffer from flood or thunderstorms. We are all very busy making nature yield as much as she can. We do not find time to quarrel with one another as we never sit idle. Our noble Queen is exceedingly fond of botany; it is her ambition to convert the whole country into one grand garden.'

'The idea is excellent. What is your chief food?'

'Fruits.'

'How do you keep your country cool in hot weather? We regard the rainfall in summer as a blessing from heaven.'

'When the heat becomes unbearable, we sprinkle the ground with plentiful showers drawn from the artificial fountains. And in cold weather we keep our room warm with sun-heat.'

She showed me her bathroom, the roof of which was removable. She could enjoy a shower bath whenever she liked, by simply removing the roof (which was like the lid of a box) and turning on the tap of the shower pipe.

'You are a lucky people!' ejaculated I. 'You know no want. What is your religion, may I ask?'

'Our religion is based on Love and Truth. It is our religious duty to love one another and to be absolutely truthful. If any person lies, she or he is . . .'

'Punished with death?'

'No, not with death. We do not take pleasure in killing a creature of God, especially a human being. The liar is asked to leave this land for good and never to come to it again.'

'Is an offender never forgiven?'

'Yes, if that person repents sincerely.'

'Are you not allowed to see any man, except your own relations?'

'No one except sacred relations.'

'Our circle of sacred relations is very limited; even first cousins are not sacred.'

'But ours is very large; a distant cousin is as sacred as a brother.'

'That is very good. I see purity itself reigns over your land. I should like to see the good Queen, who is so sagacious and far-sighted and who has made all these rules.'

'All right,' said Sister Sara.

Then she screwed a couple of seats on to a square piece of plank. To this plank she attached two smooth and well-polished balls. When I asked her what the balls were for, she said they were hydrogen balls and they were used to overcome the force of gravity. The balls were of different capacities to be used according to the different weights desired to be overcome. She then fastened to the air-car two wing-like blades, which, she said, were worked by electricity. After we were comfortably seated she touched a knob and the blades began to whirl, moving faster and faster every moment. At first we were raised to the height of about six or seven feet and then off we flew. And before I could realize that we had commenced moving, we reached the garden of the Queen.

My friend lowered the air-car by reversing the action of the machine, and when the car touched the ground the machine was stopped and we got out.

I had seen from the air-car the Queen walking on a garden path with her little daughter (who was four years old) and her maids of honour.

'Halloo! You here!' cried the Queen addressing Sister Sara. I was introduced to Her Royal Highness and was received by her cordially without any ceremony.

I was very much delighted to make her acquaintance. In the course of the conversation I had with her, the Queen told me that she had no objection to permitting her subjects to trade with other countries. 'But,' she continued, 'no trade was possible with countries where the women were kept in the zenanas and so unable to come and trade with us. Men, we find, are rather of lower morals and so we do not like dealing with them. We do not covet other people's land, we do not fight for a piece of diamond though it may be a thousand-fold brighter than the Koh-i-Noor, nor do we grudge a ruler his Peacock Throne. We dive deep into the ocean of knowledge and try to find out the precious gems which nature has kept in store for us. We enjoy nature's gifts as much as we can.'

After taking leave of the Queen, I visited the famous universities, and was shown some of their manufactories, laboratories and observatories.

After visiting the above places of interest we got again into the air-car, but as soon as it began moving, I somehow slipped down and the fall startled me out of my dream. And on opening my eyes, I found myself in my own bedroom still lounging in the easy-chair!

Edith Nesbit

THE FIVE SENSES

Edith Nesbit (1858–1924) was a remarkable woman. Remarkable enough that she was prepared to accept her husband, Hubert Bland, taking her best friend, Alice, as his mistress, with them all living in the same house, and for Edith to raise Alice's two children by Hubert as her own. Edith was clearly liberal minded and had affairs of her own, yet the Bland household remained remarkably happy and tolerant. But she was remarkable, too, for her work in the development of the socialist movement, founding the Fabian Society with her husband in 1884. And perhaps also remarkable in that, although she became one of Britain's most popular writers for children, with such perennial favourites as The Railway Children *(1906),* Five Children and It *(1902) and* The Wouldbegoods *(1901), she produced a steady flow of horror stories throughout her career, many of them genuinely macabre and grim – indeed, she called one of her collections* Grim Tales *(1893). Since childhood she had had a morbid fascination for churchyards and particularly church memorials, a fear of masks and a dread of being buried alive. Several of these macabre stories draw on the potential of science for creating even more grim circumstances. For the anthology* The Darker Sex: Tales of the Supernatural and Macabre by Victorian Women Writers *I chose Nesbit's 'The Third Drug', which concerned a dangerous drug that might just make you superhuman. The following story concerns another drug, this time one that enhances the senses. But what happens if you try to enhance all five senses at once?*

The Five Senses

PROFESSOR BOYD THOMPSON'S services to the cause of science are usually spoken of as inestimable, and so indeed they probably are, since in science, as in the rest of life, one thing leads to another, and you never know where anything is going to stop. At any rate, inestimable or not, they are world-renowned, and he with them. The discoveries which he gave to his time are a matter of common knowledge among biological experts, and the sudden ending of his experimental activities caused a few days' wonder in even lay circles. Quite unintelligent people told each other that it seemed a pity, and persons on omnibuses exchanged commonplaces starred with his name.

But the real meaning and cause of that ending have been studiously hidden, as well as the events which immediately preceded it. A veil has been drawn over all the things that people would have liked to know, and it is only now that circumstances so arrange themselves as to make it possible to tell the whole story. I propose to avail myself of this possibility.

It will serve no purpose for me to explain how the necessary knowledge came into my possession; but I will say that the story was only in part pieced together by me. Another hand is responsible for much of the detail and for a certain occasional emotionalism which is, I believe, wholly foreign to my own style. In my original statement of the following facts I dealt fully, as I am, I may say without immodesty, qualified to do, with all the scientific points of the narrative. But these details were judged, unwisely as I think, to be needless to the expert, and unintelligible to the ordinary reader, and have therefore been struck out; the merest hints have been left as necessary links in the story. This appears to me to destroy most of its interest, but I admit that the elisions are perhaps justified. I have no desire to assist or encourage callow students in such experiments as those by which Professor Boyd Thompson brought his scientific career to an end.

Incredible as it may appear, Professor Boyd Thompson was once a little boy who wore white embroidered frocks and blue sashes; in that state he caught flies and pulled off their wings to find out how they flew. He did not find out, and Lucilla, his little girl-cousin, also in white frocks, cried over the dead, dismembered flies, and buried them in little paper coffins. Later, he wore a holland blouse with a belt of leather, and watched the development of tadpoles in a tin bath in the stable yard. A microscope was, on his eighth birthday, presented to him by an affluent uncle. The uncle showed him how to surprise the secrets of a drop of pond water, which, limpid to the eye, confessed under the microscope to a whole cosmogony of strenuous and undesirable careers. At the age of ten, Arthur Boyd Thompson was sent to a private school, its Headmaster an acolyte of Science, who esteemed himself to be a high priest of Huxley and Tyndal, a devotee of Darwin. Thence to the choice of medicine as a profession was, when the choice was insisted on by the elder Boyd Thompson, a short, plain step. Inorganic chemistry failed to charm, and under the cloak of Medicine and Surgery the growing fever of scientific curiosity could be sated on bodies other than the cloak-wearer's. He became a medical student and an enthusiast for vivisection.

The bow of Apollo was not always bent. In a rest-interval, the summer vacation, to be exact, he met again the cousin – second, once removed – Lucilla, and loved her. They were betrothed. It was a long, bright summer full of sunshine, garden-parties, picnics, archery – a decaying amusement – and croquet, then coming to its own. He exulted in the distinction already crescent in his career, but some half-formed wholly unconscious desire to shine with increased lustre in theeyes of the beloved caused him to invite, for the holiday's ultimate week, a fellow student, one who knew and could testify to the quality of the laurels already encircling the head of the young scientist. The friend came, testified, and in a vibrating interview under the lime-trees of Lucilla's people's garden, Mr Boyd Thompson learned that Lucilla never could, never would, love or marry a vivisectionist.

The moon hung low and yellow in the spacious calm of the sky; the hour was propitious, the lovers fond. Mr Boyd Thompson vowed that his scientific research should henceforth deal wholly with departments into which the emotions of the non-scientific cannot enter. He went back to London, and within the week bought four dozen frogs, twelve guinea-pigs, five cats, and a spaniel. His scientific aspirations met his love-longings, and did not fight them. You cannot fight beings of another world. He took part in a debate on 'Blood Pressure', which created some little stir in medical circles, spoke eloquently, and distinction surrounded him with a halo.

He wrote to Lucilla three times a week, took his degree, and published that celebrated paper of his which set the whole scientific world by the ears; 'The Action of Choline on the Nervous System' I think its name was.

Lucilla surreptitiously subscribed to a press-cutting agency for all snippets of print relating to her lover. Three weeks after the publication of that paper, which really was the beginning of Professor Boyd Thompson's fame, she wrote to him from her home in Kent.

ARTHUR, you have been doing it again. You know how I love you, and I believe you love me; but you must choose between loving me and torturing dumb animals. If you don't choose right, then it's goodbye, and God forgive you.

Your poor Lucilla, who loved you very dearly.

He read the letter, and the human heart in him winced and whined. Yet not so deeply now, nor so loudly, but that he bethought himself to seek out a friend and pupil, who would watch certain experiments, attend to the cutting of certain sections, before he started for Tenterden, where she lived. There was no station at Tenterden in those days, but a twelve-mile walk did not dismay him.

Lucilla's home was one of those houses of brave proportions and an inalienable bourgeois stateliness, which stand back a little from the noble High Street of that most beautiful of Kentish towns. He came there, pleasantly exercised, his boots dusty, and his throat dry, and stood on the snowy doorstep, beneath the Jacobean lintel. He looked down the wide, beautiful street, raised eyebrows, and shrugged uneasy shoulders within his professional frock-coat.

'It's all so difficult,' he said to himself.

Lucilla received him in a drawing-room scented with last year's rose leaves, and fresh with chintz that had been washed a dozen times. She stood, very pale and frail; her blonde hair was not teased into fluffiness, and rounded over the chignon of the period but banded Madonna-wise, crowning her with heavy burnished plaits. Her gown was of white muslin, and round her neck black velvet passed, supporting a gold locket. He knew whose picture it held. The loose bell sleeves fell away from the slender arms with little black velvet bracelets, and she leaned one hand on a chiffonier of carved rosewood, on whose marble top stood, under a glass case, a Chinese pagoda, carved in ivory, and two Bohemian glass vases with medallions representing young women nursing pigeons. There were white curtains of darned net, in the fireplace white ravelled muslin spread a cascade brightened with threads of tinsel. A canary sang in a green cage, wainscoted with yellow tarlatan, and two red rosebuds stood in lank specimen glasses on the mantelpiece.

Every article of furniture in the room spoke eloquently of the sheltered life, the iron obstinacy of the well-brought-up.

It was a scene that invaded his mental vision many a time, in the laboratory, in the lecture-room. It symbolized many things, all dear, and all impossible.

They talked awkwardly, miserably. And always it came round to this same thing.

'But you don't mean it,' he said, and at last came close to her.

'I do mean it,' she said, very white, very trembling, very determined.

'But it's my life,' he pleaded; 'it's the life of thousands. You don't understand.'

'I understand that dogs are tortured. I can't bear it.'

He caught at her hand.

'Don't,' she said. 'When I think what that hand does!'

'Dearest,' he said very earnestly, 'which is the more important, a dog or a human being?'

'They're all God's creatures,' she flashed, unorthodoxly unorthodox. 'They're all God's creatures.' With much more that he heard and pitied and smiled at miserably in his heart.

'You don't understand,' he kept saying, stemming the flood of her rhetorical pleadings. 'Spencer Wells alone has found out wonderful things, just with experiments on rabbits.'

'Don't tell me,' she said. 'I don't want to hear.'

The conventions of their day forbade that he should tell her anything plainly. He took refuge in generalities. 'Spencer Wells, that operation he perfected, it's restored thousands of women to their husbands – saved thousands of women for their children.'

'I don't care what he's done – it's wrong if it's done in that way.'

It was on that day that they parted, after more than an hour of mutual misunderstood reiteration. He, she said, was brutal. And, besides, it was plain that he did not love her. To him she seemed unreasonable, narrow, prejudiced, blind to the high ideals of the new science.

'Then it's goodbye,' he said at last. 'If I gave way, you'd only despise me, because I should despise myself. It's no good. Goodbye, dear.'

'Goodbye,' she said. 'I know I'm right. You'll know I am, some day.'

'Never,' he answered, more moved and in a more diffused sense than he had ever believed he could be. 'I can't set my pleasure in you against the good of the whole world.'

'If that's all you think of me,' she said, and her silk and her muslin whirled from the room.

He walked back to Staplehurst, thrilled with the conflict. The thrill died down, went out, and left as ashes a cold resolve.

That was the end of Mr Boyd Thompson's engagement.

*

It was quite by accident that he made his greatest discovery. There are those who hold that all great discoveries are accident – or Providence. The terms are, in this connection, interchangeable. He plunged into work to wash away the traces of his soul's wounds, as a man plunges into water to wash off red blood. And he swam there, perhaps, a little blindly. The injection with which he treated that white rabbit was not compounded of the drugs he had intended to use. He could not lay his hand on the thing he wanted, and in that sort of frenzy of experiment, to which no scientific investigator is wholly a stranger, he cast about for a new idea. The thing that came to his hand was a drug that he had never in his normal mind intended to use – an unaccredited, wild, magic medicine obtained by a missionary from some savage South Sea tribe and brought home as an example of the ignorance of the heathen.

And it worked a miracle.

He had been fighting his way through the unbending opposition of known facts, he had been struggling in the shadows, and this discovery was like the blinding light that meets a man's eyes when his pick-axe knocks a hole in a dark cave and he finds himself face to face with the sun. The effect was undoubted. Now it behoved him to make sure of the cause, to eliminate all those other factors to which that effect might have been due. He experimented cautiously, slowly. These things take years, and the years he did not grudge. He was never tired, never impatient; the slightest variations, the least indications, were eagerly observed, faithfully recorded.

His whole soul was in his work. Lucilla was the one beautiful memory of his life. But she was a memory. The reality was this discovery, the accident, the Providence.

Day followed day, all alike, and yet each taking almost unperceived, one little step forward; or stumbling into sudden sloughs, those losses and lapses that take days and weeks to retrieve. He was Professor, and his hair was grey at the temples before his achievement rose before him, beautiful, inevitable, austere in its completed splendour, as before the triumphant artist rises the finished work of his art.

He had found out one of the secrets with which Nature has crammed her dark hiding-places. He had discovered the hidden possibilities of sensation. In plain English, his researches had led him thus far; he had found – by accident or Providence – the way to intensify sensation. Vaguely, incredulously, he had perceived his discovery; the rabbits and guinea-pigs had demonstrated it plainly enough. Then there was a night when he became aware that those results must be checked by something else. He must work out in marble the form he had worked out in clay. He knew that by this drug, which had, so to speak, thrust itself upon him, he could intensify the five senses of any of the inferior animals. Could he intensify those senses in man? If so, worlds beyond the grasp of his tired mind opened themselves before him. If so, he would have achieved a discovery, made a contribution to the science he had loved so well and followed at such a cost, a discovery equal to any that any man had ever made.

Ferrier, and Leo, and Horsley; those he would outshine. Galileo, Newton, Harvey; he would rank with these.

Could he find a human rabbit to submit to the test?

The soul of the man Lucilla had loved, turned and revolted. No: he had experimented on guinea-pigs and rabbits, but when it came to experimenting on men, there was only one man on whom he chose to use his new-found powers. Himself.

At least she would not have it to say that he was a coward, or unfair, when it came to the point of what a man could do and dare, could suffer and endure.

His big laboratory was silent and deserted. His assistants were gone, his private pupils dispersed. He was alone with the tools of his trade. Shelf on shelf of smooth stoppered bottles, drugs and stains, the long bench gleaming with beakers, test tubes, and the glass mansions of costly apparatus. In the shadows at the far end of the room, where the last going assistant had turned off the electric lights, strange shapes lurked: wicker-covered carboys, kinographs, galvanometers, the faintly threatening aspect of delicate complex machines all wires and coils and springs, the gaunt form of the pendulum myographs, and certain well-worn tables and copper troughs, which for the moment had no use.

He knew that this drug with others, diversely compounded and applied, produced in animals an abnormal intensification of the senses; that it increased – nay, as it were, magnified a thousandfold, the hearing, the sight, the touch – and, he was almost sure, the senses of taste and smell. But of the extent of the increase he could form no exact estimate.

Should he tonight put himself in the position of one able to speak on these points with authority? Or should he go to the Royal Society's meeting and hear that ass Netherby maunder yet once again about the secretion of lymph?

He pulled out his notebook and laid it open on the bench. He went to the locked cupboard, unfastened it with the bright key that hung instead of seal or charm at his watch-chain. He unfolded a paper and laid it on the bench where no one coming in could fail to see it. Then he took out little bottles, three, four, five, polished a graduated glass and dropped into it slow, heavy drops. A larger bottle yielded a medium in which all mingled. He hardly hesitated at all before turning up his sleeve and slipping the tiny needle into his arm. He pressed the end of the syringe. The injection was made.

Its effect, though not immediate, was sudden. He had to close his eyes, staggered indeed and was glad of the stool near him, for the drug coursed through him as a hunt in full cry might sweep over untrodden plains. Then suddenly everything seemed to settle; he was no longer helpless but was once again Professor Boyd Thompson, who had injected a mixture of certain drugs and was experiencing their effect.

His fingers, still holding the glass syringe, sent swift messages to his brain. When he looked down at his fingers, he saw that what they grasped was the smooth, slender tube of clear glass. What he felt that they held was a tremendous cylinder, rough to the touch. He wondered, even at the moment, why, if his sense of touch were indeed magnified to this degree, everything did not appear enormous – his ring, his collar. He examined the new phenomenon with cold care. It seemed that only that was enlarged on which his attention, his mind, was fixed. He kept his hand on the glass syringe, and thought of his ring, got his mind away from the tube, back again in time to feel it small between his fingers, grow, increase, and become big once more.

'So *that's* a success,' he said, and saw himself lay the thing down. It lay just in front of the rack of test tubes, to the eye, just that little glass cylinder. To the touch it was like a water-pipe on a house side, and the test tubes, when he touched them, like the pipes of a great organ.

'Success,' he said again, and mixed the antidote. For he had found the antidote in one of those flashes of intuition, imagination, genius, that light the ways of science as stars light the way of a ship in dark waters. The action of the antidote was enough for one night. He locked the cupboard, and, after all, was glad to listen to the maunderings of Netherby. It had been lonely there, in the atmosphere of complete success.

One by one, day by day, he tested the action of his drugs on his other senses. Without being technical, I had perhaps better explain that the compelling drug was, in each case, one and the same. Its action was directed to this set of nerves or that by means of the other drugs mixed with it. I trust this is clear?

The sense of smell was tested, and its laboratory, with its mingled odours, became abominable to him. Hardly could he stay himself from rushing forth into the outer air to wash his nostrils in the clear coolness of Hampstead Heath. The sense of taste gave him, magnified a thousand times, the flavour of his after-dinner coffee, and other tastes, distasteful almost beyond the bearing point.

But 'Success,' he said, rinsing his mouth at the laboratory sink after the drinking of the antidote, 'all along the line, success.'

Then he tested the action of his discovery on the sense of hearing. And the sound of London came like the roar of a giant, yet when he fixed his attention on the movements of a fly all other sounds ceased, and he heard the sound of the fly's feet on the shelf when it walked. Thus, in turn, he heard the creak of boards expanding in the heat, the movement of the glass stoppers that kept imprisoned in their proper bottles the giants of acid and alkali.

'Success!' he cried aloud, and his voice sounded in his ears like the shout of a monster overcoming primeval forces. 'Success! Success!'

There remained only the eyes, and here, strangely enough, the Professor hesitated, faint with a sudden heart-sickness. Following all intensification there must be reaction. What if the reaction exceeded that from which it reacted, what if the wave of tremendous sight, stemmed by the antidote ebbing, left him blind? But the spirit of the explorer in science is the spirit that explores African rivers, and sails amid white bergs to seek the undiscovered Pole.

He held the syringe with a firm hand, made the required puncture, and braced himself for the result. His eyes seemed to swell to great globes, to dwindle to microscopic globules, to swim in a flood of fire, to shrivel high and dry on a beach of hot sand. Then he saw, and the glass fell from his hand. For the whole of the stable earth seemed to be suddenly set in movement, even the air grew thick with vast overlapping shapeless shapes. He opined later that these were the microbes and bacilli that cover and fill all things in this world that looks so clean and bright.

Concentrating his vision, he saw in the one day's little dust on the bottles myriads of creatures, crawling and writhing, alive. The proportions of the laboratory seemed but little altered. Its large lines and forms remained practically unchanged. It was the little things that were no longer little, the invisible things that were now invisible no longer. And he felt grateful for the first time in his life for the limits set by Nature to the powers of the human body. He had increased those powers. If he let his eye stray idly about, as one does in the waltz, for example, all was much as it used to be. But the moment he looked steadily at any one thing it became enormous.

He closed his eyes. Success here had gone beyond his wildest dreams. Indeed he could not but feel that success, taking the bit between its teeth, had perhaps gone just the least little bit too far.

And on the next day he decided to examine the drug in all its aspects, to court the intensification of all his senses, which should set him in the position of supreme power over men and things, transform him from a Professor into a demi-god.

The great question was, of course, how the five preparations of his drug would act on or against each other. Would it be intensification, or would they neutralize each other? Like all imaginative scientists, he was working with stuff perilously like the spells of magic, and certain things were not possible to be foretold. Besides, this drug came from a land of mystery and the knowledge of secrets which we call magic. He did not anticipate any increase in the danger of the experiment. Nevertheless he spent some hours in arranging and destroying papers, among others certain pages of the yellow notebook. After dinner he detained his man as, laden with the last tray, he was leaving the room.

'I may as well tell you, Parker,' the Professor said, moved by some impulse he had not expected, 'that you will benefit to some extent by my will. On conditions. If any accident should cut short my life, you will at once communicate with my solicitor, whose name you will now write down.'

The model man, trained by fifteen years of close personal service, drew forth a notebook neat as the Professor's own, wrote in it neatly the address the Professor gave.

'Anything more, sir?' he asked, looking up, pencil in hand.

'No,' said the Professor, 'nothing more. Goodnight, Parker.'

'Goodnight, sir,' said the model man.

The next words the model man opened his lips to speak were breathed into the night tube of the nearest doctor.

'My master, Professor Boyd Thompson; could you come round at once, sir. I'm afraid it's very serious.'

It was half past six when the nearest doctor – Jones was his unimportant name – stooped over the lifeless body of the Professor.

He shook his head as he stood up and looked round the private laboratory on whose floor the body lay.

'His researches are over,' he said. 'Yes, he's dead. Been dead some hours. When did you find him?'

'I went to call my master as usual,' said Parker; 'he rises at six, summer and winter, sir. He was not in his room, and the bed had not been slept in. So I came in here, sir. It is not unusual for my master to work all night when he has been very interested in his experiments, and then he likes his coffee at six.'

'I see,' said Doctor Jones. 'Well, you'd better rouse the house and fetch his own doctor. It's heart failure, of course, but I daresay he'd like to sign the certificate himself.'

'Can nothing be done?' said Parker, much affected.

'Nothing,' said Dr Jones. 'It's the common lot. You'll have to look out for another situation.'

'Yes, sir,' said Parker; 'he told me only last night what I was to do in case of anything happening to him. I wonder if he had any idea?'

'Some premonition, perhaps,' the doctor corrected.

The funeral was a very quiet one. So the late Professor Boyd Thompson had decreed in his will. He had arranged all details. The body was to be clothed in flannel, placed in an open coffin covered only with a linen sheet, and laid in the family mausoleum, a moss-grown building in the midst of a little park which surrounded Boyd Grange, the birthplace of the Boyd Thompsons. A little property in Sussex it was. The Professor sometimes went there for weekends. He had left this property to Lucilla, with a last love-letter, in which he begged her to give his body the hospitality of the death-house, now hers with the rest of the estate. To Parker he left an annuity of two hundred pounds, on the condition that he should visit and enter the mausoleum once in every twenty-four hours for fourteen days after the funeral.

To this end the late Professor's solicitor decided that Parker had better reside at Boyd Grange for the said fortnight, and Parker, whose nerves seemed to be shaken, petitioned for company. This made easy the arrangement which the solicitor desired to make – of a witness to the carrying out by Parker of the provisions of the dead man's will. The solicitor's clerk was quite good company, and arm in arm with him Parker paid his first visit to the mausoleum. The little building stands in a glade of evergreen oaks. The trees are old and thick, and the narrow door is deep in shadow even on the sunniest day. Parker went to the mausoleum, peered through its square grating, but he did not go in. Instead, he listened, and his ears were full of silence.

'He's dead, right enough,' he said, with a doubtful glance at his companion.

'You ought to go in, oughtn't you?' said the solicitor's clerk;

'Go in yourself if you like, Mr Pollack,' said Parker, suddenly angry; 'anyone who likes can go in, but it won't be me. If he was alive, it 'ud be different. I'd have done anything for *him*. But I ain't going in among all them dead and mouldering Thompsons. See? If we both say I did, it'll be just the same as me doing it.'

'So it will,' said the solicitor's clerk; 'but where do I come in?'

Parker explained to him where he came in, to their mutual consent.

'Right you are,' said the clerk; 'on those terms I'm fly. And if we both say you did it, we needn't come to the beastly place again,' he added, shivering and glancing over his shoulder at the door with the grating.

'No more we need,' said Parker.

Behind the bars of the narrow door lay deeper shadows than those of the ilexes outside. And in the blackest of the shadow lay a man whose every sense was intensified as though by a magic potion. For when the Professor swallowed the five variants of his great discovery, each acted as he had expected it to act. But the union of the five vehicles conveying the drug to the nerves, which served his five senses, had paralysed every muscle. His hearing, taste, touch, scent, and sight were intensified a thousandfold – as they had been in the individual experiments – but the man who felt all this exaggerated increase of sensation was powerless as a cat under kurali. He could not raise a finger, stir an eyelash. More, he could not breathe, nor did his body advise him of any need of breathing. And he had lain thus immobile and felt his body slowly grow cold, had heard in thunder the voices of Parker and the doctor, had felt the enormous hands of those who made his death-toilet, had smelt intolerably the camphor and lavender that they laid round him in the narrow, black bed; had tasted the mingled flavours of the drug and its five mediums; and, in an ecstasy of magnified sensation, had made the lonely train journey which coffins make, and known himself carried into the mausoleum and left there alone. And every sense was intensified, even his sense of time, so that it seemed to him that he had lain there for many years. And the effect of the drugs showed no sign of any diminution or reaction. Why had he not left directions for the injection of the antidote? It was one of those slips which wreck campaigns, cause the discovery of hidden crimes. It was a slip, and he had made it. He had thought of death, but in all the results he had anticipated death's semblance had found no place. Well, he had made his bed, and he must lie on it. This narrow bed, whose scent of clean oak and French polish was distinct among the musty, intolerable odours of the charnel house.

It was perhaps twenty hours that he had lain there, powerless, immobile, listening to the sounds of unexplained movements about him, when he felt with joy, almost like delirium, a faint quivering in the eyelids.

They had closed his eyes, and till now, they had remained closed. Now, with an effort as of one who lifts a grave-stone, he raised his eyelids. They closed again quickly, for the roof of the vault, at which he gazed earnestly, was alive with monsters; spiders, earwigs, crawling beetles, and flies, far too small to have been perceived by normal eyes, spread giant forms over him. He closed his eyes and shuddered. It felt like a shudder, but no one who had stood beside him could have noted any movement

It was then that Parker came – and went.

Professor Boyd Thompson heard Parker's words, and lay listening to the thunder of Parker's retreating feet. He tried to move – to call out. But he could not. He lay there helpless, and somehow he thought of the dark end of the laboratory, where the assistant before leaving had turned out the electric lights.

He had nothing but his thoughts. He thought how he would lie there, and die there. The place was sequestered; no one passed that way. Parker had failed him, and the end was not hard to picture. He might recover all his faculties, might be able to get up, able to scream, to shout, to tear at the bars. The bars were strong, and Parker would not come again. Well, he would try to face with a decent bravery whatever had to be faced.

Time, measureless, spread round. It seemed as though someone had stopped all the clocks in the world, as though he were not in time but in eternity. Only by the waxing and waning light he knew of the night and the day.

His brain was weary with the effort to move, to speak, to cry out. He lay, informed with something like despair – or fortitude. And then Parker came again. And this time a key grated in the lock. The Professor noted with rapture that it sounded no louder than a key should sound, turned in a lock that was rusty. Nor was the voice other than he had been used to hear it, when he was man alive and Parker's master. And –

'You can go in, of course, if you wish it, miss,' said Parker disapprovingly; 'but it's not what I should advise myself. For me it's different,' he added, on a sudden instinct of self-preservation; 'I've got to go in. Every day for a fortnight,' he added, pitying himself.

'I will go in, thank you,' said a voice. 'Yes, give me the candle, please. And you need not wait. I will lock the door when I come out.' Thus the voice spoke. And the voice was Lucilla's.

In all his life the Professor had never feared death or its trappings. Neither its physical repulsiveness, nor the supernatural terrors which cling about it, had he either understood or tolerated. But now, in one little instant, he did understand.

He heard Lucilla come in. A light held near him shone warm and red through his closed eyelids. And he knew that he had only to unclose those eyelids to see her face bending over him. And he could unclose them. Yet he would not. He lay there, still and straight in his coffin, and life swept through him in waves of returning power. Yet he lay like death. For he said, or something in him said:

'She believes me dead. If I open my eyes it will be like a dead man looking at her. If I move it will be a dead man moving under her eyes. People have gone mad for less. Lie still, lie still,' he told himself; 'take any risks yourself. There must be none for her.'

She had taken the candle away, set it down somewhere at a distance, and now she was kneeling beside him and her hand was under his head. He knew he could raise his arm and clasp her – and Parker would come back perhaps, when she did not return to the house, come back to find a man in grave-clothes, clasping a mad woman. He lay still. Then her kisses and tears fell on his face, and she murmured broken words of love and longing. But he lay still. At any cost he must lie still. Even at the cost of his own sanity, his own life. And the warmth of her hand under his head, her face against his, her kisses, her tears, set his blood flowing evenly and strongly. Her other arm lay on his breast, softly pressing over his heart. He would not move. He would be strong. If he were to be saved, it must be by some other way, not this.

Suddenly tears and kisses ceased; her every breath seemed to have stopped with these. She had drawn away from him. She spoke. Her voice came from above him. She was standing up.

'Arthur!' she said. 'Arthur!' Then he opened his eyes, the narrowest chink. But he could not see her. Only he knew she was moving towards the door. There had been a new quality in her tone, a thrill of fear, or hope was it? or at least of uncertainty? Should he move; should he speak? He dared not. He knew too well the fear that the normal human being has of death and the grave, the fear transcending love, transcending reason. Her voice was further away now. She was by the door. She was leaving him. If he let her go, it was an end of hope for him. If he did not let her go, an end, perhaps, of reason, for her. No.

'Arthur,' she said, 'I don't believe . . . I believe you can hear me. I'm going to get a doctor. If you *can* speak, speak to me.'

Her speaking ended, cut off short as a cord is cut by a knife. He did not speak. He lay in conscious, forced rigidity.

'Speak if you can,' she implored, 'just one word!'

Then he said, very faintly, very distinctly, in a voice that seemed to come from a great way off, 'Lucilla!'

And at the word she screamed aloud pitifully, and leaped for the entrance; and he heard the rustle of her crape in the narrow door. Then be opened his eyes wide, and raised himself on his elbow. Very weak he was, and trembling exceedingly. To his ears her scream held the note of madness. Vainly he had refrained. Selfishly he had yielded. The cold band of a mortal faintness clutched at his heart.

'I don't want to live now,' he told himself, and fell back in the straight bed.

Her arms were round him.

'I'm going to get help,' she said, her lips to his ear; 'brandy and things. Only I came back. I didn't want you to think I was frightened. Oh, my dear! Thank God, thank God!' He felt her kisses even through the swooning mist that swirled about him. Had she really fled in terror? He never knew. He knew that she had come back to him.

That is the real, true, and authentic narrative of the events which caused Professor Boyd Thompson to abandon a brilliant career, to promise anything that Lucilla might demand, and to devote himself entirely to a gentlemanly and unprofitable farming, and to his wife. From the point of view of the scientific world it is a sad ending to much promise, but at any rate there are two happy people hand in hand at the story's ending.

There is no doubt that for several years Professor Boyd Thompson had had enough of science, and, by a natural revulsion, flung himself into the full tide of commonplace sentiment. But genius, like youth, cannot be denied. And I, for one, am doubtful whether the Professor's renunciation of research will be a lasting one. Already I have heard whispers of a laboratory which is being built on the house, beyond the billiard-room.

But I am inclined to believe the rumours which assert that, for the future, his research will take the form of extending paths already well trodden; that he will refrain from experiments with unknown drugs, and those dreadful researches which tend to merge the chemist and biologist in the alchemist and the magician. And he certainly does not intend to experiment further on the nerves of any living thing, even his own. The Professor had already done enough work to make the reputation of half-a-dozen ordinary scientists. He may be pardoned if he rests on his laurels, entwining them, to some extent, with roses.

The bottle containing the drug from the South Seas was knocked down on the day of his death and swept up in bits by the laboratory boy. It is a curious fact that the Professor has wholly forgotten the formulae of his experiment, which so nearly was his last. This is a great satisfaction to his wife, and possibly to the Professor. But of this I cannot be sure; the scientific spirit survives much.

To the unscientific reader the strangest part of this story will perhaps be the fact that Parker is still with his old master, a wonderful example of the perfect butler. Professor Boyd Thompson was able to forgive Parker because he understood him. And he learned to understand Parker in those moments of agony, when his keen intellect and his awakened heart taught him, through his love for Lucilla, the depth of that gulf of fear which lies between the quick and the dead.

Clotilde Graves

LADY CLANBEVAN'S BABY

Clotilde Inez Mary Graves (1863–1932), or 'Clo' as she was usually known, was born into a military family, the daughter of Major W.H. Graves of the 18th Royal Irish Regiment, and she spent all her infant years at the barracks in County Cork. She was the second cousin of the poet and novelist Robert Graves. She clearly had a good sense of humour, as her early days were spent drawing cartoons and writing sketches for the comic papers and subsequently for the stage. In the end she had sixteen plays produced in London and New York between 1887 and 1913 starting with Nitocris, *a tragedy in blank verse. She also wrote the book of the pantomime* Puss in Boots *(1888). Her life was anything but conventional. Perhaps her upbringing in a military establishment had its effect, but she frequently dressed as a man and enjoyed smoking in public. She apparently had a temper –* The Times' *obituarist remarked that rehearsals of her plays were apt 'to be marked by unconventional incidents'. Alongside her plays she wrote several novels, mostly humorous, such as* A Well-Meaning Woman *(1896), about the consequences of a busybody's matchmaking plans.*

Suddenly, in 1910, Clo took on a new persona and, as Richard Dehan, she wrote The Dop Doctor. *The book was a huge bestseller in its portrayal of a city under siege during the Boer War and of a disgraced London doctor who redeems his honour. Graves wished to keep the identity of Dehan secret, although it soon leaked out, but thereafter Graves retained the Dehan personality. Grant Overton, writing in* Authors of Today *in 1923, who knew Graves, made the perceptive observation that it was as if Dehan was Graves's son, which makes the following story, published under the Dehan name, all the more pertinent.*

Lady Clanbevan's Baby

THERE WAS A grey, woolly October fog over Hyde Park. The railings wept grimy tears, and the damp yellow leaves dropped soddenly from the soaked trees. Pedestrians looked chilled and sulky; camphor chests and cedar-presses had yielded up their treasures of sables and sealskin, chinchilla and silver fox. A double stream of fashionable traffic rolled west and east, and the rich clarets and vivid crimsons of the automobiles burned through the fog like genial, warming fires.

A Baby-Bunting six-horse-power petrol car, in colour a chrysanthemum yellow, came jiggeting by. The driver stopped. He was a technical chemist and biologist of note and standing, and I had last heard him speak from the platform of the Royal Institution.

'I haven't seen you,' said the Professor, 'for years.'

'That must be because you haven't looked,' said I, 'for I have both seen and heard you quite recently. Only you were upon the platform and I was on the ground floor.'

'You are too much upon the ground floor now,' said the Professor, with a shudder of a Southern European at the dampness around and under foot, 'and I advise you to accept a seat in my car.'

And the Baby-Bunting, trembling with excitement at being in the company of so many highly varnished electric victorias and forty-horse-power auto cars, joined the steadily flowing stream going west.

'I wonder that you stoop to petrol, Professor,' I said, as the thin, skilful hand in the baggy chamois glove manipulated the driving-wheel, and the little car snaked in and out like a torpedo-boat picking her way between the giant warships of a Channel Squadron.

The Professor's black brows unbent under the cap-peak, and his thin, tightly gripped lips relaxed into a mirthless smile.

'Ah, yes; you think that I should drive my car by radio-activity, is it not? And so I could and would, if the pure radium chloride were not three thousand times the price of gold. From eight tons of uranium ore residues about one gramme, that is, fifteen grains, can be extracted by fusing the residue with carbonates of soda, dissolving in hydrochloric acid, precipitating the lead and other metals in solution by the aid of hydrogen sulphide, and separating from the chlorides that remain – polonium, actinium, barium, and so forth – the chloride of radium. With a single pound of this I could not only drive an auto-car, my friend' – his olive cheek warmed, and his melancholy dark eyes grew oddly lustrous – 'I could stop the world!'

'And supposing it was necessary to make it go on again?' I suggested.

'When I speak of the world,' exclaimed the Professor, 'I do not refer to the planet upon which we revolve; I speak of the human race which inhabits it.'

'Would the human race be obliged to you, Professor?' I queried.

The Professor turned upon me with so sudden a verbal riposte that the Baby-Bunting swerved violently.

'You are not as young as you were when I met you first. To be plain, you are getting middle-aged. Do you like it?'

'I hate it!' I answered, with beautiful sincerity.

'Would you thank the man who should arrest, not the beneficent passage of Time, which means progress, but the wear and tear of nerve and muscle, tissue, and bone, the slow deterioration of the blood by the microbes of old age, for Metchnikoff has shown that there is no difference between the atrophy of senility and the atrophy caused by microbe poison? Would you thank him – the man who should do that for you? Tell me, my friend.'

I replied, briefly and succinctly: 'Wouldn't I?'

'Ha!' exclaimed the Professor, 'I thought so!'

'But I should have liked him to have begun earlier,' I said. 'Twenty-nine is a nice age, now . . . It is the age we all try to stop at, and can't, however much we try. Look there!'

A landau limousine, dark blue, beautifully varnished, nickel-plated, and upholstered in cream-white leather, came gliding gracefully through the press of vehicles. From the crest upon the panel to the sober workman-like livery of the chauffeur, the turn-out was perfection. The pearl it contained was worthy of the setting.

'Look there!' I repeated, as the rose-cheeked, sapphire-eyed, smiling vision passed, wrapped in a voluminous coat of chinchilla and silver fox, with a toque of Parma violets under the shimmer of the silken veil that could only temper the burning glory of her wonderful Renaissance hair.

'There's the exception to the rule . . . There's a woman who doesn't need the aid of science or of Art to keep her at nine and twenty. There's a woman in whom "the wear and tear of nerve and muscle, tissue and bone" goes on – if it does go on – imperceptibly. Her blood doesn't seem to be much deteriorated by the microbe of old age, Professor, does it? And she's forty-three! The alchemistical forty-three, that turns the gold of life back into lead! The gold remains gold in her case, for that hair, that complexion, that figure, are,' I solemnly declared, 'her own.'

At that moment Lady Clanbevan gave a smiling gracious nod to the Professor, and he responded with a cold, grave bow. The glow of her gorgeous hair, the liquid sapphire of her eyes, were wasted on this stony man of science. She passed, going home to Stanhope Gate, I suppose, in which neighbourhood she has a house; I had barely a moment to notice the white-bonneted, blue-cloaked nurse on the front of the landau, holding a bundle of laces and cashmeres, and to reflect that I have never yet seen Lady Clanbevan taking the air out of the society of a baby, when the Professor spoke:

'So Lady Clanbevan is the one woman who has no need of the aid of art or science to preserve her beauty and maintain her appearance of youth? Supposing I could prove to you otherwise, my friend, what then?'

'I should say,' I returned, 'that you had proved what everybody else denies. Even the enemies of that modern Ninon de l'Enclos, who has just passed.'

'With the nurse and the baby?' interpolated the Professor.

'With the nurse and the baby,' said I. 'Even her enemies, and they are legion, admit the genuineness of the charms they detest. Mentioning the baby, do you know that for twenty years I have never seen Lady Clanbevan out without a baby? She must have quite a regiment of children of all ages, sizes, and sexes.'

'Upon the contrary,' said the Professor, 'she has only one!'

'The others have all died young, then?' I asked sympathetically, and was rendered breathless by the rejoinder: 'Lady Clanbevan is a widow.'

'One never asks questions about the husband of a professional beauty,' I said. 'His individuality is merged in hers from the day upon which her latest photograph assumes a marketable value. Are you sure there isn't a Lord Clanbevan alive somewhere?'

'There is a Lord Clanbevan alive,' said the Professor coldly. 'You have just seen him, in his nurse's arms. He is the only child of his mother, and she has been a widow for nearly twenty years! You do not credit what I assert, my friend?'

'How can I, Professor?' I asked, turning to meet his full face, and noticed that his dark, somewhat opaque brown irises had lights and gleams of carbuncle-crimson in them. 'I have had Lady Clanbevan and her progeny under my occasional observation for years. The world grows older, if she doesn't, and she has invariably a baby – *toujours* a new baby – to add to the charming illusion of young motherhood which she sustains so well. And now you tell me that she is a twenty-years' widow with one child, who must be nearly of age or it isn't proper. You puzzle me painfully!'

'Would you care,' asked the Professor after a moment's pause, 'to drive back to Harley Street with me? I am, as you know, a vegetarian, so I will not tax your politeness by inviting you to lunch. But I have something in my laboratory I should wish to show you.'

'Of all things, I should like to come,' I said. 'How many times haven't I fished fruitlessly for an invitation to visit the famous laboratory where nearly twenty years ago –'

'I traced,' said the Professor, 'the source of phenomena which heralded the evolution of the Rontgen Ray and the ultimate discovery

of the radio-active salt they have christened radium. I called it protium twenty years ago, because of its various and protean qualities.
Why did I not push on, perfect the discovery and anticipate Sir
William C and the X's? There was a reason. You will understand it
before you leave my laboratory.'

The Baby-Bunting stopped at the unfashionable end of Harley
Street, in front of the dingy yellow house with the black front door,
flanked by dusty boxes of mildewed dwarf evergreens, and the
Professor, relieved of his fur-lined coat and cap, led the way upstairs
as lightly as a boy. Two garret-rooms had been knocked together for
a laboratory. There was a tiled furnace at the darker end of the long
skylighted room thus made, and solid wooden tables, much stained
with spilt chemicals, were covered with scales, glasses, jars, and
retorts – all the tools of chemistry. From one of the many shelves
running round the walls, the Professor took down a circular glass
flask and placed it in my hands. The flask contained a handful of
decayed and mouldy-looking wheat, and a number of peculiarly
offensive-looking little beetles with tapir-like proboscides.

'The perfectly developed beetle of the *Calandria granaria*,' said
the Professor, as I cheerfully resigned the flask, 'a common British
weevil, whose larvae feed upon stored grain. Now look at this.' He
reached down and handed me a precisely similar flask, containing
another handful of grain, cleaner and sounder in appearance, and
a number of grubs, sharp-ended chrysalis-like things buried in the
grain, inert and inactive.

'The larvae of *Calandria granaria*,' said the Professor, in his drawl-
ing monotone. 'How long does it take to hatch the beetle from the
grub? you ask. Less than a month. The perfect weevils that I have
just shown you I placed in their flask a little more than three weeks
back. The grubs you see in the flask you are holding, and which, as
you will observe by their anxiety to bury themselves in the grain so
as to avoid contact with the light, are still immature, I placed in the
glass receptacle twenty years ago. Don't drop the flask. I value it.'

'Professor!' I gasped.

'Twenty years ago,' repeated the Professor, delicately handling

the venerable grubs, 'I enclosed these grubs in this flask, with sufficient grain to fully nourish them and bring them to the perfect state.
In another flask I placed a similar number of grubs in exactly the
same quantity of wheat. Then for twenty-four hours I exposed flask
number one to the rays emanating from what is now called radium.
And as the electrons discharged from radium are obstructed by
collision with air-atoms, I exhausted the air contained in the flask.'

He paused.

'Then, when the grubs in flask number two hatched out,' I anticipated, 'and the larvae in flask number one remained stationary, you
realized –'

'I realized that the rays from the salt arrested growth, and at the
same time prolonged life to an almost incalculable extent,' said the
Professor 'for you will understand that the grubs in flask number one
had lived as grubs half a dozen times as long as grubs usually do . . .
And I said to myself that the discovery presented an immense, a
tremendous, field for future development. Suppose a young woman
of, say, twenty-nine were enclosed in a glass receptacle of sufficient
bulk to contain her, and exposed for a few hours to my protium
rays, she would retain for many years to come, until she was a
great-grandmother of ninety, the same charming, youthful appearance.'

'As Lady Clanbevan!' I cried, as the truth rushed upon me and I
grasped the meaning this astonishing man had intended to convey.

'As Lady Clanbevan presents today,' said the Professor, 'thanks to
the discovery of a . . .'

'Of a great man,' said I, looking admiringly at the lean, worn
figure in the closely buttoned black frock-coat.

'I loved her . . . It was a delight to her to drag a disciple of Science
at her chariot-wheels. People talked of me as a coming man. Perhaps
I was . . . But I did not thirst for distinction, honours, fame . . . I
thirsted for that woman's love . . . I told her of my discovery as I
told her everything. Bah!' His lean nostrils worked. 'You know the
game that is played when one is in earnest and the other at play. She
promised nothing; she walked delicately among the passions she

sowed and fostered in the souls of men, as a beautiful tigress walks among the poison plants of the jungle. She saw that rightly used, or wrongly used, my great discovery might save her beauty, her angelic, dazzling beauty that had as yet but felt the first touch of Time. She planned the whole thing, and when she said, 'You do not love me if you will not do this, ' I did it. I was mad when I acceded to her wish, perhaps; but she is a woman to drive men frenzied. You have seen how coldly, how slightingly she looked at me when we encountered her in the Row? I tell you, you have guessed already, I went there to see her. I always go where she is to be encountered, when she is in town. And she bows, always; but her eyes are those of a stranger. Yet I have had her on her knees to me. She cried and begged and kissed my hands.'

He knotted his thin hands, their fingers brown-tipped with the stains of acids, and wrung and twisted them ferociously.

'And so I granted what she asked, carried out the experiment, and paid what you English call the piper. The giant glass bulb with the rubber-valve door was blown and finished in France. It involved an expense of three hundred pounds. The salt I used of protium (christened radium now) cost me all my savings – over two thousand pounds – for I had been a struggling man.'

'But the experiment?' I broke in. 'Good Heavens, Professor! How could a living being remain for any time in an exhausted receiver? Agony unspeakable, convulsions, syncope, death! One knows what the result would be. The merest common sense.'

'The merest common sense is not what one employs to make discoveries or carry out great experiments,' said the Professor. 'I will not disclose my method; I will only admit to you that the subjects were insensible; that I induced anaesthesia by the ordinary ether-pump apparatus, and that the strength of the ray obtained was concentrated to such a degree that the exposure was complete in three hours.' He looked about him haggardly. 'The experiment took place here nineteen years ago. Nineteen years ago, and it seems to me as though it were yesterday.'

'And it must seem like yesterday to Lady Clanbevan whenever

she looks in the glass,' I said. 'But you have pricked my curiosity, Professor, by the use of the plural. Who was the other subject?'

'Is it possible you don't guess?' The sad, hollow eyes questioned my face in surprise. Then they turned haggardly away. 'My friend, the other subject associated with Lady Clanbevan in my great experiment was Her Baby!'

I could not speak. The dowdy little grubs in the flask became for me creatures imbued with dreadful potentialities . . . The tragedy and the sublime absurdity of the thing I realized caught at my throat, and my brain grew dizzy with its horror.

'Oh! Professor!' I gurgled, 'how, how grimly, awfully, tragically ridiculous! To carry about with one wherever one goes a baby that never grows older, a baby . . .'

'A baby nearly twenty years old? Yes, it is, as you say, ridiculous and horrible,' the Professor agreed.

'What could have induced the woman!' burst from me.

The Professor smiled bitterly. 'She is greedy of money. It is the only thing she loves except her beauty and her power over men; and during the boy's infancy – that word is used in the Will – she has full enjoyment of the estate. After he 'attains to manhood' – I quote the Will again – hers is but a life-interest. Now you understand?'

I did understand, and the daring of the woman dazzled me. She had made the Professor doubly her tool.

'And so,' I gurgled between tears and laughter, 'Lord Clanbevan, who ought to be leaving Eton this year to commence his first Oxford term, is being carried about in the arms of a nurse, arrayed in the flowing garments of a six-months baby! What an astonishing conspiracy!'

'His mother,' continued the Professor calmly, 'allows no one to approach him but the nurse. The family are only too glad to ignore what they consider a deplorable case of atavistic growth-arrest, and the boy himself . . .' He broke off. 'I have detained you,' he said, after a pause.' I will not do so longer. Nor will I offer you my hand. I am as conscious as you are that it has committed a crime.' And he bowed me out with his hands sternly held behind him. There were few more words between us, only I remember turning on the threshold of the laboratory, where I left him, to ask whether protium radium, as it is now christened, checks the growth of every organic substance? The answer I received was curious: 'Certainly, with the exception of the nails and the hair!'

A week later the Professor was found dead in his laboratory . . . There were reports of suicide hushed up. People said he had been more eccentric than ever of late, and theorized about brain-mischief; only I located the trouble in the heart. A year went by, and I had almost forgotten Lady Clanbevan, for she went abroad after the Professor's death, when, at a little watering-place on the Dorset coast, I saw that lovely thing, as lovely as ever she who was fifty if a day!

With her were the blue-cloaked elderly nurse and Lord Clanbevan, borne, as usual, in the arms of his attendant, or wheeled in a luxurious perambulator. Day after day I encountered them – the lovely mother, the middle-aged nurse, and the mysterious child – until the sight began to get on my nerves. Had the Professor selected me as the recipient of a secret unrivalled in the records of biological discovery, or had he been the victim of some maniacal delusion that cold October day when we met in Rotten Row? One peep under the thick white lace veil with which the baby's face was invariably covered would clear everything up! Oh! for a chance to allay the pangs of curiosity!

The chance came. It was a hot, waspy August forenoon. Everybody was indoors with all the doors and windows open, lunch-ing upon the innutritive viands alone procurable at health resorts – everybody but myself, Lord Clanbevan, and his nurse. She had fallen asleep upon a green-painted esplanade seat, gratuitously shielded by a striped awning. Lord Clanbevan's C-springed, white-hooded, cane-built perambulator stood close beside her. He was, as usual, a mass of embroidered cambric and cashmere, and, as always, thickly veiled, his regular breathing heaved his infant breast; the thick white lace drapery attached to his beribboned bonnet obscured the features upon which I so ardently longed to gaze! It was the chance, as I have said; and as the head of the blue-cloaked nurse dropped reassuringly upon her breast, as she emitted the snore that gave assurance of the soundness of her slumbers, I stepped silently on the gravel towards the baby's perambulator. Three seconds, and I stood over its apparently sleeping inmate; another, and I had lifted the veil from the face of the mystery and dropped it with a stifled cry of horror!

The child had a moustache!

Muriel Pollexfen

MONSIEUR FLY-BY-NIGHT

Muriel Pollexfen (1877–1927) was related to greatness but never got much chance to shine in her own light. Her paternal aunt, Susan Pollexfen, had married John B. Yeats and became the mother of Jack Yeats and W.B. Yeats. Although the Pollexfen family came from Ireland, they were of Cornish descent. Muriel's father, John, was a sea captain and spent much of his time away. Muriel was born in Liverpool but later moved to London, where she married a surveyor and land agent, Adrian Tresidder, in 1907. Alas, the marriage ended in divorce in 1919. Muriel lived only a few years more, dying in Godstone in Surrey in 1927, aged just fifty.

Both she and her sister Claire turned their hand to writing but neither with any great success. Muriel showed an interest in the advent of the aeroplane and wrote a series of stories collected as Grey Ghost *(1910) about the exploits of a daring adventurer, Algy Brett, versus the scoundrel Alsop Ostermann, master of a giant aircraft. She returned to the idea but this time with a giant airship, featuring another daring villain, Monsieur Fly-By-Night.*

Monsieur Fly-by-Night

'THE GENTLEMAN, BY appointment, to see you, sir,' murmured the boy's voice from the door as he opened it and ushered in the visitor.

A big, stout, florid man of sixty or so; slightly bald beneath the Homburg hat; bird-like, restless eyes peering from under fleshy lids topped by thick white brows – their alertness dimmed by a pair of slightly smoked pince-nez. A foreigner without a doubt, but a foreigner aping English.

He was obviously nervous and waited a full moment while the door closed behind him before he spoke. Then he turned to the slim, slender, colourless youth awaiting him, held out a podgy hand, and bowed in undisguised uncertainty.

'Monsieur Fly-by-Night?' he asked, cautiousness in his voice, incredulity leaping to life behind the dull glasses. 'Monsieur himself?' he emphasized.

Maxtone Domville had risen from the depths of a luxurious chair on the announcement of the visitor, but now he sank back into it again and with a wave of a hand thin to attenuation motioned his guest to another seat beside his own.

'Yes,' he said languidly, in response to the other's question, 'I am that same notorious person, at your service. I am that Monsieur Fly-by-Night whom Paris has so honoured as to baptize in a hundred toasts, and so loves as to talk foolishly about my cleverness! But, after all, I am only just the rather poor fellow you see before you and who disappoints you so! . . . But I am Monsieur Fly-by-Night all the same, and you – who are you? . . . if I may presume to ask?'

'I am Confidential Minister to the Court of Travonia; I am

Rachinov – Count Rachinov, sir, and I have come to ask you for your help, your advice – but –'

Domville smiled appreciation.

'But you're aghast! You're afraid to trust me! I'm so young, so fragile, so unlike the hawk-like creature you had conjured up in your mind's eye! The bull-dog jaw! The flashing eye! The bellicose attitude all conspicuous by their absence, and you are non-plussed. You came expecting a berserker, and you see an emaciated, consumptive-looking youth! Isn't that the situation, eh, dear count?'

The count smiled weakly, and sat down in the indicated chair. His eyes behind the glasses scanned the thin face of his host as though trying to find the hidden personality beneath the presentment of effeteness.

'You are very astute, at any rate, Mr Domville,' he said finally, a firmer tone distinct beneath the pleasantry. 'But you admit I have cause for surprise? I have heard of you as the most daring adventurer of modern times, as the most marvellous airman in the world. I have heard you spoken of as something not quite human, something of a mystery, yet something too authentic to be despised. You make a mystery of your airship. One tells of you speeding over the dome of St Paul's, leaving London on a secret errand; then news comes that you are sweeping the deserts of China for a hiding foe; then news comes that you are in Africa. Ah! I heard the most wonderful things of you, monsieur!'

Domville smiled inwardly at the other's acceptance of him, and in the smile there was a faint suspicion of braggart consciousness.

'Taking me on trust, count? How good of you. And I do not even know your business yet.'

'You have me on the thigh, monsieur, and I am at your feet. I, of course, should have explained that before I permitted myself to be patronizing! Pray pardon me and let us cry off this play and parry business and get down to rock bottom. First, though, are you free – are you willing to help me, or am I merely wasting both my time and yours?'

'That depends. I'm an adventurer purely and above everything else. I earn a good living at it, incidentally, and have a good time. I'm top-dog at the moment and can pick my own business. What's yours?'

'One that not another man I know of would undertake. If you want adventure, then you are my servant, for I can . . . oh! sir! sir! I come to you on an errand of the utmost importance, an errand of life and death, to ask you to take your life in your hands, and save a nation.'

'And shall I figure as a smouldering corpse atop the ruins, or am I crowned with laurels and proclaimed king of Travonia by a crowd of insane revolutionists, and bucking soldiers and statesmen?'

Domville's breath caught slightly at the last few words. It was the only sign of the excitement that had begun to breed in him, but the count seized on it with eagerness, and, whisking the glasses from his eyes, looked hungrily into Domville's face.

'I'm on an honest errand,' he said, trying to speak quietly. 'I'm not with them, and you're to believe it! How has the news come over here into this little London room of yours? Or was it a chance shot? Have you learned that the red cloud of revolution is clotting up the sky over Travonia, or are you guessing?'

'One doesn't guess such things from choice, dear count! Nay, 'tis Rumour, the jade, escaped from beneath the crimson mantle and confiding in me. I heard the news yesterday. Er – how soon?'

'At the most in three nights from now – or it may burst the last bond that binds it, and be tonight! My God, if it should be!'

'Tell me about it – from the beginning.'

'It would have been months ago if it had not been for one of the gun-running steamers being captured as she was entering the private harbour below the Duke Renzi's château, and causing a volley of enquiries to be set afoot. Renzi was all for going ahead, but Raunay and Schweps got frightened, and advised – insisted on – delay. So far they have worked so quietly that not a breath of suspicion has dimmed the glass; there was only the incident of the gun-runner, and Renzi got rid of it in time. He's clever, and they allowed him a free hand. He's the best man in the thing; there's been no friction as yet between him and Raunay and Co., but it's bound to come. If only one could, in arranging partnerships of this sort, accurately gauge the rising and sinking values of their fellow conspirators, there would be an end to traitors, eh?'

Domville laughed dryly. 'You yourself –' he commented.

'Yes, even I. I deliberately went under that heading knowing what men would say of me. But it bears out what I have just said to you. If Raunay and Schweps and the rest of them had accurately gauged the heights and depths of my villainy, I should not be here now.'

'They suspect you?'

'Not when I left, but they may do so from my absence from the meeting tonight. With Renzi the thought will be welcome! He hates me, sets traps for me, and waits – waits . . .'

He leaned forward to scan Domville's face. 'What do you think?' he asked.

'I think you'd better cut the cackle and get to the beasts. If they suspect then our task is re-doubled in dangers, whatever it may be. Tell me.'

'Here it is then, as bare as your hand. We've been governed for fifteen rotten, barren, godless years by Peter VII, and bribed, cajoled, threatened, and tricked by Peter's half-brother, Osric Renzi, acting as Peter's right hand. Osric claims that God and Nature have better fitted and equipped him to grace the throne than they have his half-brother Peter, and in a measure he is right. He would be strong and brutal where Peter is weak and despicable. A fool never yet brought a nation to prosperity, whereas there is a chance that a brute might. With us the country is tired of the fool and would try the brute. I cannot blame them when I look on the fifteen lean, ignoble years that have gone; any state would be an improvement on the present! Travonians are the most loyal of people, but Osric has won them at last, and they will follow his battle-cry, acclaiming him, on the third night from now – if not before!'

'Why not fifteen years ago? Why wait till the third night from now? Pure loyalty? The fear of a brute's whip?'

'Neither. Something much more simple . . . and more inconceivable. The fact that the Duke Osric's mother was the Court washerwoman! Quite farcical, isn't it? And yet so true that it has kept a kingdom loyal to a fool. The people dislike him for it, and for the fact that the discovery of the intrigue – if such an alliance could be so named – was the cause of the Queen's sudden and mysterious death. It was given out at the time that the cause of her Majesty's illness was a fever, but the story got abroad that the fever was the fever of a poisoned glass of wine. She had been dearly beloved, and the sting of her death rankles still, and Osric suffers for the sin of his father.'

'And your allegiance to the reigning Fool – is what? The soap-suds on the escutcheon? A short cut to honours? What?'

Domville was looking clear into Rachinov's face as he whipped out the question, and was quick to read the dull red flush which shot into his cheeks and stained his forehead.

'Ah!' he cried, triumphantly, 'the woman in the case!'

Rachinov stood up nervously. The red colour flamed in his face.

'If one can call Her Serene Highness the Grand Duchess Eva by such a name!' he said, half shyly, half stiffly, yet with a look in his eyes which gave away the man's middle-aged heart.

'But she *is* the woman in the case for all her rank!' repeated Domville, 'and you would save her from the red terror of Revolution? You want me to get her out of Travonia before three nights hence, eh?'

'There is another motive, and perhaps it is one which will not appeal to your English mind; perhaps one that will stamp me as a madman, a medieval fool, a mountebank of a minister! Listen . . . I, too, desire to humble Peter! I, too, desire to dethrone him, banish him for ever, supplant him and exile him! I also, like the revolting populace, desire to set another on the throne of Travonia . . . But that other is not the Duke Osric!'

Domville was suddenly interested. His eyes flickered.

'No?' he said.

'No! I would have a Queen! A Queen! The Duchess Eva . . . she's only a bit of a girl, but what a woman she'll make! What a Queen!

Man, the people will rally round her like the loyalists they are! She's of the old stock. The dignity and daring of her bravest ancestors are in her veins, and her fingers would be like iron on the reins of government. There are tried and trusty ministers, men who have advised her grandfather, and engineered the era of prosperity we enjoyed before Peter succeeded, who are not yet too old to advise and guide a young girl's ignorance, and who would be willing to emerge from the obscurity of premature retirement forced upon them by Peter in his headstrong wilfulness. With such men at the helm, and such a queen at the prow, the Argosy of Travonia would sail into triumphant prosperity!'

'And I come in – where? If your Travonians will turn loyalists when you offer them a queen, why not proclaim your intention to them without delay? Why wait? Why come to me?'

'Because Renzi stepped in. I was imagining he intended including her in the fate he was preparing for her parents. I made a mistake.'

Domville rammed another cigarette into the amber holder, and lit it.

'You made a big mistake. One unworthy of you. Why, the man's success rests upon the dullness of the people's brains! They have been made to forget the daughter in the hatred of the King! Your Duke has seen to it that their fevered memories do not recollect her. He would be the last to conjure her memory to their minds by an act so mad, so horrible, as the inclusion of her in the carnage he purposes for the night of the tragedy. To bring her so hideously to their notice, to their remembrance, by putting her to so cruel a death in the turbulence of insane rebellion would be the act of a fool – and you say he is no fool. So he has done what?'

Rachinov swore as he answered, and Domville could see that the words were as bitter on his tongue as the thought of his checkmate was to his memory.

'He has kidnapped her. She is missing from the palace. The King is frightened and suspicious, and is trying to keep her absence a secret . . . an easy matter, seeing that she was always in the background. But they are frightened. It came as a shock to them, but it was a tonic to me. I knew what had happened. I guessed where she was, and I realized I was powerless to help her alone.'

'So you came to me.'

'So I came to you. Yes.'

II

Something swept silently through the still air.

In the clinging midnight mist it looked like a mammoth moth entrapped, encircled with grey fog that shaped like the thousand fingers of drifting wraiths. Here and there a pale star, penetrating the mists, gleamed a guidance for a space. A soughing wind sighed in the belt of trees crowding the mountain sides, and whistled down the heights topping the valley.

Below, the lights of Sordenburg, the capital of Travonia, twinkled and winked and disappeared one by one as the night waned.

The Palace in the Central Square looked like a big spreading blot, and was wrapped in sleep; its dark turrets struck up into the sky like so many fixed bayonets, and its long rows of dark windows blinded in white linen were eyes, sightless and ghostly, peering out upon the ceaseless striding to and fro of the sentries on the pavement outside the gilt-spiked railings girding the Palace grounds.

If ever a town was synonymous with peace and security, it was Sordenburg that night, as it lay asleep under the mist-laden sky. The Thing sailing above the Palace dropped lower for a brief spell, taking stock of the lightless windows, the empty streets, the pacing sentries in the Central Square.

Then, as though suddenly satisfied that a slumbering city meant peace at least for a period, the thing in the air swerved upwards once more, and became one again with the clinging mists and the racing clouds and the shrilling wind.

One sentry pricked his ears and listened. Afterwards he told of the sound of a mysterious rush through space, and the faint, faint humming from far above him, and spoke of it as an uninterpreted omen of events.

'Quiet so far!'

Maxtone Domville said the words over his shoulder to the man who sat crouched down beside him in the narrow wheel-house.

'Quiet so far!' Rachinov assented thickly, his voice muffled in the folds of a white woollen throat wrap. 'Quiet so far, but under the orders of a clever villain, remember. One light left burning into the small hours – one window left uncurtained – one fire unraked, and a gust of suspicion might be fanned into being and wreck the work of months. Our Duke is a connoisseur in plots and plans, and he is not the man to leave a fire unraked or a blind undrawn. He ever looks to his straws lest the smallest of them should betray him. See, that way his stronghold lies! The château is the most impregnable of fortresses, the eyrie of the most cunning vulture in Europe!'

Domville pulled round, and the great, ghost-like airship veered into a vast gap in the two walls of granite peaks which blocked the sky-line.

Beyond the gap a narrow, tortuous valley twisted like a writhing snake, ending in a formless waste of grey – clouds and valleys and giant boulders all mingling and merging into each other, and crowned in floating veils of mist, forming and breaking and gathering and scattering on the undistinguishable line where the sea and land met.

And then there came above the mist, as though forced upwards from the invisible foundations, a solitary bastion, clear and distinct for a long, inspired moment, and then swallowed up again in wallowing clouds, which parted a second later to spume up a second turret, separated from the first by a wide abyss of fog.

And cradled in the billowing heavens, like an enormous phantom, the airship Fly-by-Night patrolled in circles, marking the bearings as the fog lifted and fell and disclosed the spreading outline of the unseen castle on the edge of the sea. A castle of dreams, half discerned – now hid; now a flying buttress winging visibly against high heaven, then the smothering, drifting mist blotting it all out save perhaps for the glimpse of a gargoyle, grotesque, gigantic, looming like a nightmare into unfathomable space.

Domville spun the steering-wheel, and Fly-by-Night winged heavily over, and a pin-head of light glowed like a yellow star across its path.

He noted it with quick eagerness.

'So that's where your Duchess is a prisoner, is it?' he asked.

Rachinov nodded grimly.

'I could stake my life on it,' he said violently, his eyes straining into the grey smother ahead. 'Where else could a scheming villain find a stronger hiding-place? Inaccessible from every quarter. Guarded by two of the grimmest sentinels that ever watched a prison-house – sea and illimitable space unbridged! Look at that tower yonder! One could swear they could read a motto written in tears in the mist above it! . . . Abandon Hope!'

Domville grinned cheerfully, and swung the ship's nose round again, beating back up the valley again in the direction from which they had come.

'That old welcome doesn't apply to Fly-by-Night,' he laughed, whipping up his speed as the breeze strengthened in their wake. 'Your friend is a bit behind the times. The march of science has made a mockery of such things! Space is the airman's friend! The two great bridges, wireless and the power to fly, have spanned it at last, and Renzi is no more safe in his eagle's nest down there than he will be in the heart of the revolution tonight.'

They were above the Palace again before the count could realize it.

'The Palace?' he cried. 'Why the Palace? The Duchess is not at the Palace!'

'But you've got your key? You can get in?'

'Certainly, I could get in. I have apartments in the East Wing and a private entrance from the East Gate and the rose-garden. But why?'

'I've an odd aversion to slaughter, that's all,' said Domville, coming down lower and lower. 'My idea is that you get into the Palace and warn the King and Queen – save 'em if you can, or die with 'em if you can't, and leave me to –'

'And leave you to what?'

Rachinov was wrathful and his voice full of bluster, but there was a realization of impotency in it that betrayed his weakness.

'And leave you to – what?' he cried a second time as his companion did not answer.

'To mind my own business,' said Domville shortly, hitching round on his swaying seat. 'Look here, I see this adventure through an apparently different pair of goggles than you do. I'm used to adventures and you are only used to intrigues, and there's nothing of intrigue in the game that's going to be played tonight by our friend the Duke Osric! Nothing! It's civil war and red murder. That's what it's going to be, and you know it. It's war, plain and simple, and no hanky hidden by smooth faces and fair words. Those chaps down there are going to meet face to face and fight for their lives, if they've got the pluck not to run away! And two of the unfortunate beggars are your King and Queen. They may be rotten rulers – I don't care a button. But they're human beings – a man and a woman – and I'm damned if I'm going to sit down and twiddle my thumbs while your ruffianly countrymen hack them up into mincemeat. You've got to help 'em save their lives if you can – not necessarily by standing shoulder to shoulder when the rush comes, but at least by warning them of the danger and giving them the chance of getting away. And now to drop you. Where is it to be?'

Count Rachinov hesitated. There was a look on his face that betrayed the emotion he felt. He stooped over close to Domville and peered into his face. Both looked ghastly and unreal in the grey light, and the silence was so great that the nervous chattering of the count's teeth sounded through the tiny cabin like a phantom knocking.

Far away in the east the mist evaporated, and a faint smear of palest orange veiled in rose tinged the atmosphere.

Domville gazed at the signal over the count's stooping head.

If revolution was to stalk forth, breathing retribution and swift murder, then the moment must be coming even as he stared at the spreading pink. Rachinov was trying to speak, but his words were a jumble of trash. Domville, shouting suddenly, called out that there was no time to listen.

'Save your breath, man; you'll want it soon enough, God knows! I'm going down . . .'

Fly-by-Night swooped – a rush of cold, wet cloud smacked their faces through the open casing, a shrilling whine of bitter, racing wind stung their ears, an upwards rise sickened Rachinov, and then they were on the flat once more and the level beating of the motors acted like a sedative to their excitement.

Trees and marble figures and fantastically trimmed hedges spread out beneath them, distinct and weird – apparitions of the dawn. A flight of white steps made a quick landmark, and Domville pointed to them with a hastily uplifted hand. 'There,' he said, but the count plucked his sleeve and his shaking finger showed another direction.

'No, no,' he said. 'Over there – that gap in the hedge will do – But the Duchess? What of her? You're making a fool of me! The King and Queen can go to hell for all I care, and I'll go there with them if you like – *but afterwards*! Not now! The Duchess must come first!'

'Get out and get into the Palace. I'll meet you here in an hour, or in less than an hour, but at the most not more than an hour. See, here at this pagoda – by the Diana, yonder: be here at all costs, and wait for me, mind. Wait for me.' Then, even as Maxtone spoke, the dull boom of a single gun rolled a muffled call through the night air, and the sound of it came surging towards them in voluminous waves . . . It was followed by a single cry that seemed to come from close beside them – and was echoed by a second one from behind the dark mass of a clipped yew. It seemed the garden was the shelter of unseen watchers, waiting there in the darkness.

Lights flew, frightened sentinels into a hundred houses across the square. The sound of running feet became the sound of rushing water bursting through dams. White blazes of space told of the great hotels awake and alert: dark spaces of black silence told of desertion and panic.

And in the middle of it all the Palace itself stood up, a great, black heap in the middle of a square that was filling – that was almost full, almost overflowing – with a horde of crying, struggling, yelling people that had gone mad with the lust for blood.

Not a single light glowed, even as the long moments fled past. It was almost as though the noise and savagery of the rabble had failed to penetrate the thick grey walls. The long rows of windows, one atop the other, still looked like sightless eyes shrouded in white linen staring out into night. The empty flagstaff still stood stalwart in the sky like an emblem of arrogant power guarding the sleeping King and Queen beneath the roof it stood on.

But at last – at last the clamour beat down the silent pride, and two feeble lights, side by side, fluttered up behind shuttered windows, and the shutters themselves were timidly pushed open from within.

All the savage rose in Rachinov. He pointed to the open window with triumphant gesture.

'Their Majesties are alarmed!' he scoffed. 'See how alone they are! Not a man or woman under the same roof! Not a creature left but themselves! Two rats in a gilded cage – gilded by blood-money, gilded by crime and harshness and the trampling under foot of human souls! – and they're alive in it! – trapped!'

Domville came down to a man's height from the dew-sodden lawn. Touching a switch he lowered a steel ladder and bade the count descend.

'If, within five minutes,' he said coarsely, 'you are not in the rat-trap helping those two wretched creatures to escape I shall go straight back to London. If within five minutes you are still in this garden I shall leave your Duchess to rot for ever in her prison. You're helpless to rescue her, remember that. You're not in the picture, except as a man being pitchforked into that Palace to try and save two poor devils who, after all, are your Duchess's father and mother. Now get!'

Rachinov gripped his arm in a fever of anxiety.

'Swear you'll save her! Swear to bring her here to me! Here!'

'Here. By this Diana. In one hour.'

III

With the dawn the mist faded, but so slowly that its going was barely apparent.

But here and there a pink streak zagged like a scratch across the heavens, and once a pale orange glowed above a bank of grey.

Up the ravine a scurrying wind whimpered and whined, impinging on Domville's face and forcing an added, erratic weight against the wide-spread wings out-standing from Fly-by-Night's sleek sides, barring progress and making direct coursing difficult.

Shortly before, the journey from the Palace to the castle on the cliff had barely taken twenty minutes. Now, with the snappy, choppy wind, it was likely to take twice that time. Domville swore softly and shot up into the higher air-ways, trying for less wind.

But the buffeting was continual, and Fly-by-Night jibbed dangerously more than once, as though calling attention to the reckless uselessness of its master's persistency in endeavouring to make direct headway down a narrow gully which acted as a trap for every puff of wind heaven held.

But, with a fool's daring, Domville fought on.

'I'll be too late, old Fly-by-Night, if you go and bust yourself to bits in a tantrum!' he cried loudly, as though to someone close to him. 'Come on, old chap, come on – you're pulling the arm out of me! Make a try for it, old man. Don't you know that this is the most romantic adventure of my life? It's all about a real, live princess shut up in a tower, and we've got to get her out – in time – IN TIME, boy! Come on. Make a try for it, old man!'

He spoke cajolingly to the slipping steering-wheel, bent lower over it as though whispering some tender exhortation for more speed and more strength to hold on against the onslaught of the elements.

Then, like a fractious spirit giving in with a bad grace to a stronger will, the airship shook itself sullenly, hung quivering against the wind for a moment as though undecided still as to what to do, then, taking advantage of a lull, shot down the ravine with the speed of a giant sea-bird which has sighted prey and is racing for it against an enemy.

200 | THE DREAMING SEX

Even the wind seemed to give in against the onslaught. The clouds of enveloping mist parted and ebbed as the great, gleaming bows of the ship cleft them, and the dim outlines of the prison-house on the heights of the abyss came nearer and became clearer with startling suddenness, frowning through the pale light, a creature of infamy and ill-omen.

To Domville, gazing down at it from above, it looked like an evil toad, squat and misshapen and ugly; and far beneath, crawling at the base of the giant cliffs, a black and sluggish tide lapped and gurgled below the rocks, sounding sullenly like the roar of watching enemies.

'My friend Renzi knew a good safe lair when he met it, evidently!' decided the airman in audible meditation. 'He's chosen a pretty ugly nest for his captive dove, I must say. Nice and cheerful inside and out, I should guess. I wonder whereabouts the lady is. It's a fair bulky parcel to have to look through in a hurry . . . Ah!'

The pin-head of yellow light he had seen before was gleaming still from the narrow lancet slit far up a bulging tower. It was as likely a place – by gad, it was –

He slid down through the clouds with a swift rush. His noiseless motors made but a faint sound like a sob in a whiff of wind; there was nothing but the cry in the air as the colossal wings cut through it.

He came to an anchor a few feet from the soft and velvety grass of a wide lawn that led towards ramparts. The pin-head of light still glimmered through the pale dawn. Down in a sunken quadrangle before the armoured entrance two watchmen were sunk in depth-less slumber, their arms reversed and their heads sunk upon their hands.

'Sure sign that their masters are away and that they are not in exactly immediate danger of observation. Good old Fly-by-Night, you're a good boy to be so quiet! So the Duke and his merry men are kicking up the dust of revolution in Sordenburg and the little lady is left behind that little lancet lattice . . . Well, Duke Osric, while you're away getting a crown for yourself, I might as well try my hand at rescuing the real claimant? But how? That's the deuced awkwardness of the damn thing! How!'

Everything seemed dead against luck. A wizard could only escape from that ridiculously mediaeval lancet by squeezing through it, certainly not a young woman who must be eighteen or nineteen years of age! He shook his fist up at the impassivity of it, and swore softly as he paced to and fro in the chilly morning air.

'If something would only happen! If a bit of luck would only hop over to me! If only those towers weren't so utterly impossible! . . . Lord! send help that a miracle may happen! 'Tis in a good cause, anyhow.'

And then, wonder of wonders, in the very moment of his beseeching, a miracle indeed happened – or was wrought. And it was so extraordinarily simple and unbelievable that at first Domville could do nothing but stare, and then his boyish face all crinkled up into grins, and he wanted badly to laugh out loudly, so intense was his amazement and amusement.

'What a girl!' he said, half audibly. 'What a girl! No wonder the old boy wants her as his Queen and has a sneaking passion for her in his tough old savage's heart!'

The miracle was after all but very simple indeed. It was this. A tiny door in the base of the swelling tower opened heavily as though a delicate arm pulled at its iron strength, and a girl stepped out from the blackness into the fresh greenness of the garden and the sharp clearness of the dawning day. She looked from right to left with a half-scared swiftness and then walked across the rough stone path on to the dew-spangled grass. She walked erect with chin held high and seemed to revel in the sweetness of the damp turf and the sea-drenched air blowing up from the coast below. For the moment she seemed to have escaped from the memory of the turreted walls rising up so relentlessly on all sides of her, barring her from freedom.

Then she reached the wall and leaned over. Domville knew that sheer down for a thousand feet there was not the foothold for a mouse; and from those depths the water sent up a dull noise like something evil laughing.

With a jerking, backward movement, as though suddenly afraid, the girl drew away from the wall, and Maxtone could see her face go white, and her hand clasp over her ears as though to shut out the horrible sound of the evil laughter. She stood absolutely still, thinking, and there was fear dark in her blue eyes, and despair in the trembling of the curving lips.

Domville came close to her, and whispered to her. She sprang round, at bay, her fingers on her lips to keep back the cry that rose to them.

'What is it?' she cried, her voice strangled. 'Who are you?'

'First, tell me, mademoiselle, who you are. For I must be sure that I make no mistake. I am on an errand that means life or death. Will you tell me who you are?'

Reassured, she looked at him, the tears sparkling on her white cheeks and the goldenness of her hair, making her beautiful.

'I am the Grand Duchess Eva of Travonia – I'm a prisoner here in this awful place! I don't know why . . . I don't even know who is my gaoler, but I have suffered, oh, I've suffered so cruelly all these hours!'

She was so utterly unlike a royal duchess and an imminent queen that Domville forgot that she was anything else but a frightened child; and perhaps it was just as well, for he patted her very shaky little hands in his, and talked to her in a funny wheedling way that was rather nice, and not at all familiar to the many people who knew him.

'If you'll take the news gently, Your Highness, I'll tell you. It appears you were somewhat in the way of a certain relative of yours –'

'Osric?'

'Osric – yes.'

'I want to see him; take me to him!'

Domville smiled and took her hand in his, leading her almost unobserved in the direction of the airship.

'Listen to me. I came in my airship – there she is yonder, and I propose that we go back in her to Sordenburg – you and I. Will you trust me? It sounds like a romance, doesn't it, but it's a perfectly safe romance, and it's the one and only way of escape from this gaol-house. Will you come?'

'I want to see my Uncle Osric! I must see him first!'

'Then you must come with me, for he is not in the castle here. He is at this moment busy in Sordenburg.'

'Busy in Sordenburg? Busy?'

The girl's eyes were staring at him, distrust and belief dilating them.

'Very busy,' he answered laconically, taking out his watch and holding it up so as to clearly see the exact time. 'The revolution is just about halfway through, I should think.'

The girl's gasping cry stopped him. He felt he had been brutal, but there had been no time for Court manners. It was now or never, and he had to force the pace. But for a moment he felt that the blow had been too severe, and that the child's nerve wouldn't hold. But it did! Of a sudden he felt her hand grip his arm, and he told from the pressure her absolute acceptance of the bitter truth.

Looking into her face he saw it ashy pale, but in her eyes the reliance that Rachinov had boasted was already springing to vivid life. The pale face grew regal, and a sudden wisdom straightened the lines of girlish fear from her lips; her body that a few short minutes since was a fairy vision in its green trailing gown was now statuesque – the figure of a Queen.

She looked a Queen, a woman who loved her country, and would fight for it to the death!

She stepped towards the seat Domville was silently indicating, and allowed him to place her in it.

And not until they were off, beating their way down the valley with the cold sea-drenched wind racing behind them, and the dawn growing a deeper and deeper pink before them, and the singing whine of the motors sounding like a song of victory in their ears, did the little Grand Duchess utter one word, and then it was one which compassed all things.

'Revolution!'

Domville told her everything, as he knew it, and watched her face go whiter and whiter, as the cruelty of it all became horrible realization.

'My father and my mother! They will murder them! . . . Oh, dear God, no!'

'Rachinov was to warn them, and try and get them away. He will do all he can; he has promised – See, there is Sordenburg! . . .'

Sordenburg! A Sordenburg wrapped in blood-red flames, crowned by a blood-red dawn!

The boom of the heavy cannon sounded like dulled thunder in the stillness of the first hours of day.

Osric Renzi had chosen his time well.

IV

They leaned over Fly-by-Night's side, gazing downwards at the things which were happening on the earth beneath them in struggling Sordenburg.

The streets were alive with men and women, running and running, to and fro, backwards and forwards, like ants on a disturbed hill. Some of them carried swords, antique and cumbersome, the blades flashing in the lamp-light; some of them carried guns, which every now and again puffed little jets of smoke; some of them waved hideous knives, with hideous gestures that bespoke the insane rebel. All of them shrieked with the lust for blood and the thirst for battle, and the frenzy of the kill. Here and there a squad of men in bright red coats marched towards the Central Square, and behind them the riff-raff fell in, cheering, cursing, jeering, waving the red flag of revolution. Carts filled with guns and ammunition made slow way through the masses, and a man handed out arms to all who asked for them. Man, woman, and child had the blood-coloured cockade in their hats, and some had leaped back into savagery, and had smeared red in gruesome streaks across their hideous cheeks.

The Palace in the Central Square was a lodestone. It drew a

magnetic sinew from every street and square; and men in Sordenburg that night turned in that direction in obedience to an unspoken command.

A black swarm seethed and writhed outside the gilt-spiked railings until they swayed and waved and bent inwards. Another onslaught, and they were down, and the black swarm with them, seething and writhing and roaring, sheer up to the Palace doors. The squads of red coats pressed through and over the black swarms, and the cheering and groaning and roaring burst forth again like a volley of infantry.

The boom of the guns sounded again, deafening the shouts of the surging crowds, and the Grand Duchess covered her ears till the dulled echoes died away. It was the first time her bravery showed sign of weakening. She clung to Maxtone with trembling hands clutched about his arm, her ashen face fixed with shrinking intensity upon that heaving, snarling, struggling mass beneath them.

'Why don't the guards answer them?' she cried bitterly, her voice a sob. 'Have they also deserted? Are they traitors, too?'

'Every mother's son of them,' said Domville. 'But you mustn't expect anything else. They're all mad drunk with the desire for blood and revolution, and they've been tuned up to this for months and months past. Renzi is a cunning leader, and a strong one. Men are fore-doomed to follow where he leads. Do you think you are brave enough, strong enough, to go down there and try and check all that riot and murder that is going on?'

The little Duchess turned and looked into Domville's eyes; they were on a level, and the blue and grey met squarely.

'I am ready. What do you want me to do?'

'I want you to forget that the man and woman in the Palace are your father and mother. You must forget it if you would save Travonia; you must think only of Travonia! For Travonia you must proclaim yourself Queen, leaving the fate of your parents to Rachinov, believing that he will do his utmost to save them. It is a duel between you and the Count Osric, and you must win! For the sake of Travonia and Fly-by-Night's honour you must win!'

'I will win!' she answered, her eyes blazing, her voice an anguished whisper. 'I will win.'

'Do you understand that down there it is running red with blood, that there will be gruesome things to step over; that murder will be done at your very feet, and that you must not so much as shudder or turn aside? Can you do it? Think –'

'I will wade through blood if need be! I will be brave! I will be brave! For Travonia I will be brave!'

'Then come. The time is here.'

Fly-by-Night sank slowly – slowly – slowly. Smoke, smelling of gunpowder and dense as fog, rose up in clouds, shielding them from view. The cries of the maddened populace came nearer and nearer, a deafening roar like a jungle of beasts starving for food, ravenous for it. The guns spat shrill commands, and the booming of cannon sounded the knell of the fugitives within the beleaguered Palace.

Domville was stricken suddenly with fear for his little comrade, and his strength failed him.

'I'm wrong to bring you here!' he said, his voice filled with grave anxiety. 'I'm a fool . . . it's death . . .'

'Death or victory, I'm going on with it!' announced the Duchess, and Domville brought the airship to a stop.

More by chance than memory he had come down in the quiet of the rose-garden, almost in the spot where he had parted from Rachinov. Barely ten yards to the right of them the Diana gleamed purely white, and beyond the Diana the little pagoda, smothered in roses, peaceful as a painted picture.

But it was peaceful only for a single moment, and its sweetness was nothing but a hollow jest – a jest of roses covering a death-mask!

For on the floor, clinging to each other in death as they had never done in life, Peter, the King of Travonia, embraced his Queen, and in the hearts of both a rebel knife was buried.

'Don't look, don't look!' Domville called in agony over his shoulder, and with his arm he pushed the Duchess behind him. 'Don't look! You will need all your courage, little girl, all your bravery.'

What came afterwards came rushing on them, scene after scene, all crowded and jostled and jumbled together, smothered in an unreal haze. Minutes were hours, and hours but the flash of time! Memory, afterwards, was a merciful blur; just a confused massing together of a thousand horrors crammed and squeezed into five minutes!

Domville pushed the Duchess away from the pagoda door with all his might, pulling a tangle of crimson rambler over the entrance as he did so, that she might not remember afterwards what had lain there, and how they had looked. Then with all the strength of his lungs he called for Rachinov.

'Rachinov!'

And at once, as in answer to the call, Rachinov came running.

'Rachinov!'

Domville sprang to meet him, and stopped dead as he saw that something had happened.

Rachinov was wounded, badly wounded. The sleeve was ripped from his shoulder, and a great gash spurted redly over the braided tunic of his brilliant uniform; his arm swung helplessly and his face was grey, like spent ashes.

He came quickly, but his feet swayed as he turned by the Diana and caught sight of the two waiting for him.

'Go!' he panted, his good arm supporting him as he leaned against the statue. 'Go, go, for God's sake, go! Renzi is searching the rose-garden for me – he knows – he knows –'

As he spoke, the sound of a heavy man running thudded above the noise of the mob, who were apparently surging slowly round to the garden side of the Palace, and were almost within view. Rachinov lifted his head. Then he spoke again, stuttering.

'Go! Go quickly. Through the arbour there. Get into the Palace by my little private door; here is the key. Take the passage to the right; it leads to the balcony over the central door – take her there and let them see her! – little Duchess – little Queen – only let them see her!'

The Duchess tore her fingers from Domville, and ran towards him, taking his wounded hand in hers, and looking into his filming eyes with a world of remorse and pity in her own.

'Dear, dear friend, you are dying for me – for me! Oh, die happy if it will make you so to know that I will be the Queen you have dreamed of so often! All the old friends shall be my friends and remember you always, always, dear, dear friend!'

'Your Majesty – to please me – go now! Quickly, he is here!'

Renzi came like a bull, sword unsheathed in his gripping fingers, and the red ribbons of revolution flying from his military cap in mad defiance.

At sight of Rachinov he stopped for a second, and then rushed forward like a whirlwind, the sword swirling aloft.

'Traitor! Traitor! Traitor!'

And before Domville could prevent it, even if he had desired to do so, the two men were fighting in unequal combat, two gladiators filled with the frantic state of hate and passion. Rachinov seemed to fight only to give time to two retreating figures whose progress he watched with wary eyes until he saw them reach and pass within the portals of a little door half hid under the roses growing on the Palace wall. He watched them unlock the door and push it open, turn lingeringly in the open space, and look back towards him with pitiable indecision – then he saw Domville lead the little Duchess gently in, and saw the door shut behind them –

His part in it all was over. He turned suddenly to Renzi.

'In three minutes,' he shouted abruptly, his voice amazingly strong. 'Listen!'

'In less than that time you will be beyond listening to anything on this side of heaven!' roared the Duke in answer, and lunged clumsily.

Rachinov shook his head, and parried feebly.

'In two minutes,' he said more gently; 'listen.'

And, ere he had ceased speaking, a lull fell in the storm of riot beyond the rose-garden, a lull so sudden and unanimous that Renzi was taken aback. His sword quivered aimlessly in the air and his eyes sought the count's.

'What is it?' he said thickly. 'What is it?'

Rachinov only smiled.

'In one minute – in less – now! Listen!'

His voice dropped on the words, and the glaze stiffened over the life in his eyes. His sword arm slipped lower and lower.

Against his will the Duke was listening.

Then it came. The great volley of cheering, the roar upon roar of cheering, the thrill of laughter, the sound of sobbing, the wild joyousness of tragedy turned to happiness. Clearly the words 'Long live the Queen!' swept like a gust of pure air into the stifling atmosphere of the rose-garden.

Renzi stood still, listening.

'God bless Her Majesty!' said Rachinov very, very softly.

Greye La Spina

THE ULTIMATE INGREDIENT

Greye La Spina (1880–1969) was born Fanny Greye Bragg and became Baroness La Spina with her second marriage, in 1910, to Robert La Spina, Barone di Savuto. She was born in Wakefield, Massachusetts, but lived for many years in Pennsylvania and, for all I know, may have known Gertrude Barrows. When she later moved to New York as possibly the first woman newspaper photographer, she found it difficult to sleep unless she played a tape of the sound of crickets to remind her of home. She was also a Master Weaver and won prizes for her rugs and tapestries. In the 1920s she became a regular contributor to the legendary pulp magazine Weird Tales, *which serialized her novels* Invaders from the Dark *(1925) and* Fettered *(1926). Her first sales were to the now very rare adventure pulp,* The Thrill Book, *which ran for just sixteen issues during 1919 and was where the following story appeared. It deals with invisibility, a topic which had proved popular in H.G. Wells's* The Invisible Man *(1897) but one with which scientists are only just starting to come to terms.*

The Ultimate Ingredient

'IT HAS ALWAYS appeared plausible to me,' observed Dr Wilson thoughtfully, 'that some day there may be discovered – perhaps entirely by accident – a combination of chemicals which will possess the property of raising the vibrations of the human body to such an extent that solid flesh will become invisible to the eye.'

'That is a ridiculous supposition in my opinion,' objected Burton Howe contemptuously, flicking the ash from his monogrammed cigarette.

'Not as ridiculous as you claim,' cut in Philip Lindsay.

'How do you make that out?' laughed Howe, his eyebrows lifted incredulously.

'How? My dear fellow, between ourselves, I know of an actual case where just such a discovery was made.'

Howe and the doctor laughed outright in unison. Lindsay looked at them more seriously than the occasion warranted in the doctor's opinion.

'Well, tell us about it,' invited the latter, smiling quizzically.

'Do you remember the man I had so many years?' enquired Lindsay abruptly. 'The nervous fellow? Of course you do! Well, that man had reason to be nervous; he went through an experience once that was quite sufficient to unnerve any one permanently.'

'I observed the chap particularly, I remember,' said the doctor interestedly. He leaned forward in his chair. 'Do you mean to tell me that he had a story?'

'That is just what I am trying to tell you,' retorted Lindsay a bit impatiently. 'You may remember what a nervous wreck he was. He would not remain alone in the dark under any circumstances; he jumped like a timid hare at the slightest rustle;

he continually glanced backwards, peering behind doors and draperies.

'In spite of his efficiency he got me keyed up to such a pitch that one night I fairly yelled at him to stop pawing the air as if he were warding off an invisible menace.

'"Confound you, Mallett. If you don't quit your nervous tricks we'll have to part. You're getting me to jumping, too!' 'He gave me a reproachful look.

'"I'm sorry I annoyed you, Mr Lindsay," said he. "But my nerves are ruined. It's the effects of a ghastly experience I had several years ago. I don't believe I'll ever recover from it entirely," he finished mournfully.

'You fellows may understand that it interested me considerably to discover that Mallett had a story, for he had appeared such a colourless individual. I finally got him to tell me the story. I may as well tell it to you, for it is of a nature strange enough to be of considerable interest to lovers of the unusual.

'Mallett used to be secretary to old Ebenezer Starr, of Starr & Co. Mr Starr had two motherless children, Paul, thirty, and Constance, twenty, at the time he died.'

The doctor settled himself more comfortably in his armchair. Howe lit another cigarette and leaned his elbows on the table, his eyes on Lindsay.

'Go on!' he commanded. 'Let's have the story!'

Lindsay's Story

Paul Starr seemed an estimable young man, devoted to chemical research. He frequently worked into the small hours in his laboratory, following out some obscure experiment. He utilized the willing and interested Mallett as an assistant, and many were the strange and eccentric experiments the young chemist made. Up to a certain point he had the complete confidence of the secretary, who was doubly devoted to his service because he adored the young mistress of the house hopelessly. Finally, however, Paul began to dabble in the forbidden arts; his requirements grew more and more exacting until Mallett found it incumbent upon himself to refuse further assistance in experiments which bore the stamp of demonism and witchcraft.

Mallett had permitted himself to be hypnotized on several occasions by his young master, who – as unscrupulous, learned and clever – now took advantage of the weakness of will which frequent submission had brought about on Mallett's part. The unfortunate secretary awoke one day from a trance to find that he had written in his own handwriting a document purporting to be a confession of a crime so heinous that he shuddered at the remembrance of it when he told me his story. Shocked and horrified beyond measure, Mallett enquired falteringly what this meant.

'Mallett,' Paul said unconcernedly, 'it is necessary for my experiments that I have someone attached to me so irrevocably as to carry out whatever directions he may receive, no matter what the cost to him. I assure you, my good Mallett, that I have no intention of injuring you, unless you attempt to deceive me or refuse to aid me in my work. But if such an occasion arises I shall feel obliged to put your confession into the hands of the proper authorities, and I regret to state that they will find full circumstantial evidence of its truth, since to have been confessed, a crime must have been committed.' He smiled at Mallett with a significance that made the unfortunate secretary's blood run cold.

From that time Mallett became a weak, terrified tool in the unscrupulous hands of Paul Starr. No matter how strange or how unusual were the young man's wishes, the secretary was compelled to carry them out. Finally the experiments arrived at a stage where they required careful, undisturbed attention and an absence of the constant jarring that is not to be avoided in a city house. The chemist decided that he would carry them to a conclusion in a more secluded spot than could be afforded by the laboratory he maintained in his residence, where his sister was continually disturbing him and the servants constantly intruded.

Young Starr owned a hunting lodge in the woods of Maine. He

made arrangements to fit up this bungalow for the conclusion of his work. The place was situated twelve miles from the railroad station, and the village was fourteen miles away. One had to make one's way by wagon over a primitive country road to reach it. An automobile would have been racked to pieces after a single trip over that road; only a bicycle or a rude country wagon could make the trip. From the road a narrow path branched off through the woods to the lodge.

Mallett was an indifferent cook, but Paul would take no one else with him in his retirement. Large supplies of canned food and of chemicals were transported to the lodge, and arrangements made for Mallett to make a weekly trip to the station for other necessaries, small quantities of which he could carry in a wire basket attached to the handlebars of his bicycle. Mail was held for these weekly trips, as the place was out of the way of the rural mail delivery.

After arriving at the lonely lodge, Paul began to shut himself up for days at a stretch in the room which he had equipped as a laboratory, only opening the door to admit Mallett with meals. He ate, slept, worked with the enthusiasm of a man completely under the domination of an absorbing idea. Once or twice, when something had to be watched continuously for a longer time than he could remain awake, he called upon Mallett while he snatched a few moments of sleep.

Weekly Mallett went to the station for letters. There was always more than one in the handwriting of the young lady. Mallett knew that his master had written to no one since his arrival at the lodge. He therefore took the liberty of sending her a short, respectful note, informing her of her brother's preoccupation with his work. Paul Starr laughed shortly when Mallett told him of this bit of thoughtfulness.

'You may be a fool, Mallett,' said he scornfully, 'but even a fool has his uses. And you will shortly be of great use to me, as you shall see. It may interest you to learn that my sister has written me of her engagement to our next-door neighbour – Jack Allison, the pigeon fancier,' and he curled his lip with a sneer, while his sharp eyes seemed to probe the other man's heart.

Mallett soon found that he was destined to be useful indeed to his master. He was summoned one day to the laboratory to assist in an experiment. Paul wore a clumsy bandage around his left wrist; through it the blood had seeped, and there was blood on the table and the floor. The secretary gave an alarmed exclamation.

'You have injured yourself!' he cried.

'It was intentional,' replied the other shortly. 'I've taken all I dared from my own veins, as you may observe. Now I'll thank you to give me a little of your blood.'

So commanding was his manner as he made this astounding demand, so little did it brook of contradiction, that the dazed assistant mechanically held out his arm and permitted the enthusiastic inquisitor to open a vein and help himself to sufficient blood to continue the experiment, whatever it was. It was not until afterwards that the wretched man realized how completely he had fallen under the hypnotic influence of his unscrupulous master. But worse was yet to follow.

A couple of days after this experience Mallett knocked at the laboratory door as usual and it swung open before him as though by invisible hands. He walked in after a moment's hesitation, put the breakfast tray on the table where his master usually ate, and then turned to enquire if there were any special orders for the day. To his vast astonishment there was no one in the room with him.

In spite of the testimony of his eyes, something gave him to understand definitely that he was not alone. He saw no one; he heard nothing. There was no hiding place for an intruder in that room, bare except for the shelves and the experiment tables. Yet that there was someone else in the laboratory Mallett was absolutely convinced.

His hair slowly rose on his scalp with a prickling sensation as he realized that he had to deal with a something unearthly, a something uncanny and strange, in close contact with himself. He felt hands that touched his shoulders from behind. He whirled around, his breath almost quitting his body with the awful horror and fear of he knew not what, and he saw that there was nothing behind him. But when he had turned abruptly he felt that he had brushed against something palpable that retarded his movement, just as might have been done by another human body. He could not bear the awfulness of his sensations. With hands stretched fearfully before him he fled from that haunted room and out of the house. Mechanically he followed his impulse to escape by mounting the bicycle and starting down the path that led to the road.

Why he fled he could not have explained, for he knew that somewhere inside the lodge was Paul Starr. But he felt that he was fleeing from something menacing, something unutterably frightful. He pedalled with all possible speed. He had begun to recover in a measure from his unreasoning fear when he heard a bicycle bell behind him. He turned to look.

Horror upon horror! The other bicycle sometimes ridden by his master was pedalling down the path behind him, apparently of its own volition. It swayed from side to side as though the invisible rider were in haste. Whatever the Unknown Thing was, it was undoubtedly pursuing Mallett. As it approached, the poor secretary's brain began to whirl; he could bear no more; he felt his consciousness leaving him, and with a wild and terrible cry he fell from his wheel to the ground.

When he came to himself again he was lying on his bed in the lodge. Evidence that he had not dreamed he found on a sheet of paper lying on the table beside the bed. The writing was in his master's hand, and ran much as follows:

MY GOOD MALLETT, you should really know better than to try giving me the slip. As you must now realize, it is futile for you to attempt an escape. As I don't wish you to be alarmed needlessly, however, I will explain that in the course of my experiments I have compounded a salve which makes the user invisible. I have discovered a combination of chemical substances that produces a higher rate of vibration in the atoms of the human body, thus making them swing farther apart in their motion, which results in the body becoming invisible, just as by applying heat to certain substances they become invisible gases. Unfortunately, in raising the rate of vibration in this way, I find that the vibrations of the vocal chords have been accelerated to such an extent that they can make no impression upon the etheric waves that will be reproduced upon the tympanum of the human ear. I am unable to make my voice heard, although I can make a noise by moving articles about me. In future, until I shall have solved the *immediate* problem before me, of compounding a salve that will restore me to my original state of vibration, I will write out your orders daily. Don't, I beg of you, distinguish yourself by another piece of idiocy such as this morning's. With the sole exception that you cannot hear or see me, I am quite the same as yesterday.

To claim that the secretary was entirely reassured by this astounding document would be taking too much for granted. On the contrary, he began to fear that either he or his master had gone quite mad. Warned by his vain attempt at flight he did his best to accept the situation, putting his mind on his daily tasks without pondering too much over the wild statements in the letter. He did debate much over the wisdom of notifying Miss Starr of her brother's strange discovery, but even had he written to her he could not have stolen away for the trip to the station without discovery.

So each day Mallett carried Paul's meals to the laboratory door, controlling as best he could his shrinking repulsion for the strange and unhallowed conditions he felt prevailed within that mysterious room. Each day he watched the door swing open by hands unseen that he might place the tray on the table within. On one occasion those unseen hands took the tray from him, causing him to jump with an uncontrollable cry backwards out of the room.

Even with the passing of weeks he could not accustom himself to that silent, ominous presence. He found himself dwelling with terror upon the memory of the last demand the bold experimenter had made upon him, and imagination ran riot over the possibilities of future demands. Every night the poor trembling secretary implored Providence to spare him from the untold horrors that he felt were slowly developing around him, and every morning he braced himself anew to face that gruesome ordeal of the laboratory with its invisible inmate.

His nerves went back on him to such an extent that he developed habits which were to cling to him the rest of his life. He never knew when that invisible presence would be near him; when a hand would reach out of the luminous daylight invisibly to touch him as he worked about the house or walked about the grounds. His life became a living agony, filled with the most terrible apprehensions, the more dreadful because he knew not what he had to fear. At last these intangible misgivings were justified.

A letter addressed to him lay on the laboratory table one morning when he went in with the breakfast tray. He was to present himself in the afternoon for a repetition of the blood-letting operation. His terror was extreme. Who knew how much of the precious fluid would be required of him? How long would this slow draining of his life-blood last? Would he ever see the outside world again?

He realized with poignant despair that the recent development of Paul Starr's character left him no grounds for hope; he knew intuitively that he would be sacrificed in the interests of Paul's experiments as pitilessly as a dog is sacrificed by the vivisectionist. He spent the remainder of the morning locked in his room, on his knees, in a mental condition that was most unenviable. His powers of resistance had become so atrophied that he did even contemplate a dash for freedom. The hours flew. The appointed moment arrived when he must make another unwilling sacrifice on the altar of his master's insatiable Baal.

He entered the laboratory with dragging feet and thudding heartbeats that shook him with their violence. Invisible hands took him by the hand. Again the vein was opened and a quantity of blood drawn into a vessel held by an invisible hand.

Fainting with weakness, loathing his cowardliness, and hating with all his soul the man who dared rob him in this unparalleled manner, the poor fellow permitted the unseen hands to bind up his wrist As he staggered from the room a paper was thrust into hand.

He gained his room and sank upon his bed, weeping tears of silent, impotent outrage and humiliation. It seemed to him that he had fallen to the lowest depths of degradation. For a man to give up without a good fight his very life-blood to a phantom – it seemed as though he could die with shame.

At last he opened the paper to see what fresh trouble was brewing. It was as he had dreaded. The chemist wrote that if the blood already drawn did not suffice he would need yet more from 'his good Mallett'.

The wretched man lay weakly on his bed, vainly praying for deliverance. With the afternoon came the dear voice of a woman halloing outside the bungalow. And the voice was the voice of Constance Starr.

He walked to the window and leaned out. He wanted to warn her not to enter the accursed and fatal house. She did not see him. And then hands were laid on Mallett's shoulders; he felt himself being propelled towards the door. He knew, as though he had been directed in so many words, just what he was expected to do. He was to open the door to the young lady and he was to give no sign or warning that would frighten her away. He cried out from the depths of his heart: 'No! No! I cannot!' The pressure of those terrible hands on his shoulders urged him forward; in the very touch there was a threat. He weakened, and gave in.

She stood on the low porch, a travelling bag at her feet, in her right hand a wooden cage in which cooed four pigeons.

'Letter carriers,' she explained smilingly as she turned it for him to look in. 'Mallett, what's the matter with my brother? He has not written for weeks. I've been awfully anxious about him. I thought I would just run down to see how he was getting on with his mysterious experiments.'

The secretary incoherently explained that his master was engaged on some work behind locked doors, and that the experiment would undoubtedly be completed by the following day, when she could see him for herself. With all his heart he hoped his words would be true prophets.

Constance caught a glimpse of the poor fellow's face. It was drawn and absolutely colourless.

'Why, Mallett, you look as if you hadn't a drop of blood in you!' she exclaimed in amazement. 'Your face is terribly white. Have you been ill?'

Again the secretary was forced to dissemble. His brain was whirling with his enforced blood-letting. He felt that he must get away to think in quiet; otherwise he knew he could not cope with this new condition. He dared not surmise just what the young lady's dramatic entrance might mean at this critical juncture, but he still had hopes that Paul had been able to complete the experiment successfully and that further sacrifices would be unnecessary.

Directly after supper Constance retired to her room, and while it was yet light wrote a little note to her betrothed. She fastened it to one of the carrier pigeons, which she took to the window and sent on its way. As she sat fondling the other three birds her door opened softly and an envelope whirled through the air, to alight on the table before her. The door closed again with suspicious caution. Mallett had received his orders to lock her in, and with a vague feeling that in so doing he was safeguarding her he tried to slip the key into his pocket, but no sooner had he started back to his room than the invisible horror was upon him, and he felt the unseen hand searching his pocket and abstracting the key. The omnipresent had guessed at his wish to help Constance.

Mallett fell on his knees outside her door. He dared not speak. His agony of mind was intense. But he felt that his presence near her might help when the blow fell, for that there was a blow to be dealt he now felt intuitively.

He heard the young lady strike a match and light the lamp. Then there was a short silence, followed by her exclamation.

'Impossible!' she cried. 'Why, he has gone absolutely mad! My poor brother! This is what comes of brooding too long over forbidden mysteries.'

She paced the room restlessly. The man lying outside her door felt the rustle of the letter as she picked it up to reread it. She threw it down upon the table, apparently in a sudden rush of unreasoning terror, and ran to the door, rattling the handle with a cry that rang with growing fear and dismay.

'Mallett, Mallett!' she cried desperately, and began to beat upon the panels of the door.

A restraining hand made itself felt upon Mallett's bowed shoulder, and he dared not reply. The hand was removed, but the poor wretch lay on the floor beside the young girl's door, sobbing softly in his helpless weakness, his hands stretched out before him as if to implore silently her forgiveness.

All night he lay there. All night he heard the poor girl pacing back and forth. He dared not speak for fear of attracting the attention of Paul Starr. But he decided to make a last attempt to communicate with Constance. He got up quietly, went to his room, and wrote her a few hasty lines, begging her to dispatch another pigeon at once, as the situation was critical. He asked her to do it immediately, before her brother was up, for a sight of the liberated bird might hasten designs that were odious to consider. This note he slipped under her door, tapping cautiously to attract her attention. .

After a moment the note was withdrawn from under the door. There was a moment's pause, then another letter was pushed out to him. It was Paul's letter of the night before.

'I will do what you suggest at once,' she said very low and guardedly. 'I have been too confused to think of it myself. Thank you, Mallett.'

Mallett hid the letter under, his coat, returned to his room, locked himself in, and read it.

I have seen the letter myself. Mallett slipped it back into his pocket after reading it, so that it was preserved for record in this narrative. Here follows that unutterably selfish and astounding document:

MY DEAR CONSTANCE: I have at last discovered, in the course of my experiments, a compound that, used as a salve, will render the user invisible to ordinary rays of light. This may seem strange to you, but it is a very simple matter to understand for one who has studied even superficially ether vibration as a carrier of light. Unfortunately, I have not as yet been able to find the exact combination of chemicals that will restore the user to visibility again. I used all I dared of my own blood in my first experiment, but I need other blood for the anti-compound; and Mallett's blood has not done what I expected of it. I need blood from a young and healthy woman and I need it in large quantities. I am sure you, my dear sister, will hasten to offer yourself to science, as it will mean the establishment of one of the most epoch-making discoveries in the world's history. I shall not take *all* your blood immediately; only what I need now to restore myself to visibility, for I labour under a disadvantage inasmuch as my vibrations are now raised to a point where I cannot make my vocal organs start ether waves of sufficient force to vibrate upon the tympanum of others in a different state of vibration. As soon as I have returned to visibility, I will gladly accept the balance of the blood your fine young body can offer me so that I may make up sufficient quantities of the compound to serve my purposes for some time to come. You can therefore plan for two more days of life. I need only remind you that in case you should be so selfish and unreasonable as to refuse to offer such a trifling sacrifice on the altar of science, I shall be obliged to take from you by force what you refuse to yield of your own free will. This I trust I shall not be obliged to do. I infinitely prefer that you offer yourself freely.

Paul

'Monstrous!' cried the secretary aloud. His blood – what there was left of it, poor fellow – ran cold in his veins. The sacrifice of that beautiful, vital young creature by a madman was too dreadful to contemplate. He hoped the pigeon was on its way!

He moved to the window, and leaned out to get a good look at her adjoining one. As he watched he saw Constance's hand emerge, and a pigeon stepped mincingly from it to the window ledge and began to strut there, arching its neck.

'Go, go!' he whispered with hoarse impatience.

The pigeon's pride proved its downfall. A shot rang out, and the poor bird fell, scarlet-breasted, to the ground. Mallett saw the letter being disengaged from the bleeding body, opened by invisible hands. He knew unseen eyes were scanning that frantic call for help. The little paper fluttered to the ground.

Then came a sound of hurrying feet, the sound of a key in the lock of Constance's door, which sprang open under the impetus of an invisible body that flung itself furiously into the young lady's room.

The secretary unlocked his door and ran towards the other room. Before his eyes the plucky girl was struggling with an unseen something that held high a pigeon, wringing its neck ruthlessly, while under the shower of crimson drops fluttered in terror the last bird, its plumage all flecked with its companion's blood.

'How could you kill that innocent thing?' cried Constance, her indignation getting the better of her fear. 'Let it go, I tell you.'

She tried to protect the last pigeon, beating against the invisible intruder with puny fists. The window closed down suddenly with force; the bird could not issue from there. Constance caught up her hairbrush from the dressing table and flung it with all her nervous force against the pane. With the crash and the tinkle of falling glass she laughed triumphantly, for the pigeon, seeing the way clear to liberty, darted like an arrow out of the broken window, and in a moment disappeared among the trees.

Miss Starr's triumph was short-lived. Mallett saw her caught up from the floor. Struggling and calling to him for help, she was borne past him down the hall. The fury of the exodus convinced the secretary that his master was in no mind to wait for a calmer moment to continue his experiment; he undoubtedly intended to make sure of the ultimate ingredient before further complications ensued. With an access of nervous strength, Mallett sprang after them and clutched the air in a vain attempt to seize the madman by the throat. He missed and fell heavily to the floor. Without pausing, the invisible Paul carried the poor girl, shrieking, into the laboratory, and the door closed behind the pair. Mallett, picking himself dizzily from the floor, heard the key turning in the lock.

There was a short and furious struggle within, Constance's screams ringing out wildly, until there came the sound of a blow or a fall, and her voice dying away in a choked-off moan, then silence.

Mallett, wringing his hands in despair, stood outside the terrible door that had closed upon that innocent victim to Paul Starr's mad projects. After a few moments that seemed hours to him the door suddenly opened, a sheet of paper, which he took mechanically, was extended. The door closed again with ominous grinding of the key.

The secretary read the paper. It contained directions for him to meet the two o'clock train that afternoon and to bring back a box of chemicals that were absolutely essential for the prosecution of the experiment. Hope sprang up in Mallett's heart. Perhaps the young lady would be safe for a few hours at least. And what might not happen in those hours of respite from the dread sentence? He began planning wildly all manner of schemes for her rescue. In spite of the warning to remember the confession which had held him for so long, Mallett took courage from the very desperateness of the situation, and made up his mind to risk all in an attempt to save his adored young mistress.

He could hardly contain his impatience for the afternoon to come, that he might get out his bicycle and go, ostensibly to the station, actually to seek help in the village. When he found himself finally on his way, it seemed too good to be true, and he almost felt that the whole happening had been a terrifying nightmare. Three miles out on the main road, he saw an automobile coming towards him at a speed that was reckless considering the condition of the road. As be neared it he waved one hand to stop the driver. Then he gave a cry of relief and joy; the driver was Jack Allison, Constance's betrothed.

The situation needed but few words to make it clear. The face of the young lover grew whiter and sterner as he listened. He pulled Mallett's bicycle upon the running board, and they went rocking and plunging along the road to the side path that led through the dense woods to the hunting lodge. As they rode, Allison expressed his fear that Paul had sent Mallett to the station merely to get him out of the way. He related the feeling of premonition he had had when he received Constance's first letter. Then the blood-spattered pigeon arrived which bore no message. This was sufficient for the lover; he was on his way within the half-hour, at breakneck speed, to rescue or avenge the girl he loved.

Leaving the automobile at the edge of the woods, the two men plunged down the path, fear lending wings to their feet. They burst out of the woods into the clearing and ran across to the lodge. They went down the hall to the laboratory door. It was wide open! Paul had not expected intrusion.

Stretched out upon an operating table lay Constance, gagged. Her hands and feet had been secured to the table legs. One hand – they could see it as they stood for an instant in the doorway – was covered with blood, and blood was running from an open vein in the wrist into a test tube held under it by invisible hands. She turned her head towards them with an agony of appeal in her eyes that fell upon their blanched faces.

Allison leaped towards her, his eyes aflame, his face ashen. He came in contact with something as he neared her, something that pushed him aside roughly, following up the push with a sudden blow. He staggered under the unexpected attack, and put his hand in his pocket instinctively. A revolver fell clattering upon the floor. But he did not stop to recover it; of what use was a revolver against an invisible foe? He had seen a knife lying on a stand near by, and with a quick motion possessed himself of it, and in another moment Constance was freed from her bonds. Allison flung the knife to one side to help her to her feet She stood, sobbing dreadfully, leaning half on him and half on the table, for she was weak with loss of blood. He tied his handkerchief about her wrist, and would have gotten her at once from the room, but she seemed unable to stir, so weak was she from her fearful experience.

In the doorway, Mallet picked up the revolver warily and held it behind him stealthily. He believed his action had gone unnoted, for the invisible experimenter had carried the test tube across the room with a haste which showed that he did not care to be disturbed at this critical point The secretary watched the visible manifestations of that invisible force, while Jack Allison freed his sweetheart from the cords that had bound her.

Mallett saw the blood poured into a vessel partly filled with liquid which bubbled over a Bunsen burner. He saw a wad of absorbent cotton lifted from the table and dipped lightly into the boiling liquid, squeezed out into a dish to cool it, and then – the cotton began to make circular sweeps in the air.

From behind it there emerged a face, a horrible, rage-distorted countenance with furious eyes and bared, gnashing teeth. The cotton was flung aside. Mallett, staring, fascinated, as though hypnotized, realized that Paul Starr had successfully completed his experiment. He had found the ultimate ingredient that could restore his body to its normal rate of vibration. His face and hands, having come into contact with the anti-invisible mixture, developed as it were from the air; they floated as though supported by their own buoyancy; then they turned, those burning eyes, in the direction of the drooping girl and her lover.

Paul Starr flung himself across the room at the couple standing there. He gave vent to hoarse cries of savage fury as he went. His face, all stained with his sister's blood, leered at young Allison, who turned to protect Constance, warned by her weak cry of horror at the sight of her brother's face.

That face and those hands, that seemed to float in the air, now flung themselves at Allison with a raging strength, tenfold that of an ordinary man. Allison was forced backwards, for added to the impetus of the sudden attack was the contracting horror and loathing his heart felt at that frightful sight. He was obliged to battle with a something which fought with a savagery hard to resist, a something he could not see, against whose attacks he could not protect himself. And while he fought, that horrible leering face, ugly with its crazed fury, pressed itself upon him out of the air, and the two bloodstained hands caught at him and tore at him, those terrible hands that came out of nothingness.

Weak and trembling, with foreboding clutching at her fluttering heart, Constance leaned against the wall, to which she had shrunk to make way for the terrific struggle going on before her wide-opened, agonized eyes.

In the doorway the secretary watched silently, tensely, Allison's revolver hidden behind him.

Back and forth the man and the horror swung and balanced, fell, and rose to fall again. Paul's hoarse exclamations burst out spasmodically as he dealt blow upon blow to his opponent.

'Miserable fool! Wretched bird breeder! Do you think I can be balked by you? We shall see whether your interference will do you any good – or her, either!'

Now they swayed down the room, locked in a mutual embrace of fierce and desperate hatred. They fell against the table that held the vessel with its unholy contents. Jarred by the shock, it fell, staining the floor crimson in all directions. The Bunsen burner was upset as well, and the issuing flame began to lick the surface of the table, seizing upon the chemicals spread over it.

Paul gave a wild cry of outraged desperation as he saw the fate of his precious mixture. With a tremendous effort he threw Allison upon the floor, and with both hands at the young man's throat he bent his whole weight and strength in a last attempt to beat his Nemesis.

Constance shrieked.

The only calm person was the secretary. He came close up behind the writhing figures on the floor. He pulled the revolver from behind him, pointed it at the head that seemed floating there in the air above the prostrate Allison, and pulled the trigger. The was a loud report, followed by ghastly silence

Constance staggered towards the combatants, catching at tables and wall to support herself. Mallett dropped the smoking revolver as though it burned his hand. The horrible head wavered a moment in mid-air, then slowly described an arc that finished on the floor almost at the secretary's feet.

From Allison, in answer to Constance's 'Jack, Jack, are you hurt?' came a long, painful, gasping breath as he drew the air slowly into his tortured lungs. He put his hand uncertainly to his throat, drawing himself to a sitting posture and looking about him dazedly.

On the floor lay Paul Starr, or what they could see of him. His head was steeped in his own blood, as well as in that of his sister. Mallett's timely shot had put an end for all time to the experiments of the unscrupulous, ambitious chemist. His eyes were open yet; although he could not speak, the light of such a triumph shone in his terrible smile that Allison was filled with fresh apprehension. He looked hastily behind him, and realized their imminent danger.

The flame of the Bunsen burner had ignited the chemicals, and the blaze had made headway that in their preoccupation they had not noticed. If they wished to escape with their lives they would have to be quick. Allison put his arm about Constance, and the two lovers, mutually helping, swayed from the room. Mallett stood looking at the Thing on the floor. If he tried to pull it out he himself would beyond all doubt be caught in the swiftly advancing flames. The secretary shrank away in horror and dread, and fled while was yet time.

And not a moment too soon. Hardly had the three gained the open when a loud explosion thundered on their ears, followed by a series of smaller ones. Paul Starr and his unhallowed secret had disappeared together in the flames.

Clare Winger Harris

THE MIRACLE OF THE LILY

Clare Winger Harris (1891–1968) has the distinction of being the first woman contributor to the world's first science fiction magazine, Amazing Stories. *Had Gertrude Bennett continued to write she might have earned that honour, but the baton was now passed on. Harris was a housewife raising three children when she sold her first story, 'A Runaway World' to* Weird Tales, *where it appeared in July 1926. For a first story this was fairly extreme. It built on the popular idea that a solar system is like an atom and the planets like the sub-atomic particles and that just as we are experimenting with atoms so some greater cosmic being starts manipulating the planets. She then entered a story contest run by* Amazing Stories *and came in third with 'The Fate of the Poseidonia', published in June 1927. A little more down to earth, so to speak, it dealt with Martians who, needing water, start to draw it away from earth. Harris was to write eleven stories in all during the years 1926 to 1930 before she laid down her pen. All of them were later collected as* Away from the Here and Now *(1947). The best of her stories were those that questioned the nature of being human. 'The Artificial Man', for example, had a man who, following two near-fatal accidents, receives two artificial limbs and an artificial kidney. It makes him wonder how many such replacements he could have and yet still remain human, and he has almost his entire body rebuilt. The same question arises in the following, which many regard as her best story.*

The Miracle of the Lily

I

SINCE THE COMPARATIVELY recent résumé of the ancient order of agriculture I, Nathano, have been asked to set down the extraordinary events of the past two thousand years, at the beginning of which time the supremacy of man, chief of the mammals, threatened to come to an untimely end.

Ever since the dawn of life upon this globe, life which it seemed had crept from the slime of the sea, only two great types had been the rulers: the reptiles and the mammals. The former held undisputed sway for aeons, but gave way eventually before the smaller, but intellectually superior mammals. Man himself, the supreme example of the ability of life to govern and control inanimate matter, was master of the world with apparently none to dispute his right. Yet, so blinded was he with pride over the continued exercise of his power on earth over other lower types of mammals and the nearly extinct reptiles, that he failed to notice the slow but steady rise of another branch of life, different from his own; smaller, it is true, but no smaller than he had been in comparison with the mighty reptilian monsters that roamed the swamps in Mesozoic times.

These new enemies of man, though seldom attacking him personally, threatened his downfall by destroying his chief means of sustenance, so that by the close of the twentieth century strange and daring projects were laid before the various governments of the world with an idea of fighting man's insect enemies to the finish. These pests were growing in size, multiplying so rapidly and destroying so much vegetation, that eventually no plants would be left to sustain human life. Humanity suddenly woke to the realization that it might suffer the fate of the nearly extinct reptiles. Would mankind be able to prevent the encroachment of the insects?

And at last man *knew* that unless drastic measures were taken *at once*, a third great class of life was on the brink of terrestrial sovereignty.

Of course no great changes in development come suddenly. Slow evolutionary progress had brought us up to the point where, with the application of outside pressure, we were ready to handle a situation that, a century before, would have overwhelmed us.

I reproduce here in part a lecture delivered by a great American scientist, a talk which, sent by radio throughout the world, changed the destiny of mankind: but whether for good or for evil I will leave you to judge at the conclusion of this story.

> Only in comparatively recent times has man succeeded in conquering natural enemies – flood, storm, inclemency of climate, distance – and now we face an encroaching menace to the whole of humanity. Have we learned more and more of truth and of the laws that control matter only to succumb to the first real danger that threatens us with extermination? Surely, no matter what the cost, you will rally to the solution of our problem, and I believe, friends, that I have discovered the answer to the enigma.
>
> I know that many of you, like my friend Professor Fair, will believe my ideas too extreme, but I am convinced that, unless you are willing to put behind you those notions which are old and not utilitarian, you cannot hope to cope with the present situation.
>
> Already, in the past few decades, you have realized the utter futility of encumbering yourselves with superfluous possessions that have no useful virtue, but which, for various sentimental reasons, you continue to hoard, thus lessening the degree of your life's efficiency by using for it time and attention that should have been applied to the practical work of life's accomplishments. You have given these things up slowly, but I am now going to ask you to relinquish the rest of them *quickly*; everything that interferes in any way with the immediate disposal of our enemies, the insects.

At this point, it seems that my worthy ancestor, Professor Fair, objected to the scientist's words, asserting that efficiency at the expense of some of the sentimental virtues was undesirable and not conducive to happiness, the real goal of man. The scientist, in his turn, argued that happiness was available only through a perfect adaptability to one's environment, and that efficiency *sans* love, mercy and the softer sentiments was the short-cut to human bliss.

It look a number of years for the scientist to put over his scheme of salvation, but in the end he succeeded, not so much from the persuasiveness of his words as because prompt action of some sort was necessary. There was not enough food to feed the people of the earth. Fruit and vegetables were becoming a thing of the past. Too much protein in the form of meat and fish was injuring the race, and at last the people realized that, for fruits and vegetables, or their nutritive equivalent, they must turn from the field to the laboratory; from the farmer to the chemist. Synthetic food was the solution to the problem. There was no longer any use in planting and caring for food stuffs destined to become the nourishment of man's most deadly enemy.

The last planting took place in 2900, but there was no harvest, the voracious insects took every green shoot as soon as it appeared, and even trees, which had previously withstood the attacks of the huge insects, were by this time stripped of every vestige of greenery.

The vegetable world suddenly ceased to exist. Over the barren plains, which had been gradually filling with vast cities, man-made fires brought devastation to every living bit of greenery, so that in all the world there was no food for the insect pests.

II

*Extract from the diary of Delfair, a descendant of
Professor Fair, who had opposed the daring scientist.*

From the borders of the great state-city of Iowa, I was witness to the passing of one of the great kingdoms of earth – the vegetable and I cannot find words to express the grief that overwhelms me as I write of its demise, for I loved all growing things. Many of us realized that Earth was no longer beautiful; but if beauty meant death, better life in the sterility of the metropolis.

The viciousness of the thwarted insects was a menace that we had foreseen and yet failed to take into adequate account. On the state-city borderland, life is constantly imperilled by the attacks of well-organized bodies of our dreaded foe.

(*Note:* The organization that now exists among the ants, bees and other insects testifies to the possibility of the development of military tactics among them in the centuries to come.)

Robbed of their source of food, they have become emboldened to such an extent that they will take any risks to carry human beings away for food, and after one of their well-organized raids the toll of human life is appalling.

But the great chemical laboratories where our synthetic food is made, and our oxygen plants, we thought, were impregnable to their attacks. In that we were mistaken.

Let me say briefly that since the destruction of all vegetation, which furnished a part of the oxygen essential to human life, it became necessary to manufacture this gas artificially for general diffusion through the atmosphere.

I was flying to my work, which is in Oxygen Plant No. 21, when I noticed a peculiar thing on upper speedway near Food Plant No. 3,439. Although it was night, the various levels of the state-city were illuminated as brightly as by day. A pleasure vehicle was going with prodigious speed westward. I looked after it in amazement. It was unquestionably the car of Eric, my co-worker at Oxygen Plant No. 21. I recognized the gay colour of its body, but to verify my suspicion beyond the question of a doubt I turned my volplane in pursuit and made out the familiar licence number. What was Eric doing away from the plant before I had arrived to relieve him from duty?

In hot pursuit, I sped above the car to the very border of the state-city, wondering what unheard-of errand took him to the land of the enemy, for the car came to a sudden stop at the edge of what had once been an agricultural area. Miles ahead of me stretched an enormous expanse of black sterility; at my back was the teeming metropolis, five levels high – if one counted the hangar-level, which did not cover the residence sections.

I had not long to wait, for almost immediately my friend appeared. What a sight he presented to my incredulous gaze! He was literally covered from head to foot with the two-inch ants that, next to the beetles, had proved the greatest menace in their attacks upon humanity. With wild incoherent cries he fled over the rock and stubble-burned earth.

As soon as my stunned senses permitted, I swooped down towards him to effect a rescue, but even as my plane touched the barren earth, I saw that I was too late, for he fell, borne down by the vicious attacks of his myriad foes. I knew it was useless for me to set down upon the ground, for my fate would be that of Eric. I rose ten feet and, seizing my poison-gas weapon, let its contents out upon the tiny black evil things that swarmed below. I did not bother with my mask, for I planned to rise immediately, and it was not a moment too soon. From across the wasteland, a dark cloud eclipsed the stars and I saw coming towards me a horde of flying ants interspersed with larger flying insects, all bent upon my annihilation. I now took my mask and prepared to turn more gas upon my pursuers, but, alas, I had used every atom of it in my attack upon the non-flying ants! I had no recourse but flight, and to this I immediately resorted, knowing that I could outdistance my pursuers.

When I could no longer see them, I removed my gas mask. A suffocating sensation seized me. I could not breathe! How high had I flown in my endeavour to escape the flying ants? I leaned over the side of my plane expecting to see the city far, far below me. What was my utter amazement when I discovered that I was scarcely a thousand feet high! It was not altitude that was depriving me of the life-giving oxygen.

A drop of three hundred feet showed me inert specks of humanity lying about the streets. Then I knew; *the oxygen plant was not in operation*! In another minute I had on my oxygen mask, which was attached to a small portable tank for emergency use, and I rushed for the vicinity of the plant. There I witnessed the first signs of life. Men equipped with oxygen masks were trying to force entrance into the locked building. Being an employee, I possessed knowledge of the combination of the great lock, and I opened the door, only to be greeted by a swarm of ants that commenced a concerted attack upon us.

The floor seemed to be covered with a moving black rug, the corner nearest the door appearing to unravel as we entered, and it was but a few seconds before we were covered with the clinging, biting creatures, who fought with a supernatural energy born of despair. Two very active ants succeeded in getting under my helmet. The bite of their sharp mandibles and the effect of their poisonous formic acid became intolerable. Did I dare remove my mask while the air about me was foul with the gas discharged from the weapons of my allies? While I felt the attacks elsewhere upon my body gradually diminishing as the insects succumbed to the deadly fumes, the two upon my face waxed more vicious under the protection of my mask. One at each eye, they were trying to blind me. The pain was unbearable. Better the suffocating death-gas than the torture of lacerated eyes! Frantically I removed the headgear and tore at the shiny black fiends. Strange to tell, I discovered that I could breathe near the vicinity of the great oxygen tanks, where enough oxygen lingered to support life at least temporarily. The two vicious insects, no longer protected by my gas-mask, scurried from me like rats from a sinking ship and disappeared behind the oxygen tanks.

This attack of our enemies, though unsuccessful on their part, was dire in its significance, for it had shown more cunning and ingenuity than anything that had ever preceded it. Heretofore, their onslaughts had been confined to direct attacks upon us personally or upon the synthetic-food laboratories, but in this last raid they had shown an amazing cleverness that portended future disaster, unless they were checked at once. It was obvious they had ingeniously planned to smother us by the suspension of work at the oxygen plant, knowing that they themselves could exist in an atmosphere containing a greater percentage of carbon-dioxide. Their scheme, then, was to raid our laboratories for food.

III

A continuation of Delfair's account

Although it was evident that the cessation of all plant-life spelled inevitable doom for the insect inhabitants of Earth, their extermination did not follow as rapidly as one might have supposed. There were years of internecine warfare. The insects continued to thrive, though in decreasing numbers, upon stolen laboratory foods, bodies of human beings and finally upon each other; at first capturing enemy species and at last even resorting to cannibalistic procedures. Their rapacity grew in inverse proportion to their waning numbers, until the meeting of even an isolated insect might mean death, unless one were equipped with poison gas and prepared to use it upon a second's notice.

I am an old man now, though I have not yet lived quite two centuries, but I am happy in the knowledge that I have lived to see the last living insect which was held in captivity. It was an excellent specimen of the stag-beetle (*Lucanus*), and the years have testified that it was the sole survivor of a form of life that might have succeeded man upon this planet. This beetle was caught weeks after we had previously seen what was supposed to be the last living thing upon the globe, barring man and the sea-life. Untiring search for years has failed to reveal any more insects, so that at last man rests secure in the knowledge that he is monarch of all he surveys.

I have heard that long, long ago man used to gaze with a fearful fascination upon the reptilian creatures which he displaced, and just so did he view this lone specimen of a type of life that might have covered the face of the earth, but for man's ingenuity.

It was this unholy lure that drew me one day to view the captive beetle in his cage in district 404 at Universapolis. I was amazed at the size of the creature, for it looked larger than when I had seen it by television, but I reasoned that upon that occasion there had been no object near with which to compare its size. True, the broadcaster had announced its dimensions, but the statistics concretely given had failed to register a perfect realization of its prodigious proportions.

As I approached the cage, the creature was lying with its dorsal covering towards me, and I judged it measured fourteen inches from one extremity to the other. Its smooth horny sheath gleamed in the bright artificial light. (It was confined on the third level.) As I stood there, mentally conjuring a picture of a world overrun with billions of such creatures as the one before me, the keeper approached the cage with a meal-portion of synthetic food. Although the food has no odour, the beetle sensed the man's approach, for it rose on its jointed legs and came towards us, its horn-like prongs moving threateningly; then apparently remembering its confinement, and the impotency of an attack, it subsided and quickly ate the food which had been placed within its prison.

The food consumed, it lifted itself to its hind legs, partially supported by a box, and turned its great eyes upon me. I have never been regarded with such utter malevolence before. The detestation was almost tangible, and I shuddered involuntarily. As plainly as if he spoke, I knew that Lucanus was perfectly cognizant of the situation and in his gaze I read the concentrated hate of an entire defeated race.

I had no desire to gloat over his misfortune; rather, a great pity towards him welled up within me. I pictured myself alone, the last of my kind, held up for ridicule before the swarming hordes of insects who had conquered my people, and I knew that life would no longer be worth the living.

Whether he sensed my pity or not I do not know, but he continued to survey me with unmitigated rage, as if he would convey to me the information that his was an implacable hatred that would outlast eternity.

Not long after this he died, and a world long since intolerant of ceremony surprised itself by interring the beetle's remains in a golden casket, accompanied by much pomp and splendour.

I have lived many long years since that memorable event, and undoubtedly my days here are numbered, but I can pass on happily, convinced that in this sphere man's conquest of his environment is supreme.

IV

In a direct line of descent from Professor Fair and Delfair, the author of the preceding chapter, comes Thanor, whose journal is given in this chapter.

Am I a true product of the year 2928? Sometimes I am convinced that I am hopelessly old-fashioned, an anachronism that should have existed a thousand years ago. In no other way can I account for the dissatisfaction I feel in a world where efficiency has at last reached a maximum.

I am told that I spring from a line of ancestors who were not readily acclimated to changing conditions. I love beauty, yet I see none of it here. There are many who think our lofty buildings that tower two and three thousand feet into the air are beautiful, but while they are architectural splendours they do not represent the kind of loveliness I crave. Only when I visit the sea do I feel any satisfaction for a certain yearning in my soul. The ocean alone shows the handiwork of God. The land bears evidence only of man.

As I read back through the diaries of my sentimental ancestors I find occasional glowing descriptions of the world that was; the world before the insects menaced human existence. Trees, plants and flowers brought delight into the lives of people as they wandered among them in vast open spaces, I am told, where the earth was soft beneath the feet, and flying creatures, called birds, sang among the greenery. True, I learn that many people had not enough to eat, and that uncontrollable passions governed them, but I do believe it must have been more interesting than this methodical, unemotional existence. I cannot understand why many people were poor, for I am told that Nature as manifested in the vegetable kingdom was very prolific; so much so that year after year quantities of food rotted on the ground. The fault, I find by my reading, was not with Nature but with man's economic system, which is now perfect, though this perfection really brings few of us happiness, I think.

Now there is no waste; all is converted into food. Long ago man learned how to reduce all matter to its constituent elements, of which there are nearly a hundred in number, and from them to rebuild compounds for food. The old axiom that nothing is created or destroyed, but merely changed from one form to another, has stood the test of ages. Man, as the agent of God, has simply performed the miracle of transmutation himself instead of waiting for natural forces to accomplish it, as in the old days.

At first humanity was horrified when it was decreed that it must relinquish its dead to the laboratory. For too many aeons had man closely associated the soul and body, failing to comprehend the body is merely a material agent through which the spirit functioned. When man knew at last of the eternal qualities of spirit, he ceased to regard the discarded body with reverential awe, and saw in it only the same molecular constituents which comprised all matter about him. He recognized only material basically the same as that of stone or metal; material to be reduced to its atomic elements and rebuilt into matter that would render service to living humanity; that portion of matter wherein spirit functions.

The drab monotony of life is appalling. Is it possible that man had reached his height a thousand years ago and should have been willing to resign Earth's sovereignty to a coming order of creatures destined to be man's worthy successor in the aeons to come? It seems that life is interesting only when there is a struggle, a goal to be reached through an evolutionary process. Once the goal is attained, all progress ceases. The huge reptiles of pre-glacial ages rose to supremacy by virtue of their great size, and yet was it not the excessive bulk of those creatures that finally wiped them out of existence? Nature, it seems, avoids extremes. She allows the fantastic to develop for a while and then wipes the slate clean for a new order of development. Is it not conceivable that man could destroy himself through excessive development of his nervous system, and give place for the future evolution of a comparatively simple form of life, such as the insects were at man's height of development? This, it seems to me, was the great plan; a scheme with which man dared to interfere and for which he is now paying by the boredom of existence. The Earth's population is decreasing so rapidly, that I fear another thousand years will see a lifeless planet hurtling through space. It seems to me that only a miracle will save us now.

V

The original writer, Nathano, resumes the narrative

My ancestor, Thanor, of ten centuries ago, according to the records he gave to my great-grandfather, seems to voice the general despair of humanity which, bad enough in his times, has reached the nth power in my day. A soulless world is gradually dying from self-inflicted boredom.

As I have ascertained from the perusal of the journals of my forebears, even antedating the extermination of the insects, I come of a stock that clings with sentimental tenacity to the things that made life worth while in the old days. If the world at large knew of my emotional musings concerning past ages, it would scarcely tolerate me, but surrounded by my thought-insulator I often indulge in what fancies I will, and such meditation, coupled with a love for a few ancient relics from the past, have led me to a most amazing discovery.

Several months ago I found among my family relics a golden receptacle two feet long, one and a half in width and one in depth, which I found, upon opening, to contain many tiny square compartments, each filled with minute objects of slightly varying size, texture and colour.

'Not sand!' I exclaimed as I closely examined the little particles of matter.

Food? After eating some, I was convinced that their nutritive value was small in comparison with a similar quantity of the products of our laboratories. What were the mysterious objects?

Just as I was about to close the lid again, convinced that I had one over-sentimental ancestor, whose gift to posterity was absolutely useless, my pocket-radio buzzed and the voice of my friend Stentor, the interplanetary broadcaster, issued from the tiny instrument.

'If you're going to be home this afternoon,' said Stentor, 'I'll skate over. I have some interesting news.'

I consented, for I thought I would share my 'find' with this friend whom I loved above all others, but before he arrived I had again hidden my golden chest, for I had decided to await the development of events before sharing its mysterious secret with another. It was well that I did this, for Stentor was so filled with the importance of his own news that he could have given me little attention at first.

'Well, what is your interesting news?' I asked after he was comfortably seated in my adjustable chair.

'You'd never guess,' he replied with irritating leisureliness.

'Does it pertain to Mars or Venus?' I queried. 'What news of our neighbour planets?'

'You may know it has nothing to do with the self-satisfied Martians,' answered the broadcaster, 'but the Venusians have a very serious problem confronting them. It is in connection with the same old difficulty they have had ever since interplanetary radio was developed forty years ago. You remember that, in their second communication with us, they told us of their continual warfare on insect pests that were destroying all vegetable food? Well, last night after general broadcasting had ceased, I was surprised to hear the voice of the Venusian broadcaster. He is suggesting that we get up a scientific expedition to Venus to help the natives of his unfortunate planet solve their insect problem as we did ours. He says the Martians turn a deaf ear to their plea for help, but he expects sympathy and assistance from Earth who has so recently solved these problems for herself.'

I was dumbfounded at Stentor's news. 'But the Venusians are further advanced mechanically than we,' I objected, 'though they are behind us in the natural sciences. They could much more easily solve the difficulties of space-flying than we could.'

'That is true,' agreed Stentor, 'but if we are to render them material aid in freeing their world from devastating insects, we must get to Venus. The past four decades have proved that we cannot help them merely by verbal instructions.'

'Now, last night,' Stentor continued, with warming enthusiasm, 'Wanyana, the Venusian broadcaster, informed me that scientists on Venus are developing interplanetary television. This, if successful, will prove highly beneficial in facilitating communication, and it may even do away with the necessity of interplanetary travel, which I think is centuries ahead of us yet.'

'Television, though so common here on earth and on Venus, has seemed an impossibility across the ethereal void,' I said, 'but if it becomes a reality, I believe it will be the Venusians who will take the initiative, though of course they will be helpless without our friendly cooperation. In return for the mechanical instructions they have given us from time to time, I think it no more than right that we should try to give them all the help possible in freeing their world, as ours has been freed, of the insects that threaten their very existence. Personally, therefore, I hope it can be done through radio and tele-vision rather than by personal excursions.'

'I believe you are right,' he admitted, 'but I hope we can be of service to them soon. Ever since I have served in the capacity of official interplanetary broadcaster, I have liked the spirit of good fellowship shown by the Venusians through their broadcaster Wanyana. The impression is favourable in contrast to the super-ciliousness of the inhabitants of Mars.'

We conversed for some time, but at length he rose to take his leave. It was then I ventured to broach the subject that was upper-most in my thoughts.

'I want to show you something, Stentor,' I said, going into an adjoining room for my precious box and returning shortly with it. 'A relic from the days of an ancestor named Delfair, who lived at the time the last insect, a beetle, was held in captivity. From his personal account, Delfair was fully aware of the significance of the changing times in which he lived and, contrary to the majority of his contemporaries, possessed a sentimentality of soul that has proved an historical asset to future generations. Look, my friend, these he left to posterity!'

I deposited the heavy casket on the table between us and lifted the lid, revealing to Stentor the mystifying particles.

The face of Stentor was eloquent of astonishment. Not unnaturally his mind took somewhat of the same route as mine had followed previously, though he added atomic-power units to the list of possibilities. He shook his head in perplexity.

'Whatever they are, there must have been a real purpose behind their preservation,' he said at last. 'You say this old fellow Delfair witnessed the passing of the insects? What sort of fellow was he? Likely to be up to any tricks?'

'Not at all,' I asserted rather indignantly. 'He seemed a very serious-minded chap; worked in an oxygen-plant and took an active part in the last warfare between men and insects.'

Suddenly Stentor stooped over and scooped up some of the minute particles into the palm of his hand – and then he uttered a maniacal shriek and flung them into the air.

'Great God, man, do you know what they are?' he screamed, shaking violently.

'No, I do not,' I replied quietly, with an attempt at dignity I did not feel.

'Insect eggs!' he cried, and, shuddering with terror, he made for the door.

I caught him on the threshold and pulled him forcibly back into the room.

'Now see here,' I said sternly. 'Not a word of this to anyone. Do you understand? I will test out your theory in every possible way, but I want no public interference.'

At first he was obstinate, but finally yielded to threats when supplications were impotent.

'I will test them,' I said, 'and will endeavour to keep hatchings under absolute control, should they prove to be what you suspect.'

It was time for the evening broadcasting, so he left, promising to keep our secret and leaving me regretting that I had taken another into my confidence.

VI

For days following my unfortunate experience with Stentor, I experimented upon the tiny objects that had so terrified him. I subjected them to various tests for the purpose of ascertaining whether or not they bore evidence of life, whether in egg, pupa or larva stages of development. And to all my experiments, there was but one answer. No life was manifest. Yet I was not satisfied, for chemical tests showed that they were composed of organic matter. Here was an inexplicable enigma! Many times I was on the verge of consigning the entire contents of the chest to the flames. I seemed to see in my mind's eye the world again over-ridden with insects, and that calamity due to the indiscretions of one man! My next impulse was to turn over my problem to scientists, when a suspicion of the truth dawned on me. These were seeds, the germs of plant-life, and they might grow. But, alas, where? Over all the earth man has spread his artificial dominion. The state-city has been succeeded by what could be termed the nation-city, for one great floor of concrete or rock covers the country.

I resolved to try an experiment, the far-reaching influence of which I did not at that time suspect. Beneath the lowest level of the community edifice in which I dwell, I removed, by means of a small atomic excavator, a slab of concrete large enough to admit my body. I let myself down into the hole and felt my feet resting on a soft, dark substance that I knew to be dirt. I hastily filled a box of this, and after replacing the concrete slab returned to my room, where I proceeded to plant a variety of the seeds.

Being a product of an age when practically to wish for a thing in a material sense is to have it, I experienced the greatest impatience while waiting for any evidences of plant-life to become manifest. Daily, yes hourly, I watched the soil for signs of a type of life long since departed from the earth, and was about convinced that the germ of life could not have survived the centuries, when a tiny blade of green proved to me that a miracle, more wonderful to me than the works of man through the ages, was taking place before my eyes. This was an enigma so complex and yet so simple that one recognized in it a direct revelation of Nature.

Daily and weekly I watched in secret the botanical miracle. It was my one obsession. I was amazed at the fascination it held for me – a man who viewed the marvels of the thirty-fourth century with unemotional complacency. It showed me that Nature is manifest in the simple things which mankind has chosen to ignore.

Then one morning, when I awoke, a white blossom displayed its immaculate beauty and sent forth its delicate fragrance into the air. The lily, a symbol of new life, resurrection! I felt within me the stirring of strange emotions I had long believed dead in the bosom of man. But the message must not be for me alone. As of old, the lily would be the symbol of life for all!

With trembling hands, I carried my precious burden to a front window where it might be witnessed by all who passed by. The first day there were few who saw it, for only rarely do men and women walk; they usually ride in speeding vehicles of one kind or another, or employ electric skates, a delightful means of locomotion which gives the body some exercise. The fourth city level, which is reserved for skaters and pedestrians, is kept in a smooth glass-like condition. And so it was only the occasional pedestrian, walking on the outer border of the fourth level, upon which my window faced, who first carried the news of the growing plant to the world, and it was not long before it was necessary for civic authorities to disperse the crowds that thronged to my window for a glimpse of a miracle in green and white.

When I showed my beautiful plant to Stentor he was most profuse in his apology and came to my rooms every day to watch it unfold and develop, but the majority of people, long used to business-like efficiency, were intolerant of the sentimental emotions that swayed a small minority, and I was commanded to dispose of the lily. But a figurative seed had been planted in the human heart, a seed that could not be disposed of so readily, and this seed ripened and grew until it finally bore fruit.

VII

It is a very different picture of humanity that I paint ten years after the last entry in my diary. My new vocation is farming, but it is farming on a far more intensive scale than had been done two thousand years ago. Our crops never fail, for temperature and rainfall are regulated artificially. But we attribute our success principally to the total absence of insect pests. Our small agricultural areas dot the country like the parks of ancient days and supply us with a type of food, no more nourishing but more appetizing than that produced in the laboratories. Truly we are living in a marvellous age! If the earth is ours completely, why may we not turn our thoughts towards the other planets in our solar-system? For the past ten or eleven years the Venusians have repeatedly urged us to come and assist them in their battle for life. I believe it is our duty to help them.

Tomorrow will be a great day for us and especially for Stentor, as the new interplanetary television is to be tested, and it is possible that for the first time in history we shall see our neighbours in the infinity of space. Although the people of Venus were about a thousand years behind us in many respects, they have made wonderful progress with radio and television. We have been in radio communication with them for the last half-century and they shared with us the joy of the establishment of our Eden. They have always been greatly interested in hearing Stentor tell the story of our subjugation of the insects that threatened to wipe us out of existence, for they have exactly that problem to solve now; judging from their reports, we fear that theirs is a losing battle. Tomorrow we shall converse face to face with the Venusians! It will be an event second in importance only to the first radio communications interchanged fifty years ago. Stentor's excitement exceeds that displayed at the time of the discovery of the seeds.

Well, it is over and the experiment was a success, but alas for the revelation!

The great assembly halls all over the continent were packed with humanity eager to catch a first glimpse of the Venusians. Prior to the test, we sent our message of friendship and goodwill by radio, and received a reciprocal one from our interplanetary neighbours. Alas, we were ignorant at that time! Then the television receiving apparatus was put into operation, and we sat with breathless interest, our eyes intent upon the crystal screen before us. I sat near Stentor and noted the feverish ardour with which he watched for the first glimpse of Wanyana.

At first hazy, mist-like spectres seemed to glide across the screen. We knew these figures were not in correct perspective. Finally, one object gradually became more opaque, its outlines could be seen clearly. Then across that vast assemblage, as well as thousands of others throughout the world, there swept a wave of speechless horror, as its full significance burst upon mankind.

The figure that stood facing us was a huge six-legged beetle, not identical in every detail with our earthly enemies of past years, but unmistakably an insect of gigantic proportions! Of course it could not see us, for our broadcaster was not to appear until afterwards, but it spoke, and we had to close our eyes to convince ourselves that it was the familiar voice of Wanyana, the leading Venusian radio broadcaster. Stentor grabbed my arm, uttered an inarticulate cry and would have fallen but for my timely support.

'Friends of Eearth, as you call your world,' began the object of horror, 'this is a momentous occasion in the annals of the twin planets, and we are looking forward to seeing one of you, and preferably Stentor, for the first time, as you are now viewing one of us. We have listened many times, with interest, to your story of the insect pests which threatened to follow you as lords of your planet. As you have often heard us tell, we are likewise molested with insects. Our fight is a losing one, unless we can soon exterminate them.'

Suddenly, the Venusian was joined by another being, a colossal ant, who bore in his fore-legs a tiny light-coloured object which he handed to the beetle-announcer, who took it and held it forward for our closer inspection. It seemed to be a tiny ape, but was so small we could not ascertain for a certainty. We were convinced, however, that it was a mammalian creature, and 'insect' pest of Venus. Yet in it we recognized rudimentary man as we know him on earth!

There was no question as to the direction in which sympathies instinctively turned, yet reason told us that our pity should be given to the intelligent reigning race who had risen to its present mental attainment through aeons of time. By some quirk or freak of nature, way back in the beginning, life had developed in the form of insects instead of mammals. Or (the thought was repellent) had insects in the past succeeded in displacing mammals, as they might have done here on earth?

There was no more television that night. Stentor would not appear, so disturbed was he by the sight of the Venusians, but in the morning he talked to them by radio and explained the very natural antipathy we experienced in seeing them or in having them see us.

Now they no longer urge us to construct etherships and go to help them dispose of their 'insects'. I think they are afraid of us, and their very fear has aroused in mankind an unholy desire to conquer them.

I am against it. Have we not had enough of war in the past? We have subdued our own world and should be content with that, instead of seeking new worlds to conquer. But life is too easy here. I can plainly see that. Much as he may seem to dislike it, man is not happy unless he has some enemy to overcome, some difficulty to surmount.

Alas, my greatest fears for man were groundless!

A short time ago, when I went out into my field to see how my crops were faring, I found a six-pronged beetle voraciously eating. No – man will not need to go to Venus to fight 'insects'.

Adeline Knapp

THE EARTH SLEPT: A VISION

Adeline Knapp (1860–1909) was always something of a renegade. She was a great free-thinker and long desired to be a journalist, but she was forced by the demands of the day to work in a mercantile business from which she developed a rather cynical outlook on trade and commerce. The subtitle of her collection One Thousand Dollars a Day *(1894), from which the following story comes, is* Studies in Practical Economics, *although as the story reveals there is little that is practical about it if left to the hand of man. Knapp eventually became a journalist. Indeed, after she moved to California in 1887, she not only became a regular contributor to the* San Francisco Call *and the butt of the acerbic wit of Ambrose Bierce but ran her own newspaper, the* Alameda County Express. *She was part of the bustling San Francisco literary set but soon found that the restriction of city life did not suit her. This may have led to the acrimony with the author Charlotte Perkins Stetson (later Gilman), with whom Knapp lived for a year or two in the early 1890s, and they parted on difficult terms. Knapp later travelled widely as a reporter, including to Hawaii and the Philippines, but for three years she hid herself away in the remote Californian foothills, where she built her own house and survived by her own skill and determination. Her respect for nature and her low opinion of civilization are evident in the following fable, first published in 1894, which is almost a hymn to progress and thus a fitting way to close this anthology.*

The Earth Slept: A Vision

I

THE EARTH SLEPT.

Age upon age passed over the nebulous mass that lay without form and void in space, unknowing, unfeeling, yet guided ever by the workings of inexorable law.

'Brothers! Brothers!' whispered one statoblast to the others, 'I feel a strange stirring within me, a consciousness of broader life; and, brothers, what is this shining whiteness creeping all about us? Brothers, I dreamed once, long ago, of a wonderful glory called light. I believe, brothers, that the light is breaking!'

'How foolish!' exclaimed the others. 'We have no knowledge of such stirrings or new consciousness. Why should you have? No one has ever seen light. There never has been light and there never will be light. When will you cease to trouble us?' And all the statoblasts murmured their assent to this and, gathering more closely about their offending brother, crushed him into silence.

And slowly the dawn broke, and there was light upon the face of the earth, and the statoblasts saw it and saw each other, and looked upon each other and said:

'We knew that it would come.'

II

The earth slept.

Age upon age came and went. The light grew stronger. Great green growths shot heavenward, lived their appointed time, fell back to earth and mingled with its mould. The rain fell and covered the heated world, and its vapours steamed up and fell back in rain again. The seas heaved and dashed, and approached and receded, age upon age.

250

'Brothers! Brothers!' cried one amoeboid cell to the rest, 'I feel a strange impulse within me – a stirring as of power. Brothers, I believe that we have a wonderful destiny before us. I believe that we shall have power of motion.'

'Nonsense,' replied the others. 'Why do you trouble us? We are at rest. We never have moved. We never shall move. There is nothing to move for if we did move.'

And all the cells breathed their assent to this, and grew more closely around their brother and pressed upon him and smothered him into silence.

And the ages rolled by, and presently motion came to the cells and they darted to and fro in the water, saying to each other: 'We knew that we should move, in time.'

III

The earth slept.

Age upon age passed, and through them all the impulse of life beat on. From one form to another it travelled. Mammoth creatures walked the earth, and mammoth vegetation covered its surface. From the north swept down the mighty frozen tide bearing death before it, and the mammoth passed away.

The dawning of a new life began to break upon the world, flowers bedecked the earth, and fruits multiplied and increased in the trees. Beneficent nature was planning for the good of her children.

'Friends!' cried one climbing anthropoid to the others, 'I feel a strange impulse within me – a yearning as of aspirations undefined. Friends, I believe that we shall yet walk this earth erect!'

'Nonsense,' cried the rest, 'we feel no such impulse, and why should you? We never have walked erect. We have no power to walk erect, nor desire to do so. Why do you trouble us with your imbecile folly?'

And gathering about him they drowned his voice in the chorus of their clamouring protests.

IV

The earth slept.

Age upon age passed and man dwelt upon the earth and fought and toiled and traded with his kind. Man, king of creation, walking erect, engaged in competition with his fellows, and battled fiercely with them in the struggle for existence.

Kingdoms were set up and thrown down. Dynasties arose and died out. Whole peoples came and went upon the face of the earth, but still the struggle for existence went on; still men vied with each other in the competition of trade; still the strong struggled for greater gain and the weak went down, crushed, helpless, thrown to the earth, unable to do battle in the struggle for existence. The rich grew richer, the poor poorer, and the whole world was caught in the vice-like grip of competition.

'Oh, men!' cried one man to his fellows, 'I feel the stirring of a strange impulse within me – the dawning of a great truth. We are brothers. Our lives are knit up in each other. Fraternity, and not competition, is to be the main-spring of our racial life!'

'Nonsense!' replied his fellows. 'You talk neither policy nor logic. Fraternity is a dream of the poets, an ideal for a future life. Competition is the life of trade.'

So they gathered about him and silenced him; but his light they could not quench, the truth they could not smother, hide it as they would. Up and down the earth it wanders, showing itself in a great deed here, a great thought there, the stirring of a mighty force yonder, yet beaten back by the throng of competing men.

And the earth sleeps.

Also published by Peter Owen

THE DARKER SEX
Tales of the Supernatural and Macabre by Victorian Women Writers
Mike Ashley (Ed.)

978-0-7206-1335-3 • paperback • 248pp • £9.99

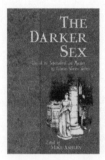

'A magnificent and terribly readable collection' – *Woman's Hour* BBC Radio 4

Ghosts, precognition, suicide and the afterlife are all themes to be found in these thrilling stories by some of the greatest Victorian women writers. It was three women who popularized the Gothic-fiction movement – Clara Reeve, Mary Shelley and Anne Radcliffe – and Victorian women proved they had a talent for creating dark, sensational and horrifying tales. This anthology showcases some of the best work by female writers of the time, including Emily Brontë, Mary Braddon, George Eliot and Edith Nesbit. Mike Ashley contextualizes each story and shows how Victorian women perfected and developed the Gothic genre.

Peter Owen books can be purchased from:
Central Books, 99 Wallis Road, London E9 5LN, UK
Tel: +44 (0) 845 458 9911 Fax: + 44 (0) 845 458 9912
e-mail: orders@centralbooks.com

www.peterowen.com